LOST ...

Two Hawks examined a big room which must have been the study of the master of the mansion. There were books on the shelves and on the floor, some destroyed by a bomb. A huge globe of Earth lay on the floor by the table from which it had been hurled by the explosion. After placing it upright on the table, heart beating hard, he verified his suspicions and cleared up some of the mysteries.

What he saw was not entirely unexpected. . . . There on the globe were Eurasia, Africa, and Australia, their shapes not quite those he was familiar with. Moreover, the lines of latitude showed the three landmasses about four hundred miles farther south than on the maps he knew.

This was alien enough. What disturbed him most was India.

It had the same triangular shape.

But it was separated by an estimated 800 miles of sea from the continent of Asia. . . .

"Ever hear of parallel universes?" Two Hawks said . . .

This is for Baron Arnold von Schindler,
ace of the freeways and
barnstormer of the smog.

Two Hawks from Earth

PHILIP JOSÉ FARMER

SF

ace books

A Division of Charter Communications Inc.
A GROSSET & DUNLAP COMPANY
360 Park Avenue South
New York, New York 10010

TWO HAWKS FROM EARTH

An ACE Book

Cover art by Boris

First Ace printing: May 1979

Foreword

This novel was first published in 1966 and then in 1971 as *The Gate of Time*. That was not my title. I have no idea why the editors changed it, since this is not a time-travel tale, and their title certainly was misleading. So I have restored the original, *Two Hawks From Earth*.

The editors of that house also rewrote a scene to bowdlerize it. This was done without my knowledge, and so I have restored that scene.

Also, I have added about ten thousand words. These include some chapters which go beyond the original ending.

—Philip José Farmer
January 1979

1

A year after the war ended, my publisher sent me to Stavanger, Norway, to interview Roger Two Hawks. I had full authority to negotiate a contract with him. The terms were very favorable, especially when the lack of printing facilities and distribution of that postwar period is considered. I had asked for the assignment, since I had heard so much about Roger Two Hawks. Most of the stories were incredible, even contradictory, yet my informants swore to the truth of their testimonies.

So high-pitched was my curiosity, I would have quit my job and gone on my own to Norway if my publisher had refused me. And this was at a time when jobs in my field were not easy to get. Rebuilding our destroyed civilization was the foremost goal; craftsmanship in steelworking or bricklaying was more desired than facility with the pen.

Nevertheless, people were buying books, and there was a worldwide interest in the mysterious stranger, Roger Two Hawks. Everyone had heard of him, but those who had known him well were either dead or missing.

I booked passage on an old steamer that took

five days to get to Stavanger. I did not even wait
to check in at the hotel, since it was late evening.
Instead, I asked directions, in my abominable
Norwegian, to the hotel at which I knew Two
Hawks was staying. I had tried to get reserva-
tions there with no success.

The taxi fare was very high, since fuel was still
being rationed. We drove through many dark
streets with unlit gaslights. But the front of the
hotel was brightly illuminated, and the lobby
was crowded with noisy and laughing guests,
still happy about having lived through the war.

I asked the desk clerk for Two Hawks' room
and was told that he was in the ballroom, attend-
ing a large party given by the mayor of
Stavanger.

I had no trouble locating Roger Two Hawks,
since I had seen many photographs of him. He
stood at one corner of the room, surrounded by
men and women. I pushed my way through
them and soon stood near him. He was about six
feet two inches tall, well-muscled, and his features were handsome, though rather aquiline.
His straight hair was black. His skin was dark.
His eyes were large and a dark hazel.

He was holding a drink of Norland in one
hand and chatting away, his frequent smiles dis-
playing very white teeth. He spoke fluently
though with a heavy accent and an occasional
lapse of correct grammar. Beside him stood a
beautiful blonde whom I also recognized from
photographs. She was his wife.

When a short pause came in the conversation,
I took the opportunity to introduce myself. He

had heard of me and my visit, of course, because
both my publisher and myself had corresponded
with him. His voice was a deep rich baritone,
very pleasant and at the same time confidence-
inspiring.

He asked me how my trip was, and I told him
that it was endurable. He smiled and said, "I
had begun to think that your publisher had
changed his mind and you weren't coming after
all. Apparently, the wireless had also broken
down on your ship."

"Everything did," I said. "The vessel was
used for coastal shipping during the war and was
bombed at least four times. Some of the repairs
were pretty hasty and done with shoddy materials."

"I'm leaving Norway in two days," he said
abruptly. "That means that I can give you about
a day and a half. I'll have to tell you the story
and depend on you to get it right. How's your
memory?"

"Photographic," I replied. "Very well, but
that means that neither of us will get much sleep.
I'm tired, but I'd like to start as soon as possible.
So . . . ?"

"Right now. I'll tell my wife we're going up to
my room and I'll be a moment explaining to my
host."

Five minutes later, we were in his room. He
put on a big pot of coffee while I got the contract
and my pen and notebook out. Then he said, "I
really don't know why I'm doing this. Perhaps
I'd like . . . well, never mind. The point is, I need
money and this book seems to be the easiest way

to get it. Yet, I may not come back to collect any royalties. It all depends on what happens at the end of my voyage."

I raised my eyebrows but said nothing. With one of the quick yet fluid motions characteristic of him, he left my side and strode across the room to a large table. On it was a globe of the world, a prewar model that did not show the change in boundaries that had taken place in the past year.

"Come here a moment," he said. "I want to show you where my story begins."

I rose and went to his side. He turned the globe slowly, then stopped it. With the point of a pencil, he indicated a spot on the land a little to the left of the central western shore of the Black Sea.

"Ploesti, Rumania," he said. "That's where I'll begin. I could start much farther back, but to do that would take time which we don't have. If you have any questions about my story before then, you'll have to insert them whenever you get the chance. However, I have a manuscript which outlines my life before I went on the mission against the oil-fields of Ploesti."

"Ploesti, Rumania?" I said.

"Ploesti, the great oil-producing and refining heart of Deutschland's new empire. The target of the 9th Air Force, based in Cyrenaica, North Africa. It took years of war before the Americans could launch an attack against the life-blood of Germany's transportation and military effectiveness. Overloaded with bombs, ammunition, and gasoline, 175 four-motored bombers set out to destroy the oil tanks and refineries of Ploesti. We did not know that it was called *Festung* Ploesti, Fortress Ploesti, that the greatest concentration of anti-aircraft guns in Europe ringed that city. Nor would it have made much difference if we had known, except that we might not have been so shocked when we found out.

"I was first pilot on the *Hiawatha;* my co-pilot was Jim Andrews. He was from Birmingham, Alabama, but the fact that I was part Iroquois Indian didn't seem to bother him any. We were the best of friends."

He stopped, then smiled, and said, "By the way, you are looking at Ye Compleat Iroquoian. I have ancestors from every existing Iroquois tribe, including great-grandparents from the Iroquoian-speaking Cherokees. But my father was part Icelandic and my mother was part Scotch."

I shrugged and said, to explain my blank look, "Can I expect to get some explanation of this from the manuscript you spoke of?"

"Yeah, sure. Anyway . . ."

2

THE MISSION leader of the group had taken the wrong turn at Targoviste. Instead of heading for Ploesti, the Circus was going toward Bucharest. First Lieutenant Two Hawks realized the error and, like some of the other pilots, he disobeyed orders by breaking radio silence. There was no reply from the mission leader, who steadfastly kept on the wrong road. Then, far to their left, Two Hawks saw a smudge in the mist and knew that this had to be smoke from burning refineries. Other groups had gotten to the correct destination and had released their bombs.

He looked at the lead bomber and wondered if the colonel had also seen the telltale smoke. Suddenly, the lead plane turned at right angles to the course and headed toward the smoke. Two Hawks, with the others, turned his plane in a maneuver so tightly executed that formation was maintained as strictly as before. The *Hiawatha*, engines straining to push at two hundred and forty-five mph, swept at only fifty feet above the ground. Sections of high green corn, alfalfa, and sheafs of wheat in gleaming stubble flashed below him. Ahead of the group, out of the smoke, the cables and elephantine bodies of bar-

rage balloons hovered. Some were rising from
the ground, and those at a high altitude were
being pulled down to counter the low altitude
attack.

Two Hawks felt dismay, although he did not
say anything to Andrews. The planes were coming in from the wrong direction, so that all the
weeks of intensive briefing on identification of
targets was wasted. Approaching from this angle
would make everything unrecognizable.

The road to Ploesti was twenty-five miles long
and took five minutes to cover. Long before the
end of the goal was reached, the Germans
sprung the trap. Sides of haystacks exploded to
reveal 20 mm. and 37 mm. guns. The freight cars
on the railway sidings fell apart, and the 37 mm.
cannons previously hidden began to flash. The
fields themselves suddenly exposed pits containing madly firing machine guns. Ahead, 88 mm.
and 105 mm. monsters, firing pointblank with
shortfused shells, made the air a white-and-
black gauntlet. The red business for which the
attackers and defenders had prepared so long
was now begun.

The *Hiawatha* shuddered at the burst of the
great shells and then trembled as her own
gunners opened fire on the AA batteries with
their twin .50's. The air was woven with a
drunken pattern of tracers and poignettes, so
thickly intertwined it seemed that no aircraft
could get through without being struck many
times. The uproar was ear-shattering with the
bellow of 134 14-cylinder motors, explosions
from 88's fired only a few yards away, the shock

of shrapnel blasts, and the insane chatter of the two hundred and thirty machine guns in the bombers.

Roger Two Hawks kept formation and the fifty-foot height from the ground, but he also managed sidelong flicks of his gaze. To one side, on a crossroad, the muzzle of an 88 flashed, and he could see the dark blurred bulk of the projectile flying towards its rendezvous. He pushed the wheel forward and dived a little, dropping to within twenty feet of the hurtling ground. The shell went harmlessly by.

Refinery tanks exploded ahead, Himalayas of flame arose, and he eased the *Hiawatha* back to fifty feet. It shook as a shell struck the tail but kept steadily on course instead of diving as he had expected. The tail gunner called in to report that the left aileron and left rudder were gone. The ship to Two Hawks' right looked as if a huge sword had slashed at it, but it was maintaining formation. The one on the left suddenly staggered, its nose enveloped in smoke, probably from a hit by an 88. It dropped like a hammer, slid burning into the ground, rose upwards in many pieces, and then was enveloped in a huge ball of fire.

Pieces of aluminum and plexiglass, bright in the sun, rode by him. The smoke ahead parted to reveal tanks and towers shrouded in flames; a bomber, on fire, headed towards an untouched tank; another plane began to turn over, its two port engines flaming; a third, also aflame, rose to gain altitude so that its crew could try to parachute. A fourth, to the right, released its bombs,

and these plummeted down striking several tanks,
all of which exploded into flame; one took the
bomber with it. The huge ship, splitting in two,
and also cartwheeling, soared out from the
smoke and smashed into an untouched tank.
This went up with a blast that seized the
Hiawatha and hurled it upwards. Two Hawks
and Andrews fought the grip of the wind and
regained control.

There was a maze of tanks, pipes, and towers
ahead. Two Hawks pulled hard on the wheel
and sent the *Hiawatha* upwards to avoid striking
the towers. He yelled at Andrews, "Dump the
bombs!"

Andrews did not question his decision to make
the release instead of waiting for the bom-
bardier. He obeyed, and the plane rose up with
increased power as the weight of the great
bombs was gone. The end of a tower tore a hole
down the center of the *Hiawatha*'s belly. But she
flew on.

O'Brien, the topturret gunner, reported in his
thick Irish brogue, "Gazzara's gone, sir! He and
his turret just went down into the smoke."

"Tail-End Charlie's gone," said Two Hawks
to Andrews.

"Hell, I didn't even feel the hit!" Andrews
said. "You feel the shell?"

Two Hawks did not reply. He had already
sent the *Hiawatha* down to avoid the murderous
barrage above the fifty-foot level. He drove the
ship between two tanks which were so close together that only a foot or so of space existed between each wingtip and a tank. But he was

forced to bring her up again so fast she seemed to stand on her tail to get over a radio tower, the tip of which was wagging like a dog's tail from the flak bursts.

Andrews said, "God! I don't think we can make it!"

Two Hawks did not reply. He was too busy. He banked the plane to lift his right wing and so avoided collision with the top of the tower.

The ship shuddered again; an explosion deafened him. Wind howled through the cockpit. A hole had appeared in the plexiglass in front of Andrews, and he was slumped forward, his face a blur of torn flesh, sheared bone, and spurting blood.

Two Hawks turned the *Hiawatha* east but, before the maneuver was completed, the ship was struck again in several places. Somebody in the aft was screaming so loudly that he could be heard even above the cacophony outside and the air shrilling through the holes in the skin of the craft. Two Hawks pulled the *Hiawatha* up at as steep an angle as he dared. Even though he had to go through the fiery lacework ahead, he had to get altitude. With his two port engines on fire and the propeller of the outermost starboard engine blown off, he could not stay airborne much longer. Get as high as possible and then jump.

He had an odd feeling, one of dissociation. It lasted for only two seconds, then it was gone, but during that time he knew that something alien, something unearthly, had occurred. What was peculiar was the sensation that the dissociation was not just subjective; he was convinced that the ship itself and all it contained had been wrenched out of the context of normality—or of reality.

Then he forgot the feeling. The spiderweb of tracers and stars of flak parted for a moment, and he was above it and through it. The roar and crump of the exploding shells were gone; only the wind whistling through the hole in the shield could be heard.

From nowhere, a fighter plane appeared. It came so swiftly, as if out of a trapdoor in the sky, that he had no time to identify it. It flashed by like black lightning, its cannon and machine guns spitting. The two craft were so close that they could not avoid each other; the German flipped one wing and dived to get away. The ship staggered again, this time struck its death blow. The left wing was sheared off; it floated away with the right wing of the German fighter.

A moment later, Two Hawks was free of the *Hiawatha*. The ground was so close that he did not wait the specified time to pull the ripcord but did so as soon as he thought he was free of the plane. He fell without turning over, and he saw that the city of Ploesti, as he knew it, was no longer there. Instead of the suburbs that had been below him, there were dirt roads, trees, and farms. Ploesti itself was so far away that it was nothing but a pillar of smoke.

Below him, the *Hiawatha*, now a globe of flame, was falling. The German craft was turning over and over; a hundred yards away from it and a hundred feet above it, the parachute of the flier was unfolding, billowing out. Then his own chute had opened, and the shock of its grip on the air had seized him.

To his left, another man was swinging below his semi-balloon of silk. Two Hawks recognized the features of Pat O'Brien, the topturret gunner. Only two had escaped from the *Hiawatha*.

3

THE SNAP of the parachute, opening like a sail to catch the wind, made the straps cut into Two Hawks' legs. Something popped in his neck, but there was no pain. If anything, he thought briefly, the jerk and the popping of vertebrae had probably been more like an osteopathic treatment and had released tension in his body and straightened out his skeleton.

Then he was examining the terrain swelling below him, the details getting larger but the field of view getting smaller. His chute had opened only two hundred feet above the ground, so he did not have much time for study and very little time to get set for the drop.

The wind was carrying him at an estimated six miles an hour over a solid growth of trees. By the time he came to earth, he would be past it and in a field of cut wheat. Beyond the wheat field was a narrow dirt road running at right angles to him. Trees grew along the road, beyond which was a thatch-roofed cottage, a barnyard, and several small barns. Past the house was a garden surrounded by a log fence. Back of the garden, the trees grew in a dense row a quarter of a mile wide. An opening in the trees permitted him to glimpse the darkness of a shadowy creek.

He came down closer to the trees than he had thought he would because there was an unexpected lull in the wind. His feet brushed the top of a tree on the edge of the woods, then he was on the ground and rolling. Immediately, he was up on his feet and going through the required procedure for disentangling himself. The trees stopped whatever wind there might be; the chute had collapsed on the ground.

He unsnapped the straps and began to roll his chute into a ball. O'Brien was doing the same thing. Having collected the silk, Two Hawks picked it up and jogged towards O'Brien, who was running towards him.

O'Brien said excitedly, "Did you see those soldiers over to the left?"

Two Hawks shook his head. "No. Were they coming our way?"

"They were on a road at right angles to this one. Must be a main road, although it wasn't paved. They were too far away for me to get many details. But they sure looked funny."

"Funny?"

O'Brien removed his helmet. He ran a thick stubby hand, freckled and covered with pale red hairs, through his orange mop. "Yeah. They had a lot of wagons drawn by oxen. There were a couple of cars at the head, but they didn't look like any cars I ever seen. One was an armored car; reminded me of the pictures of cars like in that old book my Dad had about World War I."

O'Brien grinned toothily. "You know. The Great War. The Big War. The Real War."

Two Hawks did not comment. He had heard O'Brien talk about his father's attitude towards the present conflict.

"Let's get into the woods and bury this stuff," he said. "You get a chance to bring any survival stuff with you?"

Two Hawks led the way into the thick underbrush. O'Brien shook his head, "I was lucky to get out with my skin. Did any of the others make it?"

"I don't think so," Two Hawks said. "I didn't see anybody."

He pushed on into the woods. His legs and arms were shaking, and something inside him was trembling also. Reaction, he told himself. It was natural, and he would be all right as soon as he got a chance to get hold of himself. Only thing was, he might not get a chance. The Germans or the Rumanians would be sending out search parties now. Probably, the peasants living in the house on the other side of the road had seen them drop, although it was possible that no one had. But if they had watched the big American ship burning and falling, and had seen the two chutists, they might be phoning in now to the nearest garrison or the police post.

He had been on his hands and knees, covering his chute with dirt in a depression between two huge tree-roots. Abruptly, he straightened up, grunting as if hit in the pit of his stomach. It just occurred to him that he had not seen a single telephone wire during his drop. Nor had he seen any electrical transmission towers or wires. This was strange. The absence of these would not

have been peculiar if the plane had gone down
out in the sticks. Rumania was not a very well
developed country, compared to America. But
the *Hiawatha* must not have been more than five
miles from the refineries in Ploesti when it had
encountered the German fighter.

Moreover, where were the suburbs that had
been below him only a minute before he had experienced that twisting feeling? One moment
they were there; the next, gone. And there was
something peculiar also about the suddenness
with which the German had appeared. He could
swear that it had dropped out of the sky itself.

They finished covering up the chutes. Two
Hawks stripped off his heavy suit and at once felt
cooler. There was a slight breeze, which meant
that the wind must have sprung up again outside
the woods. O'Brien already had his suit off. He
wiped his freckled forehead and said, "It sure is
quiet, ain't it? Hell of a lot quieter than it's going
to be, huh?"

"You got a gun?"

O'Brien shook his head and pointed at the .32
automatic in the holster at Two Hawks' side.
"That isn't much of a gun," he said. "How
many bullets you got?"

"Five loaded. Twenty more in my pocket,"
Two Hawks said. He did not mention the two-
barreled derringer in the little holster on the inside of his belt in back nor the switchblade knife
in his pocket.

"Well, it's better than nothing," O'Brien said.

"Not much better." Two Hawks was silent for
a moment, conscious that O'Brien was watching

him with expectation. It was evident he was not
going to offer any suggestions. That was as it
should be, since Two Hawks was the officer. But
Two Hawks doubted that O'Brien would have
anything helpful to say even if he were asked to
do so.

It struck Two Hawks then that he knew very
little about O'Brien except that he was a steady
man during a mission, had been born in Dublin,
and had emigrated to America when he was
eleven years old. Since then, he had lived in Chicago.

Finally, O'Brien said, "I'm sure glad you're
with me. You're an Indian and you been raised
in the country. I don't know what the hell to do
in all these trees. I'm lost."

By then, Two Hawks had the map out of the
pocket of his jacket. He did not think it would
help O'Brien's morale to tell him that his officer,
the Indian, had been raised in the country and
knew the woods there, but he did not know this
country or these woods.

Two Hawks spread the map out and discussed
the best routes of escape. After a half hour, during which they took off their jackets and unbut-
toned their shirts because of the heat, they had
picked several avenues of flight. Whichever one
they took, they would travel at night and hole up
during the day.

"Let's go back to the edge of the woods so we
can watch the road," Two Hawks said. "And
the farmhouse. If we're lucky, we weren't seen.
But if some peasant has told the local con-
stabulary, they'll be searching these woods for us

soon. Maybe we better get out of here. Just in
case. In fact, we will if the coast looks clear."

They sat behind a thick bush, in the shadows
cast by a huge pine, and watched the road and
the farmhouse. A half-hour passed while they
swatted at mosquitoes and midges, handicapped
by having to strike softly so they would not make
slapping noises. They saw no human beings.
The only sound was that of the wind shushing
through the treetops, the distant barking of a
dog, and the bellowing of a bull from beyond the
farmhouse.

Two Hawks sat patiently, only moving to
speed the circulation in his legs, cramped from
sitting still. O'Brien fidgeted, coughed softly,
and started to take a pack of cigarettes out of his
shirt pocket. Two Hawks said, "No smoking.
Somebody might see the smoke. Or even smell
the tobacco."

"From this distance?" O'Brien said.

"Not likely, but we don't want to take any
chances," Two Hawks replied. For another half-
hour, he continued to watch. O'Brien groaned
softly, whistled between his teeth, shifted back
and forth, then began to rock on the base of his
spine.

"You'd make a hell of a poor hunter," Two
Hawks said.

"I ain't an Indian," O'Brien said. "I'm just a
city boy."

"We're not in the city. So try practising some
patience."

He sat for fifteen minutes more, then said,
"Let's get over to the house. Looks deserted.
Maybe we could get some food and be on our

way into the woods on the other side of the house."

"Whose getting ants in their pants now?"

Two Hawks did not reply. He rose and took the switchblade from his pocket and stuck it between the front of his belt and his belly. He walked on ahead of O'Brien, who seemed reluctant to leave the imagined safety of the woods. Before Two Hawks had gone ten yards, O'Brien had run up to him.

"Take it easy," Two Hawks said. "Act as if you had every right to be here. Anybody seeing us from a long ways off might not think anything about it if we're casual."

There was a ditch between the edge of the field and the road. They leaped across the little stream in its bottom and walked across the dirt road. The ground was wet but not muddy, as if it had rained a few days ago. There were deep ruts, however, that looked like wagon tracks. And there were tracks of cattle and piles of excrement.

"No horses." Two Hawks said to himself. O'Brien said, "What?" But Two Hawks had opened the wooden gate and was ahead of him. He noticed that the hinges were also of wood, secured to the gate by wooden pins. The grass in the yards was short, kept so by several sheep with very fat tails. These raised their heads and then shied away but uttered no baas. Two Hawks wondered if they had vocal cords; it seemed unlikely that normal sheep would have been silent during the long time he had listened in the woods.

Now he could hear the clucking of hens from

behind the house and the snort of some large
animal in the barn. The house itself was built in
the shape of an L with the long part of the letter
facing the road. There was no porch. Big thick
logs, the interstices between them chinked up by
a whitish substance, formed the structure of the
house. The roof was thatched.

On the smooth wood of the door was painted
a crude representation of an eagle. Above it was
painted a large open blue eye over which was a
black X.

Two Hawks raised the wooden latch that
locked the door and pushed in. He had no
chance to follow his plan to walk boldly in. At
that moment, a woman walked around the corner of the house. She gasped and stood still, staring at them with large brown eyes. Her brown
skin turned pale.

Two Hawks smiled at her and greeted her in
what he hoped was passable Rumanian. He had
tried to gain some fluency in the language from
a fellow officer of Rumanian descent while stationed in Tobruk, but he had not had time to
master more than a few stock phrases and the
names of some common items.

The woman looked puzzled, said something in
an unfamiliar tongue, and then walked towards
them. She had a rather pretty face, although her
shape was a little too squat and her legs too thick
for Two Hawks' taste. Her hair was blue-black,
parted in the middle and plastered down with
some sort of oil. Two braided pigtails hung down
her back. She wore a necklace of red and tightly
coiled seashells, an open-necked blouse of blue

cotton, a wide belt of leather with a copper clasp, and a skirt of bright red cotton. It reached to her ankles. Her feet were bare and smeared with dirt, mud, and what looked like chicken excrement. A real peasant, thought Two Hawks. But if she's friendly, that's all that counts.

He tried some more Rumanian, got nowhere, and switched to German. She replied in the same guttural language she had used before. Although it did not sound Slavic to him, he spoke in Bulgarian. His knowledge of this was even more limited than his Rumanian. She evidently did not understand this either. However, she spoke the third time in a different speech from her first. This resembled Slavic; he tried again with Bulgarian, then with Russian, and Hungarian. She only shrugged and repeated the phrase. After hearing several more repetitions, Two Hawks understood that she was doing as he was, that is, trying out foreign languages of which she knew very little.

But when she saw that Two Hawks did not understand a word of it, she seemed to be relieved. She even smiled at him and then fell back into the first tongue she had used.

Two Hawks frowned. There was something familiar about it. Almost, he could catch a word here and there. Almost, but not quite.

He said to O'Brien, "We'll have to try sign language. I . . ."

He stopped; obviously alarmed, she was pointing past him. He turned just in time to catch the flash of sun from the metal of a vehicle through the trees. The forest was thin by the

road, and he could see across another field, perhaps three hundred yards long, to a row of trees
at right angles to him. This must line the road,
which either turned there or was crossed by another road.

"Somebody coming in a car," he said. "We'd
better take off. We'll have to trust this girl or else
take her with us. And if we do that, we may have
to kill her. In which case, we might as well do it
now."

"No!" O'Brien said. "What the hell . . . !"

"Don't worry," Two Hawks said. "If we're
captured, we might just end up in a prison
camp. But if we kill the girl, we might get executed as common criminals."

The woman placed a hand on his wrist and
pulled him towards the corner of the house while
she gestured with the other hand and talked
swiftly. It was evident that she wanted to take
them away from the approaching vehicle or perhaps hide them.

Two Hawks shrugged and decided that there
was little else to do. If they took to the woods,
they would soon be captured. There just was not
enough forest in which to hide.

They followed the woman around the corner
and to the back of the house. She led them inside, to the kitchen. There was a huge stone fireplace with a log fire and a large iron pot on a
tripod above the fire. A savory odor rose from the
simmering contents. Two Hawks had little time
to examine the kitchen; the woman lifted a trapdoor from the middle of the bare wooden floor
and gestured to them to go on down. Two

Hawks did not like the idea of placing himself
and O'Brien in a position from which he could
not escape. But he either could do that or take to
the woods, and he had already rejected that if
something else was offered. He went down a
flight of ten steps with the Irishman close behind
him. The trapdoor was shut, and they were in
complete darkness.

4

ABOVE THEM came the sound of something scraping across the floor. The woman was hiding the trapdoor with furniture. Two Hawks took out his flashlight and examined the room. His nose had already told him that there were strips of garlic and sausage and other food hanging from the roughly hewn beams above. There was a door close by; he pushed this open and then turned off the light. Enough light came through several chinks in the log wall of the house above for him to see. The large chamber was lined with shelves on which sat dust-covered glass jars. These contained preserved fruits, vegetables, and jellies. On the floor beneath the shelves were piles of junk; stuff the owner had not been able to throw away or else considered worth repairing some day. One item that particularly caught his attention was a large wooden mask, broken off at one corner. To examine it closer, he turned on his flashlight. It portrayed the face of a demon or a monster, painted in garish scarlet, purple, and a dead-white.

"I don't like being down here, Lieutenant," O'Brien said.

He came close to Two Hawks as if he found

comfort in the proximity. Although it was cool in the dark cellar, the Irishman was sweating. He stank of fear.

Then he said, "There's something funny as hell about all this. I meant to ask you, but I thought maybe you'd think I'd cracked. Did you feel as if you were being, well, sort of twisted. I got a sickish feeling, just before that German showed up. I thought I'd been hit at first. Then things got too exciting to think about it. But when we was back in the woods, sitting there, I got the same feeling. Only not so strong. Just feeling that there was something a lot more wrong than being shot down and hiding away from the Krauts."

"Yeah, I had the same feeling, too," Two Hawks said. "But I can't explain it."

"I felt like, well, like Old Mother Earth herself had disappeared for a minute," O'Brien said.

Two Hawks did not answer. He heard the vehicle approaching down the road, then stop in front of the house. The motor sounded like an old Model T. He directed the sergeant to help him pile junk beneath one of the chinks and then stood up on the unstable platform. The hole was only a little larger than his eye, but it permitted him to see the car and the soldiers getting out of it. It was a peculiar looking vehicle, perhaps not so much peculiar as old-fashioned. He remembered O'Brien's comment, when they had first landed, about the cars at the head of the ox-drawn wagon train.

Well, Rumania was supposed to be a very backward country, even if it had the largest and

most modern oil refineries in Europe. And the
soldiers certainly were not members of the
Wehrmacht. On the other hand, their uniforms
did not resemble anything in the illustrations he
had seen during his briefings in Tobruk. The officer wore a shiny steel helmet shaped to look
like a wolf's-head. There were even two steel
ears. His knee-length jacket was a green-gray,
but the collar had a strip of greyish animal fur
sewed to it. There was an enormous gold-
braided epaulette on each shoulder and a triple
row of large shiny yellow buttons down the front
of his jacket. His trousers were skintight,
crimson, and had the head of a black bull on
each leg just above the knees. He wore a broad
leather belt with a holster. A strange-looking
pistol was in his hand; he gestured with it while
giving orders to his men in a Slavic-sounding
speech. He turned and revealed that he was also
wearing a sword in a scabbard on his left side.
Shiny black calf-length boots completed his uniform.

Several of the soldiers were within Two
Hawks' range of vision. They wore helmets that
had a neck-protecting nape, but the shape above
the head was cylindrical, like a steel plug hat.
Their black coats came to the waist in front, then
curved to make a split-tail in back that fell just
below the back of the knees. They had baggy
orange trousers and jackboots. There were
swords in the scabbards hanging from broad
belts and rifles in their hands. The rifles had revolving chambers for the cartridges, like some of
the old Western rifles.

All had full beards and long hair except for the officer. He was a clean-shaven youth, blond and pale, certainly not a dark Rumanian type. However, all Rumanians weren't dark.

The men scattered. There were shouts from above, the tread of boots on the floors, and smashing sounds. The officer walked out of sight, but Two Hawks could hear him talking slowly, as if in a language he had been taught in school. The woman answered in the same speech, which had to be her native tongue. Two Hawks found himself straining to catch its meaning, almost but not quite succeeding. Ten minutes passed. The soldiers reassembled. Frightened squawks announced the "expropriation" of hens. A certain amount of stealing was to be expected, Two Hawks thought, but by the woman's own people? No, the soldiers could not be of the same nationality as she, otherwise there would be no language difficulty. Perhaps the woman belonged to one of the minorities of Rumania. It seemed logical, but he did not believe it.

Two Hawks waited. He could hear the soldiers laughing and talking loudly to each other. The woman was silent. About twenty minutes later, the officer apparently made up his mind that his men had had enough fun. He strode out of sight, and his voice came loudly to Two Hawks. Within a minute, the soldiers were lined up before him while he gave them a short but sharp lecture. Then they got into the car and drove off down the road.

"I don't think they were looking for us," Two

Hawks said. "They must know that the house has a cellar. But if not us, what were they looking for?"

He wanted to go out immediately, but he decided that the soldiers could be coming back up the road soon or another group could pass by. Better for the woman to tell them when it was safe. The day passed slowly. There was no sound from outside for a long while except for the clucking hens and mooing cows.

It was not until dusk that they heard furniture moving above the trapdoor. The door creaked open, and light from a lamp streamed through the oblong.

Two Hawks took the automatic from O'Brien and went up first, determined to shoot anybody waiting for them. Despite all the evidences of her trustworthiness, he still was not sure that she had not changed her mind and summoned the troops. It did not seem very likely since the soldiers would not have bothered waiting around until dusk. But you never knew, and it was better to take no chances.

There was a man standing in one corner of the kitchen and munching on a piece of dried meat. Two Hawks, seeing he was unarmed except for a big knife in a scabbard sheath, put his automatic in his belt. The man looked at them stonefacedly. He was as dark as the woman and had an eagle-like nose and high cheekbones. His straight black hair was cut in the shape of a helmet—a German helmet. His black shirt and dirty brown pants looked as if they were made of some coarse and tough cotton. His boots were dirty. He stank as if he had been sweating out in the fields all day. He looked old enough to be the woman's father and probably was.

The woman offered the two bowls of stew from the kettle still simmering in the fireplace. Neither was hungry, since they had been sampling the contents of the cellar. But Two Hawks thought it would be polite to accept. It was possible these people might believe that it was a gesture of hospitality and trust to offer a stranger food. They might believe that a man who ate under their roof was automatically sacrosanct. And the reverse could be true also. A stranger who accepted their bread would not break a tabu by harming them.

He explained this to O'Brien. While he was talking, he saw the farmer's expression break loose from its stony cast. He looked puzzled and frowned as if he thought there was something familiar about the language. However, he had no more success in translating than Two Hawks had had with their language.

The two aviators sat down at a five-legged table of smoothly planed but unvarnished pine. The woman served them, then busied herself working around the kitchen. She pumped water out of a handpump over the sink. Two Hawks felt a touch of nostalgia and homesickness at this, since it reminded him of the kitchen pump in his parents' farmhouse in upper New York when he had been a little boy. The man paced back and forth, talking to the woman, then sat down with the two and began eating from a large bowl. This was of ceramic with some symbols

painted in blue on it. One of them was the
likeness of the broken mask Two Hawks had
seen in the cellar.

When he had finished eating, the farmer stood
up abruptly and gestured at them to follow him.
They stepped out through a swinging screen
door with a mosquito net made of closely woven
cotton fibers. Its interstices seemed too large to
do its job, but the threads had been soaked in oil.
Suddenly, Two Hawks recognized the odor. It
was the same oil with which the woman had
plastered her hair.

Although the oil was not sunflower seed oil, it
triggered off a sequence of thought. Some of the
older women on the reservation near his father's
farm had used sunseed oil on their hair. His
mind leaped at a conclusion which he could only
reject because it was incredible. But there was
also the undeniable fact that he now recognized
the speech of the two peasants as a form of very
peculiar Iroquoian. It was still largely unin-
telligible. But it was not Rumanian nor Hungarian nor Slavic, neither Indo-European nor Ugro-
Altaic. It was a dialect related to the tongue of
the Onondaga, the Seneca, Mohawk, and the
Cherokee. Not only in its phonology but in its
structure.

He said nothing to O'Brien but silently followed the man and girl across the now dark
barnyard. They passed an outhouse, and
O'Brien made a request which Two Hawks tried
to pass on to the farmer. The man was impatient, but he agreed. A few minutes later, they
resumed their path to the barn.

O'Brien said, "We're really in the sticks. They don't have no paper; there's a pile of clean rags and a bin for dirty ones. They must wash them afterward. Geeze, and to think we was eating from food she made. I bet she doesn't even wash her hands!"

Two Hawks shrugged. He had more important matters to think about than sanitation. The man opened the barndoors, and they stepped inside.

The two large barndoors swung shut with a creaking of wooden hinges. In the darkness, Two Hawks put his hand on O'Brien's shoulder and pushed gently to urge him several feet to the left. If the farmer planned to surprise them with an attack, he would not find his victims where he had last seen them. For about thirty seconds, there was no noise. Two Hawks crouched down on the ground, O'Brien by his side. He closed his fingers around the butt of his .32 and waited.

Then the farmer moved through the straw on the ground away from Two Hawks. Slight metallic sounds made Two Hawks wonder if blades, or maybe guns, were being taken from a hiding place. Suddenly, a match flared, and he saw the farmer applying the flame to the wick of a lantern. The wick caught fire; the farmer adjusted the flow of oil; the interior of the barn was cut into light and shadows.

The farmer, seeing them crouching on the ground, smiled briefly. His smile seemed to indicate more of approval than anything else. He gestured for them to follow him. They rose and came after the farmer and the girl. Near the back of the barn, a pig grunted from a stall. Large brown eyes looked at them in the lantern light from behind wooden bars. Cows and pigs and sheep, thought Two Hawks, but no horses. Could the Germans have taken them all? Perhaps they had requisitioned all the horses of this particular farmer. But the photographs taken by reconnaissance planes before the raid had shown plenty of horses on Rumanian farms. And then there was O'Brien's brief sight of the column on the road. Cars and oxen-drawn wagons.

The farmer stopped before a shed built onto the back wall of the barn. He knocked three times, waited several seconds, knocked three times again, waited, and rapped three more times. The door swung open; the shack was dark inside. The two natives went inside, and the farmer gestured at them to come on in. As soon as the two fliers had entered, the door was closed, and the farmer turned up the lantern flame.

There were six people crowded inside the shed. The odor of dried sweat and rancid hair oil was strong. Four men, dark, eagle-faced, dressed in heavy cloth garments, were squatting or else leaning against the wall. All wore small round caps with single red feathers projecting from the top of each cap. Two had muzzle-loading, long-barreled muskets. One had a quiverful of arrows strapped to his back and a short recurved bow of horn in his fist. Two had the same type of rifles with revolving cartridge chambers that the soldiers had carried. All had long knives in scabbards at their belts; the handle of a tomahawk was thrust into the belt of one.

"Jeeze!" O'Brien said under his breath. He may have exclaimed because he was in a trap or because of the oddity and disparity of the weapons. More probably, he was startled by the sixth person, a woman. She was dressed in the same clothes as the others, but she was obviously not one of them. Her skin was very white, where there was no dirt, and her long hair was golden. She had a pretty although tired looking face with a snub nose and a sprinkling of faint freckles. Her eyes were large and deep blue.

Two Hawks, standing closer to her, knew she had been in her clothes a long time. She stank, and her hands were dirty, the fingernails half-moons of filth. The whole group had the air and looks of fugitives. Or of guerrillas who had been a long time from their base.

The leader was a tall man with hollow cheeks and burning black eyes. His coarse black hair was cut to resemble the shape of a German helmet, and he wore heavy leather boots. His shirt was of buckskin and hung outside his belt. The backs of his fists were tattooed with the faces of monsters or demons.

He spoke at length with the farmer and his daughter. Now and then he glanced sharply at the two Americans. Two Hawks listened with his ears tuned up. Occasionally, he could make a little sense out of the rapid firecracker explosions. Yes, the phonology was familiar, and so was a word or a phrase here and there. But he would never have understood anything if he had not had a fluent knowledge of all the Iroquoian languages, including Cherokee.

Once, the leader (his name was Dzikohses) turned to speak to the blonde. He used an entirely different language then, but it was one that also seemed vaguely familiar to Two Hawks. He was sure that it belonged to the Germanic family and that it was Scandinavian. Or was it? Now he could swear it was a Low German dialect.

Abruptly, Dzikohses focused his attention on O'Brien and Two Hawks. His index finger stabbing at them, occasionally indicating items of their uniforms, he rattled off one question after another. Two Hawks understood the pitches of interrogation, but he did not understand the questions themselves. He tried to reply in Onondaga, then Seneca, then Cherokee. Dzikohses listened with his eyebrows raised in a puzzled, sometimes irritated, expression. He switched to the same speech he had used with the blonde. Finding that this was not understood, he tried another language and worked his way through three others before Two Hawks could comprehend a word. The final attempt was in some form of Greek. Unfortunately, although Two Hawks had a fair reading knowledge of Homeric and Attic Greek, he had no conversational ability. Not that this knowledge would have helped him much, since Dzikohses' Greek seemed to be only distantly related to those that Two Hawks knew.

"What the hell's he gibbering about?" O'Brien growled.

"Ask him something in Gaelic," Two Hawks said.

"You nuts?" O'Brien replied, but he rattled off several sentences.

Dzikohses frowned and then threw his hands up as if to indicate that he was thrown for a complete loss. One thing Two Hawks was sure of, however. Dzikohses was no peasant. A linguist of his ability had to have traveled much or been well educated. And he bore himself as a man used to command.

Dzikohses became impatient. He gave several orders. The men checked their weapons; the girl pulled a revolver from under her loose foxskin jacket and examined the chambers. Dzikohses held out his hand for Two Hawks' automatic. Smiling, Two Hawks shook his head. Slowly, so that he would not startle the others or cause them to misinterpret his actions, he took his automatic from his holster. He ejected the clip of bullets and then reinserted them, making sure the safety was on before he put the gun back into the holster.

The eyes of the others widened, and there was a starburst of questions from them. Dzikohses told them to shut up. The farmer extinguished the lamp, and the whole group left the shed. Within two minutes, they were in the woods. The farmer and the daughter bade them a soft goodbye, then returned under the light of the half-moon to their house.

5

ALL NIGHT, the party followed a path that left the shadows of the trees only when necessary to cross fields to get from one woods to another. They saw nothing to disturb them and, shortly before dawn, they bedded down for the day in a broad hollow deep inside the forest. Their travel had been generally northeastward.

Before falling asleep under a pile of leaves, O'Brien asked Two Hawks if they were going towards Russia. Two Hawks said he thought so.

"These people ain't Russians or Rumanians either," O'Brien said. "When I was a kid in Chicago, I lived in a neighborhood that had some Russkies and Rumanians, so I know these people ain't talking neither. What in hell are these gooks?"

"They're speaking some obscure dialect," Two Hawks said. He did not think that now was the time to spring some of his speculations on O'Brien. They would only confuse him. Besides, they were so fantastic, that he could not seriously entertain them himself.

O'Brien said, "You know something else that's funny? Back there at that farmer's, and on all the other farms we seen, there wasn't a single horse. You suppose the Krauts took them all?"

"Somebody did," Two Hawks said. "Better
get to sleep. It's going to be a long tough night
tomorrow."

It was also a long tough day. The huge mosquitoes that had made their life hell during the
night did not go away with the daylight. When
he could stand it no longer, Two Hawks awoke
Dzikohses. With sign language, he made it apparent that he would now accept the offer he had
previously turned down. He took the little bottle
Dzikohses handed him and poured out a thin
liquid. It had the vilest, most stomach-turning
odor he had ever been unfortunate enough to
whiff. But it kept the mosquitoes away. He
smeared it over his face and the back of his
hands, then burrowed under the leaves. The
leaves protected the rest of him, since the needle-
suckers of the mosquitoes seemed to go through
even his clothing. He could understand now why
the others wore such heavy garments even in the
heat of summer. It was either suffer from the
heat, which was endurable, or go mad from the
unendurable stabs of the mosquitoes.

Even shielded from the insects, he did not
sleep heavily. By noon, the woods became hot,
and what with the sweat encasing him and the
sounds of men turning over, rustling the leaves,
or eliminating nearby, he woke frequently.
Once, he opened his eyes to see the hatchet face
and black eyes of Dzikohses over him. Two
Hawks grinned at him and turned over on his
side. He was helpless; he could be disarmed or
killed at any time. But, so far, Dzikohses had

shown no inclination to treat him as a possible
enemy. Plainly, he was puzzled by everything
about the two strangers. No more puzzled by us
than I am about him, Two Hawks thought, and
slid back into his bumpy sleep.

At dusk, they ate dried beef and hard black
bread and drank from canteens filled from a
nearby creek. The men then all faced east and
took from their leather provision-packs strings of
beads and various carved wooden images. They
put the strings of beads around their necks and
began telling them with the left hands while they
held the wooden images up above their heads in
their right hands. Their voices murmured what
seemed to be chants, although the chants were
not all the same. Two Hawks was startled by the
image held by the man nearest him. It was the
head of a mammoth, its proboscis curled aloft as
if trumpeting, its long tusks curving upward, its
eyes little gems that glared red.

The men were standing up and facing east.
The blonde squatted, facing westwards. She,
too, told beads, but did it with her right hand.
She had taken a silver stickpin from her bag and
driven it into the earth before her. Now, regard-
ing the image fixedly, her lips moved, and only
by getting very close to her could Two Hawks
distinguish the words of her slow measured
speech. Now he heard a language none had
spoken before. It sounded Semitic to him, and he
could have sworn that he heard more than once
words similar to the Hebrew "Ba'al" and
"Adoni." The silver image was a symbolic representation of a tree from which a man hung, the

rope around his neck tied with nine knots.

It was all very strange. O'Brien shivered and swore, crossed himself, and said a rapid Paternoster in a very low voice. Then he said, "Lieutenant, what kind of heathens have we fallen among?"

"I wish I knew," Two Hawks replied. "Anyway, let's not worry about their religion. If they get us to neutral territory, or to Russia, they've done their jobs."

The ceremonies took about three minutes. The beads and idols (if they were idols) were put away, the march was resumed. Not until midnight did they stop. Two men slipped into a village only a hundred yards away. They returned in fifteen minutes with more dried strips of beef, black bread, and six bottles of a very sour wine. All took a swig from the bottles, and then the fast walking resumed. At dawn, as they bedded down, they heard the faroff boom of big cannon. Sometime late in the afternoon, Two Hawks was awakened by O'Brien. The Irishman pointed upwards through a break in the trees, and Two Hawks saw a huge silvery sausage shape passing at about a thousand feet overhead.

"That sure as hell looks like one of them dirigibles I read about when I was a kid," O'Brien said. "I didn't know the Krauts still had 'em."

"They don't," Two Hawks said.

"Yeah? How do you account for that, then? The Russians use 'em?"

"Maybe," Two Hawks said. "They got a lot of obsolete equipment."

He did not believe that the airship was Russian or German. But he might as well keep O'Brien from panicking now. Once the full truth was known, of course, O'Brien would have to go through an inevitable terror. Two Hawks hoped he could take it. He was having enough trouble quelling his own panic.

He sat up, yawned, stretched, and pretended an indifference he did not feel. The girl was sleeping near him; her lips were slightly open. Despite the dirt and the mosquito-repelling grease on her face, she looked cute. Like a pre-adolescent child who had been too tired to wash her face before going to bed. By now he knew her name, Huskarle Ilmika Thorrsstein. Huskarle, however, might be her title, corresponding to Lady. She was treated with great respect by the others.

She did not sleep very long, however. Dzikohses woke them all up, and they began walking in the daylight now. Apparently, he felt that they were far enough from the enemy to venture out under the sun. They saw very few farms after that, and the going became rougher. For several days the hills continued to get larger and the woods thicker. Then they were in the mountains. Two Hawks consulted his map. According to it, they should not yet be in the Carpathians. But they were here, and there was no use denying the reality of the mountains. Moreover, they seemed to him to be higher than the map indicated.

Their beef and bread and wine ran out. For a whole day, they walked along the lower slopes of

the mountains without food. The next day,
Ka'hnya, the bowman, slipped away into the
forest while the others took a nap beneath the
pines or birches. It was colder up here, and the
nights were chilly enough to justify the heavy
clothing they wore. Even so, the mosquitoes
flourished during the day and part of the night.
Somehow, they managed to find and to pene-
trate thin spots in the uniforms of Two Hawks
and O'Brien, who could only escape by burying
themselves under leaves.

Two hours later, Ka'hnya reappeared. He was
a big man, but he was staggering under the
weight of the half-grown boar on his shoulders.
He smiled at the congratulations and rested
while the others busied themselves butchering
the giant porker. Two Hawks helped them, since
he had had experience on his father's farm in
such matters. He knew then that Dzikohses
might consider their location safe enough for
traveling in daylight, but he was not so confident
that he wanted to risk firing a gun. Perhaps the
bows and arrows had been brought along for just
such safety measures. He did not think so. He
got the impression from their odd assortment of
weapons that these people had to use whatever
was on hand. The two rifles with revolving
chambers had probably been taken from dead
enemies.

The pig was soon cooking over a number of
small and relatively smokeless fires. Two Hawks
ate hungrily and felt the strength flow back into
him. The meat was strong and rank and only
half-cooked, but he had no trouble wolfing it

down. Ilmika Thorrsstein, however, seemed to
have a delicate stomach. She refused the large
chunk offered her. She smiled when she rejected
it, but when she turned her face away and
thought herself unseen, she could not repress a
grimace of disgust. Then, as she watched the
others eat, she seemed to have a change of mind
—or of appetite. She took a small book from her
bag and leafed through it. Two Hawks, looking
over her shoulder, saw what appeared to be a
calendar. It was not marked with Arabic numerals, however, but with numerals derived from the
Greek alphabet. There were several that resembled runic symbols.

She asked Dzikohses a question. He came over
and pointed at the second square in a row of sev-
en figures. So, Two Hawks thought, they had a
seven-day week. Ilmika smiled at this and said
something to Dzikohses. He handed her the
same piece he had offered before, and this time
she ate.

Two Hawks could only deduce from this that
pork was tabu for her except on certain days of
the week.

"Curiouser amd curiouser," he muttered.

O'Brien said, "What?"

Two Hawks did not answer. To try to explain
the whole business would only confuse and perhaps frighten O'Brien. The sergeant looked too
happy at the moment for Two Hawks to upset
him further. Poor O'Brien, unused to such long
hard hikes and so little food, had been ready to
keel over. Now he was even humming.

O'Brien patted his stomach, belched, and

said, "Man, I feel great! If only I could get a week's sleep now, I'd be a new man; I could lick my weight in Kilkenny cats."

Several days later, they were still climbing along the lower parts of the mountains. Occasionally, they went higher to traverse a pass which would lead them down again. And then they were suddenly faced with a situation in which they had to use their firearms, noise or no noise. They had come down a mountain into a valley about six miles wide and twelve long. Part of the valley was wooded; the rest was a grassy plain and a marsh. Duck honks came from the marsh; a fox chased a hare not twenty feet in front of them. A big brown bear stood at the top of a small hill and watched them for a while before it turned and went back down the other side of the hill. The party crossed a band of trees splitting the valley in half and began to go across the wide plain. At that moment, they heard a loud bellow to their right. They whirled, their guns ready, and saw the great bull trotting towards them.

O'Brien, standing by Two Hawks, said, "Jesus, what a monster!"

The bull stood at least seven feet high at the shoulder; it was a glossy dark brown and had horns with a spread of at least ten feet.

"An aurochs!" Two Hawks said.

He gripped his gun with the eery feeling that it was the only solid thing in the universe. He was not so frightened by the enormousness of the beast itself, since there was enough firepower in the group to knock down even this huge

creature. What frightened him was that he felt as
if he had been thrust back into the dawn of mankind. This was the kind of creature that early
man had faced. Then he reassured himself that
this was also a creature that man had wiped off
the earth. Moreover, it, or something like it, was
not so ancient after all. It had survived, though
not in so great a form, up to and during World
War I in the forests of Germany and Poland.

The aurochs bellowed and trotted towards
them. Several times, it halted, threw up its head,
and sniffed the air. Its black eyes gleamed in the
sunlight, but whether it was premeditated
murder or curiosity that shone there was not yet
apparent. Fifty yards behind him, several cows
thrust their horned heads from behind bushes.
Each of these looked large enough to take care of
herself quite well, but they may have been hanging back to guard their calves. Two Hawks did
not see any young and doubted that this was
calving season. It did not matter whether or not
the bull was protecting calves. His territory was
being challenged, and he was intent on making
sure that they intruded no longer.

Dzikohses said something to the men, then
stepped out from them and shouted. The bull
slowed down, stopped, and glared about him.
Dzikohses shouted again. The aurochs wheeled
and raced away and Two Hawks breathed easier. Then, as if driven by whim or as if he had
caught a new scent which steered him around to
face them again, he stopped and wheeled. The
great head lowered; a huge hoof pawed the
ground. Another vast bellow, and the bull was

charging toward them. The ground trembled under the impact of hooves bearing a thousand pounds or more.

Dzikohses shouted more orders. His men spread out so that they could shoot at an angle at the aurochs and hit him in the body. The aurochs was not confused by this maneuver; he had evidently chosen the two Americans and Ilmika as his target. They had been standing in the center of the group and when the others went to left and right, they had stayed in the same spot as when they first saw the bull.

Two Hawks glanced at O'Brien and Ilmika and saw that they were not about to break and run. Ilmika was holding her revolver, its barrel resting on her left arm for steadiness. O'Brien did not have a weapon, but he had taken a position just to the right of Two Hawks. He was poised to run.

"I'll go one way; you go the other," he said. "Maybe it won't know which one to take after."

By then the two muzzle-loaders and the rifles were firing. Ka'hnya loosed an arrow; it plunged into the right side of the beast just behind its shoulder. This did not stop it or even make it stagger. Though it shook at the impact of bullets and arrow, it kept on with unchecked speed. Ilmika began firing with no apparent effect. If her .40 caliber bullets struck the bull, they were hitting the thick bar of bone between the horns or glancing off the massive and tough neck muscles. Two Hawks told her to quit wasting her ammunition, but she did not even glance at him. Coolly, she kept on firing.

Then another arrow plunged into the bull, this time, whether by accident or design, into his right leg. He fell to one side and skidded on the grass, his inertia making him slide right up to Two Hawks feet. Two Hawks looked down at the great head and the enormous black eye glaring at him. The long eyelashes reminded him of a girl he had known in Syracuse—later he wondered why that irrelevant thought occurred to him in such a dangerous situation. Then he stepped up to put a bullet from the .32 through the eye. The other men closed in and shot into the body. It shuddered under the impact; by now blood was spurting from at least a dozen wounds. Nevertheless, so driving was its vitality, it started to rise again. Despite the crippling arrow in its leg, it managed to get onto all four legs.

Two Hawks placed the muzzle of his automatic only an inch from the eye—he had to raise the barrel upwards—and fired. The eye exploded and left an empty socket. In the midst of a roar, the aurochs collapsed. He tried again to get up, then fell back on his side, gave a feeble bellow, and died.

Only then did Two Hawks start shaking. He thought he was going to get sick but the urge to upchuck died away and he was not forced to disgrace himself.

Dzikohses made sure that the bull was dead by cutting its throat. He arose with bloody knife and forgot about the bull for the time being. He looked all around the valley, worried that the sounds of the guns might bring unwelcome com-

pany. Two Hawks wanted to ask him whom he
might expect to find in this remote place but decided against it. He not only was not sure that he
would be understood; he thought it might be to
his advantage if their captors thought they could
speak freely in his presence. Actually, they were
not too self-deluded. He comprehended only
about one-sixteenth of what they said. But he
was learning.

The men cut out pieces of meat from the
flanks and rump. Ka'hnya started to slice away
with the intention of getting to the heart.
Dzikohses stopped him. The two argued for a
moment, then Ka'hnya sullenly obeyed. From
what he understood of the rapid conversation,
Two Hawks deduced that Ka'hnya wanted the
heart for more than its meat. Although he did
not say so, he implied that they would all eat of
the heart and so ingest the valor of the bull.
Dzikohses would have none of this. He wanted to
get across the plain and into the woods as swiftly
as possible.

They traveled by wolf-trot: a hundred paces of
fast trotting, a hundred of walking. They ate the
miles up but at a price. By the time they reached
the other end of the valley, where the woods and
the mountain began, they were breathing heavily and soaked with sweat. Dzikohses was un-
merciful. He began to climb at once. The rest of
the party looked at each other and wondered if
pleading for a rest would do any good or if it
would be better to save their breath. Two Hawks
grinned. He had his second wind by now and
was determined to prove that he was as good a
man as Dzikohses.

They had scrambled up the steep slope not more than fifty yards, going part of the way by pulling themselves up on the bushes, when a gun exploded nearby. Ka'hnya screamed and lost his hold and plunged backwards down the mountain. His head rammed into the base of a bush and stopped his descent. The rest of the party threw themselves down on the earth and looked around, but they saw nothing.

Then a gun barked again, and a bullet whistled through the leaves just over Two Hawks' head. He happened to be looking in the direction from which the fire came and saw the man lean halfway out from behind an oak. He did not try to answer the fire, since the shooter had popped back behind the tree. Moreover, at fifty yards, the automatic was too inaccurate. He might as well save his bullets.

Dzikohses called to them and began to worm towards the oaks just above him and to his left. The others followed him. Several times, guns exploded and bullets screamed above them or dug into the earth near them. By the sound, Two Hawks judged that their enemies were using muzzle-loaders. If so, they could not be too accurate at this range; Ka'hnya had been hit only because he was considerably exposed and motionless at the moment. Two Hawks decided to take a chance before the enemy could move in closer for a better shot. He jumped up and ran zigzag towards the oaks. No shots had come from that quarter. Either there were no hostiles there or else they were holding their fire. If the latter were true, then he was committing suicide, but there was only one way to find out.

Behind him and on both sides, shouts arose and guns boomed again. Bullets—or balls—ripped the air around him. He reached the oak with no near misses, although the missiles had come close enough to satisfy him. He waited, scanning the woods around him for a sight of anyone creeping close. He heard the thud of feet on the earth, and then Dzikohses was flying through the air and was down beside him. Two Hawks gestured at the big limbs above them. Dzikohses smiled, handed the rifle to Two Hawks and began climbing. On the lowest branch, he reached down and took the weapon back. He resumed climbing. Two Hawks followed him and stopped just below Dzikohses. Dzikohses was silent for a minute, then exclaimed with satisfaction. He aimed carefully, fired, and a man fell down from behind a tree. A moment later, he shot again. This time, a man began screaming. A third left the shelter of a bush to run crouching to the aid of the wounded man. Skehnaske', who probably was called Fox because of his bushy reddish hair, fired, and the running man spun around and then fell to the ground. He made the mistake of trying to get up; this time the entire party fired, and he was hurled backward by the force of several bullets.

There was silence for a while. Two Hawks saw some men dodge from one tree to another, apparently to meet behind a particularly large oak. Probably for a conference, he thought. Dzikohses did not try to shoot at them. He was waiting until he spotted somebody motionless and exposed.

He called to the others, and one by one they rose up and ran in a jagged path towards the oak. No shots were evoked by their flight. From his branch, Dzikohses gave directions to his men and also to the Huskarle Ilmika. They spread out on both sides of the oak and began working their way back down towards the mountain. Dzikohses stayed in the oak to send an occasional shot towards the tree that sheltered the enemy. Two Hawks followed Skehnaske'. O'Brien went with the men on the left. For a while, Ilmika was with Skehnaske' and Two Hawks, then she crawled off by herself.

Suddenly, a flurry of shots broke loose from the direction of the tree which sheltered the enemy. Dzikohses answered, firing as rapidly as possible. Two Hawks guessed that the hostiles had abandoned the oak and were spreading out through the woods for an ambush. He thought of how ironic it would be if he were killed in this little skirmish in an isolated valley, not knowing for whom he was fighting. For that matter, he was not sure whom he was fighting with. Or why.

Ilmika's voice cried out to their right, succeeded by three shots. Two came from muzzle-loaders; one, from a revolver. Skehnaske' and Two Hawks went towards the place from which the shots had come, but they proceeded cautiously, taking advantage of every cover and pausing to reconnoiter. Presently, they came upon a dead man, on his back, staring upward, a hole torn out of his throat and blood over his throat and chest. He wore a red handkerchief

around his head, his ears held large round silver
rings, his long-sleeved shirt had once been white.
A purple cummerbund was around his waist and
in it was stuck a single-shot breech-loading
pistol and a long slim dagger. His trousers were
baggy and knee-length, and his coarse woolen
stockings were black with scarlet clockwork. His
shoes were of a shiny black leather with huge
silver buckles.

The dead man's skin was as dark as that of a
Hindu's. He looked more like a gypsy than anything else.

The two separated and resumed their careful
search. Although there were no signs of struggle,
Two Hawks deduced that the dead man's com-
rades had taken Ilmika prisoner. A moment later, he saw the flash of a white shirt and then
Ilmika, her hands tied behind her, being shoved
ahead by one of her captors. The other, holding
a six-shooter rifle, was a few paces behind, alert
for pursuers.

Two Hawks waited until they disappeared behind a rise and then he circled to make sure he
did not crawl into an ambush. He heard faint
cries, a slap, and the deep mutter of men.

Something flashed to his left. He hugged the
ground, waited, and lifted his head cautiously.
He saw Skehnaske' signalling to him and signalled back. Then the red-haired man crawled
out of sight. Two Hawks wriggled like a snake
toward his targets, losing sight of them for a
minute when he went along a narrow trough
formed by rainwater in the dirt. The rifle of
Skehnaske' cracked; Two Hawks lifted his head

to see the guard staggering backward but still holding on to his rifle. Two Hawks jumped up and shot at him within a range of twenty yards. Then he was running forward, only to hurl himself down behind a bush as the second man stood up briefly. The enemy fired at Two Hawks with a rifle, and his bullet thudded into the dirt only an inch from his face. Two Hawks rolled away towards a larger bush.

Skehnaske' kept on firing, and the enemy did not stick his head out again. Skehnaske' was shouting something at Two Hawks, who did not understand his words. Nevertheless, he got their meaning. He was up on his feet and rushed at the hillock while Skehnaske' resumed his covering fire. He tried to make as little sound as possible, but the man must have heard the slap of his shoes against the dirt. His black-handkerchiefed head appeared and then the barrel of his rifle. He was visible to Two Hawks but not to Skehnaske'. However, he was afraid to raise his head too high, and it was this that made his shooting awkward. He missed with the first bullet, swung the barrel around to correct, and fired again.

Two Hawks heard the bullet scream by. He was not surprised that he had not been hit, since he had seen Ilmika's feet kick out and slam into the man's ribs. The man froze for a second, unable to make up his mind to shoot at Two Hawks again or kill Ilmika. Two Hawks stopped and shot twice, both bullets hitting the man. One entered his right temple; the other struck him somewhere in the body. He collapsed, seeming to shrink like a balloon with a pinprick in it.

Ilmika wept and talked hysterically while Two Hawks untied her hands. They returned to the group, which had disposed of the others. Some of the enemy had gotten away; two were dead; one was taken alive with a bullet in his left thigh and another in his right shoulder. He squatted on the ground, his eyes dull with pain.

Dzikohses asked him some questions; the man spat at him. Dzikohses put the muzzle of his rifle against the man's temple and repeated the question. Again, the man spat. The rifle cracked. His head half-blown off, the man crashed into the ground.

Another wounded prisoner was brought in by Skehnaske'. Dzikohses was about to shoot him, too, then changed his mind. The prisoner was stripped of his clothes, his hands tied behind him, and his ankles bound together. He was hoisted upside down by a rope over a branch until his head was several feet off the ground. Dzikohses took the prisoner's own long thin dagger and cut off both ears. The man fainted. The party left him hanging there. Some time later, they heard him screaming, then silence came again. He must have passed out once more. A second time, they heard him screaming just as they passed over a shoulder of the mountain. After that, they heard him no more.

O'Brien and Two Hawks were both pale, but not from exertion. O'Brien said, "Mary preserve us! These gooks play rough!"

Two Hawks was watching Lady Ilmika Thorrsstein. She seemed to have fully recovered. In fact, the incident of the tortured man had restored her color, and she seemed to have derived enjoyment from his punishment. He shuddered. Certainly, the gypsies, or whatever they were, would have done the same or worse to them if they had won. Yet he could never take vengeance in such a fashion. He would have had no compunction about shooting one in cold blood. But this! No, he might be an Iroquois Indian, but he was too civilized.

After that, he found that the blonde was not as aloof as she had been. She was grateful for his having rescued her, although the credit was only partly his. She talked with him whenever they had a chance and began to teach him her language. Now, though he wanted to learn her speech, he was the one who was constrained. It was a long time before he could forget the look on her face as she saw Dzikohses cut off the captive's ears.

6

TWO WEEKS LATER, they came down out of the mountains. They were in very flat country and among farms. They were also near the enemy, the Perkunishans, as Ilmika called them. They resumed travel by night. Forty-eight hours later, they took refuge for the day in a huge house which had been the scene of a skirmish. Six bodies lay at various positions and distances from the house, and there were even more inside. The guerrillas had taken the house, but all had died in hand-to-hand fighting along with the Perkunishan soldiers holding it. No one was left to bury the dead, now overdue to be put into the earth. The party dragged the corpses out into a nearby copse of elms and put them in two shallow graves. The muzzle-loaders were abandoned for the more modern six-shooters.

Two Hawks wondered why Dzikohses had not chosen a more hidden place for their rest. He listened to Dzikohses talk to some of his men—he was understanding at least half of the speech by now—and decided that this was a trysting place. Scouts came back to report that there were no hostiles in the neighborhood. However, cannon made thunder some miles away.

Two Hawks examined a big room which must
have been the study of the master of the mansion. There were books on the shelves and on the
floor, some destroyed by a bomb. A huge globe of
Earth lay on the floor by the table from which it
had been hurled by the explosion. He replaced it
upright on the table. His heart beating hard, he
verified his suspicions and cleared up some of the
mysteries.

What he saw was not at all entirely unexpected. He'd guessed part of the truth. He had
had all the evidence he needed to know that he
couldn't be in his own universe. At first he'd
thought that perhaps he'd been shifted somehow
to some other area of his Earth. Roger was too
well educated to persist in this theory. After
seeing the strangely clad soldiers through the
hole in that peasant's cellar, he'd known that he
wasn't on *his* Earth. Had he been shunted in
some unexplainable manner to another planet in
his own universe? It was highly improbable. It
was, or so it seemed to him, impossible. Whatever course evolution took on those non-Earths it
wouldn't be exactly the same as on Earth in all
creatures. Nor would the continents be the same
or similar shapes. Also, the languages he had
heard were too like some on his Earth. No. Not
possible. Yet this globe bore letters that were
Greek. Most were, anyway. The names would be
Hotinohsinoh. To assume so was reasonable.

There on the globe were Eurasia, Africa, and
Australia, their shapes not quite those he was
familiar with. Moreover, the lines of latitude indicated that the three landmasses were about

four hundred miles further south than on the maps he knew.

This was alien enough. What disturbed him most was India.

It had the same triangular shape.

But it was separated by an estimated 800 miles of sea from the continent of Asia.

Southwest of it was Ceylon, no longer an island but connected to India by a thin strip of land.

He muttered, "My God! His theory was right after all! There *is* such a thing as continental drift!"

O'Brien said, "What?"

Two Hawks didn't answer.

He bent down to study the relief contours.

The Iranian plateau with its bordering range of mountains, the Kunlun mountains, the Himalayas, and the Tibetan plateau were missing. There were some mountain ranges, but most of the area was relatively flat and low, if he interpreted the relief indications correctly.

He muttered again, "If India hasn't collided yet with Asia, hasn't become part of it, then . . ."

Dreading what he would see, yet having known for some time what the reality had to be, he turned the sphere westward. The Atlantic Ocean slowly spun by.

He sucked in his breath, aware that O'Brien, his jaw hanging down, was standing by him.

"What the hell?" O'Brien said, and then, "Mary, Mother of Christ!"

There was Hawaii. And there was a chain of islands starting where Alaska should be, running

southeastward gently and ending in a large island where the plateau of Mexico should be. The
Rockies and the Sierras. Rather, their islanded
peaks. A few dots in the east were the tops of the
Alleghanies. Everywhere else, water.

Central America was all blue. South America
was another chain of islands, larger than those in
the northern hemisphere, the Andes.

Two Hawks, sweating more than the heat was
responsible for, studied the western hemisphere
for a few minutes. Then he spun the globe
around to the eastern hemisphere. He bent over
to read, or to try to read, the names printed
thereon. There was a familiar enough alpha and
beta, but the gamma faced to the left. And the
digamma and koppa were still being used.
Moreover, there were no capitals. Rather, all the
letters were capitals.

O'Brien groaned and said, "I'm going to
throw up. I knew there was something wrong,
but I couldn't put my finger on it. Where in hell
are we?"

"Throwing up might make you feel better,"
Two Hawks said. "Afterwards, you'll have to
face the truth just the same."

"Which is?"

"You ever read much science-fiction?"

"Naw. That goofy stuff."

"Better for you if you had. You might have a
more flexible mind. This situation might not be
so hard for you to grasp. Or to accept. Because,
like it or not, you have to accept. Or go crazy."

"I'm going crazy. Oh, my God, where's America? Where's Chicago?"

His voice was shrill. The others in the room stopped talking to look curiously at him.

"Ever heard of parallel universes?" Two Hawks said. "I know you have because I've seen you read comic books that had just such a concept."

O'Brien looked relieved. "Yeah, I did. Only . . . hell, you telling me we're in a parallel universe? A universe that's at right angles to ours?"

Two Hawks nodded and smiled at O'Brien's "right angles." This term was no explanation, only a method of description to make the reader better comprehend. Rather, make him think he was comprehending the incomprehensible. But if the term helped O'Brien get an anchor on reality, allayed his panic, he could keep it. Any anchor was better than none.

O'Brien said, "Then that funny feeling we got back in the *Hiawatha* . . . ? That was because we were going through a . . . kind of a . . . gate?"

"You can call it a gate. The point is, the science-fiction fantasy has become for us a reality. There are parallel universes. I'd like to deny it just as much as you. But there's no denying this. Somehow, we've passed into another universe. We're on Earth, but not the one we knew."

O'Brien turned the globe to the western hemisphere. "And this Earth is one where North and South America are under water?"

He shivered and then crossed himself.

Two Hawks said, "I've known for some time that things that couldn't be nevertheless were.

Those people"—he indicated the others in the room—"speak a language that is definitely Iroquoian."

He pointed at the blonde, Ilmika. "And her speech, believe it or not, is English. A species of English, anyway. She calls it *Ingwinetalu* or *Blodland spraech.*"

"You must be kidding? I thought she was a Swede or maybe a Dutchman. English?"

Two Hawks spun the globe back to the eastern hemisphere.

"On our Earth, the ancestors of the Amerind, the so-called American Indian, migrated in prehistoric times from Siberia to North America and on to South America. Group after group came over and may have taken over ten thousand years to do it. The Eskimo, the most Mongolian of what was essentially a Caucasian-Mongolian mixture, was the last to arrive.

"But on this Earth, the Amerind had no Americas to migrate to. So he turned inwards and became a force to reckon with in the Old World. That is, Asia and Europe."

He ran his finger over the map of Europe and stopped at the peninsula of Italy. The mauve color which overlay it extended through part of northern Yugoslavia and also covered Sicily. He read aloud the large title which evidently applied to the whole area.

"Akhaivia! Achaea? If Achaea, then the ancient Greeks may have come down, for some reason, into the peninsula of what we call Italy in our world, instead of into the Hellenic peninsula!"

He looked at Greece. It was titled *Hatti*.

"Hittites?" he said aloud. "On our Earth, they conquered a part of Asia Minor, flourished for a while, contemporary with the Mycenaean Greeks, and then disappeared. What happened here? They invaded a country which the Greeks had bypassed, being shunted for some reason to the west. And the Hittites conquered the Pelasgians and gave their name to our Hellas?"

He continued talking aloud, partly to help O'Brien understand what had happened.

"I don't know the details and will have to guess at part of the outline. But I'll bet that the Iroquoians, and maybe other Amerind tribes, invaded eastern Europe and settled down. If they did so at an early date, they may have altered the course of the Indo-European migrations from the Motherland somewhere in Germany or Poland. The invasions resulted in bumping the various people—the Hittites, Hellenes, Italics, Germanics, and so forth—one country westward. Or something like that.

"Hmm! Wonder what happened to the Italics: the Sabines, Voluscans, Samnites, and the Latins? Were they bumped westwards? Or had they settled Italy before the Achaeans, only to be conquered and eventually absorbed by them?"

He placed his finger on a light green area covering approximately the area of Rumania and southern Russia. Hotinohsonih? House builders? Iroquoia? Sure! And that big cross there, 'Estokwa, would be our Earth's Odessa. Probably the capital of Hotinosonih. 'Estokwa? Paddle? It could be, though I don't know why a

place would be named after a spatula or ladle.
But then I don't know its history.

"I think we're headed for 'Estokwa, probably
because the blonde, Ilmika Thorrsstein, is an
important person. I've gathered from their conversation that her father was the Blodland ambassador to the nation of Dakota, our Hungary.
Dakota? Could it be that Dakota is Siouian-
speaking?"

He grinned and laughed and said to O'Brien,
"Doesn't that make you feel a little more at
home to know there's a state of Dakota here?"

He pointed at a river which ran from the north
southward towards 'Estokwa and into the Black
Sea. "This'll make you feel even more like home.
Our Dnester is their 'Ohiyo', that is, 'a beautiful
river'. And if I remember correctly, our Ohio
River comes fron an Iroquois word meaning
beautiful. How's that strike you, O'Brien? Dakota and Ohio! Maybe things aren't so bad after
all."

O'Brien smiled faintly and said, "Thanks for
trying to cheer me up, Lieutenant. But it's going
to take more than a couple of familiar names to
get me over this shock. I still don't believe it."

Two Hawks said, "You might as well get with
it."

He pointed at a pale red area which covered
approximately the Austria, Germany, Denmark,
Poland, Czechoslovakia, and Switzerland of his
world.

"Perkunisha. If that Greek "s" crossed with a
slanting bar indicates the "sh", and I'm sure it
does. Perkunisha. It sounds as if the word is re-

lated to or comes from the Lithuanian Perkunis. He was the chief god of the pagan Lithuanians and maybe of the Old Prussians. They spoke closely related languages of the Baltic family. Perkunis meant "thunder", just as the Norse Thor and the Old English Thonar or Thunor did. But the word has some sort of affinity with Thor's mother, Fiörgyn."

"Yeah?" O'Brien said. "I don't want no lectures, professor."

"Sorry. I find such items very interesting. Anyway, I've heard Dzikohses refer to the enemy as Pozosha. That would be his pronunciation of Borussia. The Old Prussians were called Borussians. Berlin, by the way, is an Old Prussian name. When the Germans conquered the Old Prussians, or Borussians, they used the native name for the place."

He looked at the rest of the map of Europe. The large letters naming it certainly didn't form the word "Europe" or anything like it. This was to be expected. "Europe" had come from a Greek myth. The great god Zeus had fallen in love with Europa, daughter of the Phoenician king, Agenor. Zeus changed himself into a bull and mingled with Agenor's herd. Europa, charmed by the beauty and gentleness of the disguised god, had mounted his back. Zeus had then rushed into the sea and swum with her on his back to Crete. Crete, though an island in the eastern Mediterranean, was considered to be part of the western world. And so, from Europa had come Europe, the name for the western world.

But on this Earth, there probably wouldn't be such a story. So, this world's Europe was called something else.

Khephdakh.

A Semitic name? Egyptian?

The upper third of the Scandinavian peninsula and most of Scotland and the upper fourth of Ireland were in white and marked with the black outline of a polar bear. That must mean that these areas were covered with snow and ice or perhaps with glaciers. Iceland and Greenland were similarly marked.

He whistled softly and half-turned the globe.

Those chains of little arrows surely indicated the major oceanic currents. The Japanese current, however, instead of becoming the California current, flowed eastwards undiverted by the continental mass of North America. It moved over the sunken land and across the Atlantic. Actually, in this world, there would be no separate designation for the ocean; it would just be part of the Pacific or whatever it was called. Yes. Just as he'd anticipated. *Okevanos*. If that double digamma stood for "v".

The Japanese current finally was turned southward by the shores of France and Portugal and became an equatorial current flowing westwards towards Asia.

There was no Gulf Stream, the great flow which, moving northeast out from the Gulf of Mexico, warmed northwest Europe and kept it from becoming a subarctic land. However, Europe was about four hundred miles more to the south. And the Japanese current might raise the average temperature of northern Europe.

He whistled softly again. Here was something even more significant in the history of this world's Europe than the presence of the Amerindian.

For one thing, Europe would be colder.

For another, Europe might be deeper into the Ice Age. Which meant that there should be more precipitation both in Europe and North Africa. The Sahara Desert would not be so arid and perhaps was not a desert at all. It was possible that it was as fertile as it had been in, say, 8000 B.C. This would mean that the North African states, so little populated and so politically and economically weak in his world, would be very powerful nations here. And that would have made a great difference in the history of this world.

He said, "It's hot here now. But I'll bet it'll be a hell of a long cold winter. Still, there is the difference in latitude to consider."

Two Hawks went to the shelves and looked through several books. He found an atlas with much more geographic and national details than on the globe. Moreover, the accompanying text and the names on the maps were bilingual, Greek and Iroquoian. The Greek was difficult for him, since it varied from the Homeric and Attic and also seemed to have loanwords from languages totally unknown to him. He looked for and found a bilingual dictionary, and this was some small help for him.

"O'Brien! You wondered why we saw no horses. The reason is that there just aren't any. What's more, we're not going to find any camels.

Nor tobacco, tomatoes, turkeys, peanuts, quinine, cranberries, squash, maize or Indian corn, I could go on. No American robins or bald eagles. No jaguars, ocelots, margays, tapirs, prehensile-tailed monkeys.

"But two of the most important creatures missing, in fact, the most important, are the horse and the camel. Both originated on the New World, then spread to the Old World, only to become extinct in their native land. Well, to be exact, the dromedary and the bactrian camel became extinct in the Americas. The llama, alpaca, and guanaco, which were members of the camel family, survived in South America.

"Anyway, now you know why nobody knew what you wanted when you asked for cigarettes."

"Hey!" O'Brien said. "Rubber, too! Rubber did come from South America, didn't it? Sure it did! That's why those armored cars were travelling on wooden iron-rimmed wheels. No rubber!"

"You won't have any chocolate bars or cocoa, either."

"What a hell of a world!"

Two Hawks didn't mention another item missing. It would depress O'Brien even more, especially since he was an Irishman.

Two Hawks said, "Then there's India, far more isolated from Asia than Australia since there are no islands between it and the continent. It doesn't seem likely that it would've been inhabited by human beings until fairly recent times. Does that mean that the Negro race is nonexistent in this world?"

O'Brien said, "What makes you say that?"

"Nobody knows where the Negro originated, though there have been some guesses. There's a theory, based on a few skulls found in southern India, that the race may have originated there in the Old Stone Age. Then the Negroes spread out to New Guinea and its nearby areas and also to Africa. The two branches are a slightly different variety of Negro, you know. You didn't? Anyway, between the two areas was, in very ancient times, a great gap, a distance of many thousands of miles. In between the two groups were Caucasians and Mongolians. Oh, there were Negritos, the dwarf variety, in the Malayan areas. But these had hidden in the jungles from their bigger and more numerical enemies.

"So, the anthropologists are very puzzled. How explain the mystery? If the Negro, who's probably the latest race to evolve, did originate in India, why isn't he found in India and in parts between the Melanesian area and Africa? Were Negroes exterminated or assimilated or run out of their native area in Paleolithic times? Did one group or groups go to the islands and another to Africa?"

"Maybe the theory's wrong," O'Brien said. "Never mind about the spades. What about the horse and the camel? If there ain't any here, didn't that make a hell of a difference?"

"You bet it did. It'd mean that travel and communication and trade would be much slower. Until steam engines had been invented, people would've had to travel on foot or by wa-

ter. Heavy bulk material would have been transported on the backs of humans or in ox-drawn
wagons. Maybe, though, the elephant was used
more here than in our world."

He stopped talking because a number of
strangers had come into the room. There were
twenty, most of them dark-skinned and dark-
haired, but a few had coloring pale as O'Brien's.
They were in light green uniforms and brown
leather knee-length boots. Their trousers were
skin-tight and piped with gold thread along the
seam. The coats were swallow-tailed, loose
around the chest and sleeves, with four large
button-down pockets. Their helmets were conical, like Chinese coolie hats but curving downward in back to protect the neck. The officers
wore symbolic feathers of steel affixed to the
helmet front. All carried breech-loading single-
shot rifles and slightly curving swords about four
feet long. All were beardless.

Their commanding officer talked for a while
with Dzikohses. He looked frequently at the
Americans. The officer, a kidziaskos (from the
Greek *chiliarchos*), suddenly frowned. He left
Dzikohses and strode to the fliers. He demanded
that Two Hawks hand over his gun. Two Hawks
hesitated, then shrugged. He had to comply. After making sure that the safety of the automatic
was on, he handed the gun to the officer. The
kidziaskos turned it over and over and finally
stuck it in his belt.

Dzikohses and his guerrillas left; the fliers and
Ilmika Thorrsstein were escorted from the house
by the soldiers. Again, they marched by night

and slept as well as they could during the day. Apparently, the enemy had overrun this area but did not have a tight control as yet. The party avoided all Perkunishan patrols but could not get away from the swarms of huge mosquitoes. All were forced to apply a thick coating of the stinking grease every day.

Two days after they had separated from the guerrillas, O'Brien began to suffer from chills, fever, and sweating. Two Hawks thought the sergeant had malaria. The medico with the troops confirmed his diagnosis.

"For God's sakes, don't they have any quinine?" O'Brien said. "You'd think that in a country where they have malaria, they'd . . ."

"There isn't any," Two Hawks said. "It was unknown on our Earth until after South America was discovered. So . . ."

"What'd they do before Columbus? They must've had something!"

"I don't know. Whatever they had, it wasn't very effective."

He did not tell O'Brien that malaria had been a great killer in the Mediterranean region of their Earth. In fact, it still took a large annual toll. He was worried, not only for O'Brien but for himself. The malaria parasite could kill a man if he got no medical aid, especially since the parasite of this world might be even more deadly than that of his.

The soldiers made a rude stretcher from two branches and a blanket. The sergeant was placed on it; Two Hawks took one end of the stretcher and a soldier the other. The troops re-

lieved each other at fifteen-minute intervals, but
Two Hawks had to stay at his task until his
hands could lock themselves around the
branches no more, his legs were like stone, and
his back felt as if it would unhinge at the next
step.

The medico gave O'Brien water and two large
pills, one red, one green, every hour. Whatever
the ingredients, they had little effect. O'Brien
continued to chill, burn, and sweat in turn for
four hours. Then the attacks ceased, as could be
expected. Although he was weak, he was forced
to rise and walk, with Two Hawks supporting
him. The officer made it plain that he wanted no
lagging. Two Hawks urged O'Brien to keep
going. The officer would have no compunctions
about killing a possible spy who was holding
them up. His main concern evidently was in getting the Blodland woman through the enemy
and to the capital city.

After four days of travel, during which
O'Brien became sicker and weaker, they came to
their first village. They walked during the day-
time hours the last 12 hours. The enemy must
not have advanced very near to this point. Here
Two Hawks saw the first railroad and
locomotive. The locomotive looked like an engine circa 1890, except that the huge smokestack
was shaped like a demon's face. The cars of the
train were painted scarlet and covered with good
luck signs, including the swastika.

The village was the terminus for the line.
Thirty houses and stores were parallel with both
sides of the tracks. Two Hawks gazed curiously

at the houses and the people who ran out to greet
them. The buildings reminded him of the false-
fronted structures seen in Western movies. However, each had a wooden and brightly painted
carving of a tutelary spirit in front of it and also
one like a ship's figurehead near the top of the
false front. The men wore heavy boots and shirts
of cloth or cowhide or deerskin. The shirts hung
outside their belts. The women wore bead-
fringed, low-cut blouses of cloth and ankle-
length skirts. Small stone carvings or sea shells
were sewn in various patterns on the skirts. Both
sexes had long hair falling to the shoulders; the
German-helmet haircuts of the guerrillas and
the soldiers, Two Hawks thought, must be military requirements.

There were a few old men and women, all of
whose faces and hands were tattooed in blue and
red. He supposed that this skin decoration had
been a universal custom among the Hotinosonih.
Something, possibly the influence of the white
West European nations, had caused the tattoo-
ing to die out.

The officer politely asked the Thorrsstein
woman to step aboard a passenger car. He was
not so polite to the two Americans. He shouted
at them to go three cars back. Two Hawks pretended not to understand, since he did not want
his captors to know he was gaining fluency in
their tongue. Some soldiers shoved the two
toward the car. Two Hawks, assisting the chat-
tering shaking sergeant, went up the steps and
into the mobile prison.

The car was bare of furniture and crowded

with wounded soldiers. Two Hawks found a
place for O'Brien to stretch out on the wooden
floor. Then he looked for water for O'Brien, but
discovered that it was available only in the next
car. A man with an arm in a bloody sling and a
bloody bandage around his head accompanied
Two Hawks. The wounded man held a long
knife in his good hand and promised to cut Two
Hawks' throat if he so much as looked like he
meant to escape. He did not leave the side of the
prisoners during the rest of the long trip to
'Estokwa.

This took five days and nights. Many times,
the train was shifted to a sidetrack to allow
trains loaded with soldiers to pass westwards.
During one day, nobody in the hospital car had
water. O'Brien almost died that day. But the
train finally stopped near a creek, and the bottles
and canteens were refilled.

The car was jammed, hot, noisy, and
malodorous. A man with a badly gangrened leg
lay next to the sergeant. His stench was so nau-
seating that Two Hawks could not eat. The third
day, the soldier died and was buried four hours
later in the woods near the tracks while the
locomotive puffed impatiently on a spur.

Surprisingly, O'Brien improved. By the time
they got to 'Estokwa, the fever, chill, and sweating were gone. He was pale, weak, and gaunt,
but he had beaten his sickness. Two Hawks did
not know whether the recovery was due to the
Irishman's basic toughness, the pills which the
medico had continued to dose him with, or a
combination of the two. It was also possible that

he had been afflicted with something besides malaria. It did not matter, he had health again, even if only a precarious one.

7

THE NIGHT THE TRAIN arrived in 'Estokwa, a rainstorm was lashing the city. Two Hawks could see nothing through the windows except lightning flashes, nor was he allowed to get a better look after being escorted off the car. His eyes were bound, his hands tied behind him, and he was taken through the rain to a wagon. He knew it was enclosed because he could hear the water fall on the roof, and his back was up against a wall. He sat on a bench on one side of the cabin and O'Brien, also blindfolded, sat on the other.

"Where do you think they're taking us, lieutenant?"

O'Brien sounded weak and nervous. Two Hawks replied that he did not know. Privately, he supposed that they were being taken to an interrogation station. He hoped fervently that civilization had softened the old Iroquois methods of dealing with prisoners. Not that being "civilized" necessarily meant that subtle or brutal torture was out of consideration. Look at the "civilized" Germans of his own world. Look at the Russians. Look at the Chinese. Look at the American whites in their dealings with the red man. Look at anybody, preliterate or civilized.

After an estimated fifteen minutes of travel, the wagon stopped. O'Brien and Two Hawks were roughly helped down. Ropes were put around their necks, and they were led up a long flight of steps, down a long hall, down another, then down a curving staircase. Two Hawks said nothing; O'Brien cursed. Abruptly, they were halted. A door swung open on squeaky iron hinges; they were pushed through a doorway. Again halted, they stood in silence for a while. Their blindfolds were removed, and they were blinking at the bright illumination of an electric lamp.

When his vision had come back, Two Hawks saw that the room was of polished granite. Its ceiling was far above; the light came from a huge lamp on a wooden table. Several men stood around them. These wore tight-fitting black uniforms; on the left breast of each jacket was a misshapen death's head. And, unlike any he had seen so far, these men had completely shaven heads.

He had been right. He and O'Brien were here to be interrogated. Unfortunately, they really had nothing to tell. The truth was so incredible that the questioners would not believe it. They would think that it was a fantasy concocted by

Perkunishan spies. They could not think otherwise, any more than a man of this world, caught
in a similar situation in Two Hawks' Earth,
would be believed by either Allies or Germans.

Nevertheless, there came a time when Two
Hawks told the truth, unbelievable or not.
O'Brien was the lucky one. Weakened by the
malaria, he could not endure much pain. He
kept fainting until the inquisitioners were satisfied that he was not faking. They dragged him
out by his heels, his head bobbling on the
smooth greasy-looking stone. Then they devoted
their full energies and ingenuity to Two Hawks.
Perhaps they were especially vindictive because
they believed him to be a traitor. He was obviously not a Perkunishan.

Two Hawks kept silent as long as possible. He
remembered that the old Iroquois of his Earth
had admired a man who could take it. Sometimes, though rarely, they stopped the torture to
adopt a man of great courage and endurance
into the tribe.

After a while he began wondering how his ancestors could have been so tough as to keep silent, even to sing and dance or yell insults at
their tormentors. They were better men than he.
To hell with the stoicism and with the defiance!
He began to scream. This did not make him feel
better, but it at least permitted him some expression and release of energy.

The time came when he had babbled his story
five times, insisting each time that it was true.
Six times he fainted and was revived with ice-
cold water poured over him. After a while, he did

not know what he was doing or saying. But at least he was not begging for mercy. And he was cursing them, telling them what low worthless despicable creatures they were and vowing to cut their guts out and loop them around their necks when he got a chance.

Then he began screaming again, the world was one red flame, one red scream.

When he awoke, he was in pain. But it was more like the memory of pain. The memory hurt enough but was far preferable to the actual agony inflicted on him in that stone chamber. Still, he wished he could die and get the exquisite hurt over with. Then he thought of the men who had done this thing to him, and he wished he would live. Once on his feet, give him a chance to escape, and he would somehow kill them.

Time passed. He awoke to find his head being held up and a cooling drink going down his dry throat. There were several women in the room, all clad in long black robes and with white bands around their foreheads. They shushed his croaked questions and began to change some of the bandages in which he was swathed. They did so gently but could not avoid hurting him. Afterwards, they applied soothing lotions and put fresh bandages on.

He asked where he was, and one answered that he was in a nice safe place and no one was ever going to hurt him again. He broke down and cried then. They looked to one side as if embarrassed, but he did not know if they were embarrassed by the show of emotion or by what had been done to him.

He did not stay awake long but fell into a sleep from which he awoke two days later. He felt as if he had been drugged; his head was as thick as the taste in his mouth. He managed to get out of bed that evening and to walk up and down the long hall outside his room. Nobody interfered, and he even talked—or tried to talk—to some of the other patients. Shocked, he returned to his tiny room. O'Brien was in the other bed. Weakly, O'Brien said, "Where are we?"

"In the Iroquoian version of the booby hatch," Two Hawks said.

O'Brien was too drained of strength to react violently. He did succeed in talking, however. "How come we're here?"

"I suppose our torturers, the Iroquois Gestapo, concluded we had to be insane. We stuck to our story, and our story could not possibly be true. So, here we are, and lucky at that. These people seem to have preserved the old respect for the crazed. They treat them nicely. Only, we're prisoners, of course."

O'Brien said, "I don't think I'm going to make it. I think I'm going to die. What they did to me . . . and being on this world, I . . ."

"You're too mean and ornery to die," Two Hawks said. "Where's your fighting Irish spirit? You tough mick, you'll make it all right. You just want some sympathy."

"No. But promise me one thing. When you get the chance, find those bastards and kill them. Slowly. Make them scream like they made us scream. Then kill them!"

Two Hawks said, "I felt like you did. But I've discovered something about this world. There aren't any Geneva conventions. What happened to us happens to any prisoner if the captors feel like torturing him. If we'd fallen into the hands of the Perkunishans, we'd have gotten the same treatment or worse. At least, we aren't crippled for life or permanently scarred. From now on, we've got it made. We're being treated like kings. Like captive gods. The Iroquois regard the insane as possessed by divinity. Maybe they don't really believe that any more, but the basic attitude still exists."

"Kill them!" O'Brien said, and he fell asleep again.

By the end of the following week, Two Hawks was almost back to normal. The third-degree burns were still healing, but he no longer felt as if he had been flayed alive and every exposed muscle and nerve beaten in a mortar. He met the director of the asylum, Tarhe. Tarhe was a tall thin man with a huge nose and the eyes of a gentle eagle. In addition to being the chief administrator, he was also the head *latoolats*. This word meant, literally, *he hunts,* and was the generic term for the Iroquoian equivalent of psychiatrist.

Tarhe was a kindly man and a scholar. He gave Two Hawks permission to use his library, in which Two Hawks spent hours each day learning about this world, or Earth 2, as he was beginning to call it. There were books in every major language and many in the minor tongues and over a hundred volumes of reference materi-

al. There was also a multilingual dictionary
which Two Hawks used frequently. His educa-
tion leaped ahead like a hare with a fox on its
trail.

Occasionally, Tarhe called him in for brief
therapeutic sessions. Tarhe was a busy man, but
he considered Two Hawks' case a challenge. As
time went on, he allotted an hour a day to his
patient, although for Tarhe it meant losing an
hour of sleep or of study for himself.

"Then you think that I had some experience
on the western front that was so terrible that my
mind snapped?" Two Hawks said. "I retreated
from reality into the fantasy world of this Earth
I claim to be from? I found this world unendurable?"

Two Hawks grinned at Tarhe and said, "If
that is true, why would O'Brien have exactly the
same psychosis? The same down to every minute
detail? Don't you find it strange, indeed incredible, that we could agree on a thousand details of
this fantasy world?"

Tarhe said, "He found your sickness attractive enough to want to get into it. No wonder. He
obviously depends upon you a great deal; he
would feel shut out, absolutely alone, if he were
not in this . . . this Earth 1."

Tarhe did not use the term psychosis or anything like it. His word, translated literally,
meant "possession." It was used because a
latoolats treated the insane as if they were actually possessed by a demon or an evil ghost. The
demons, however, were dealt with scientifically;
they had been categorized. One of Tarhe's medi-

cal books gave a list of one hundred and twenty-
nine types of evil spirits. Two Hawks was supposed to have been taken over by a *teotya'tya'koh*
(literally, *his body is cut in two*).

Suspecting that Tarhe was too intelligent and
too basically incredulous to believe in the existence of ghosts and demons, Two Hawks questioned him. Tarhe replied with a smile and some
carefully chosen ambiguous phrases. They satisfied Two Hawks that Tarhe used the terms only
to conform to the scientific terminology of his
profession. There may have been a time when
the categorizations were literal and not figur-
ative, but men like Tarhe no longer put credence
in them. However, the belief in demons was a
living force among the common people and the
priests of the state religion. It might be dangerous to publicly profess disbelief. So, Tarhe went
along with public opinion.

The amazing thing was that the principles of
treating the mentally sick were much the same
as those used by the Freudian practicioners of
Earth 1. The Iroquoian explanations for the gen-
esis and cure of warped minds might be different, but the therapy was similar.

"How do you account for our ignorance of
your language?" Two Hawks said to Tarhe.

"You're an intelligent man. Your *teotya'tya'koh*
is cunning. It decided to go all the way into this
dream world. So it made you forget your native
tongue. Thus, you are even more secure from
being forced back into this world."

"You have a rationalization for everything I
say," Two Hawks said. "In fact, you rationalize

so much, one might think you were the patient and I the doctor. Have you ever considered, even for one second, that I might be telling the truth? Why not conduct an experiment to determine this; take a truly scientific nonprejudicial approach? Question O'Brien and myself separately about our world. We could have agreed on a story in its broad outlines. But if you delve into it, break it down to very minor details—oh, about a thousand things: language, history, geography, religions, customs, etcetera—you'll find an absolutely astonishing agreement."

Tarhe removed his glasses and polished them.

"That would be a scientific experiment. It's true you couldn't create an entire language in all its complexities of sound, structure, vocabularly, and so forth. Or agree on details of history, architecture, and so on."

"So why don't you test us?"

Tarhe replaced his glasses and looked owlishly at Two Hawks.

"Some day, I may. Meanwhile, let's work on your possession, find out how the demon managed to invade you. Now, what were your feelings—not thoughts—when I contradicted you a moment ago?"

Two Hawks was furious at first, then he began to laugh. After all, he could not blame Tarhe for his attitude. If he were in his place, would he believe such a story?

Much of Two Hawks' time was taken up with the routine of the asylum. There were the daily sweatbaths, so long and hot that if a demon were inhabiting his body, it would have been too uncomfortable to remain. There were daily religious ceremonies, during which the priests from a nearby temple tried to exorcise the demons. Tarhe absented himself during these; apparently, he had had trouble concealing his impatience with priests. He must have felt that they were wasting time that could be better spent. It was an indication of the power of the Iroquois church that he dared not interfere with it. Two Hawks made some inquiry about the state religion and found that it was indigenous. It was based on the primitive religions of the Iroquois and had been formalized and put into writing some four hundred years ago by a prophet, Kaasyotyeetha'. The founder of the religion had made the vaguely pantheistic belief into a monotheistic one. And he had incorporated various concepts and creeds of the Western European religion into the new faith. However, all the borrowings had an Iroquoian flavor.

There was, however, religious toleration in the nation of Hotinohsonih.

In his leisure time, Two Hawks went to the library or practised conversation with the patients and staff. He intended to escape some day and would thus have to know this world well if he were to operate effectively. A children's book, printed by a house in 'Estokwa, gave him an outline of Earth 2's prehistory and history.

Over the course of several thousand years, large migrations of Amerinds (generally then referred to by Westerners as anthropophagi) from central Asia and Siberia had wandered into Europe and conquered or been conquered. The conquerers had usually been absorbed into the defeated peoples, who had then regained their national identity and integrity.

But in fairly recent times, during the past 800 years, several of the later invaders had succeeded in imposing their language and some cultural traits on the white aborigines. The area of Czechoslovakia of Earth 1 was here called Kinukkinuk. The Algonquian word for this state had originally meant *mixture* and had referred both to the differing dialects of the various conquerors and also to the fact that the Amerinds had miscegenated with the white natives.

This reminded Two Hawks of Hungary of Earth 1, where a semi-Mongolian people, speaking a Uralic tongue, had defeated the whites, imposed their language upon the whites, and then had been absorbed, losing their racial identity. Here, the Huns had never been heard of.

The Finnish speakers had been diverted eastwards, invaded and settled down in Japan, known on Earth 2 as Saariset. The Japanese, repelled when they had tried to conquer the islands, had turned instead to the area of what Two Hawks' planet knew as southern China. Northern China was inhabited by a Mongolian-type people speaking an Athabaskan tongue similar to Navaho and Apache.

The western part of India, called Mardaka here (an Arabic name?), was owned by Blodland (England) and other members of the Six Kingdoms union. Rasna had conquered most of the eastern half, though there were some Malayan and Turkic kingdoms on the northern coast and

some Arabic kingdoms in the interior. Perkunisha claimed Ceylon.

The history of India's conquest was long and
bloody, reflected by the wars in Europe among
the nations eager to seize this great and rich
land. In the beginning the New Cretans or
Kerdezh (inhabitants of the Iberian peninsula)
and some west North African nations had conquered part of the coastal regions of India or
Mardaka. Then the Six Kingdoms and Rasna
had attacked, using their west African colonies
as naval bases. The Fifty Years' War (actually a
series of wars) had resulted in the victory of the
three west European nations.

Though interested in the history of India,
Roger was fascinated by its animal and bird life.
Like Australia, Mardaka's indigenous mammals
had been all marsupials. The tiger, the elephant,
the rhinoceros, the pig, the buffalo, the dog, the
bear, and the ape were missing. But pouched
counterparts had evolved. The huge island had
marsupial beasts remarkably resembling these
creatures. It lacked, however, the kangaroo.

It also had the biggest winged and wingless
birds in the world. One of the latter was a species twenty feet high.

Snakes and crocodilians were everywhere, and
in the interior was a swamp-dwelling reptile
twenty feet high and sixty feet long. However,
the scientists were still arguing about the exact
nature of this quadruped. Though it looked like
a dinosaur, it was warm-blooded.

Asia Minor presented an alien picture. The
area of Turkey of Earth 1 spoke on Earth 2 a

language derived from an ancient tongue which
some scholars thought was distantly related to
Basque and others thought was linked to
Circassian. Pelesta (Palestine) used a speech descended from that of Cretan colonists. Hebrew
was unknown. This world lacked the rich
heritage of the Jew. The rest of Asia Minor and
Persia, Afghanistan, and lands eastward spoke a
language which Roger guessed was descended
from Tocharian. In his world, this had been the
furthest eastward extension of Indo-European.
Its speakers had built a high civilization in Chinese Turkestan but had become assimilated in
the 11th century A. D. by the Mongolian or Turkic peoples.

Arabic was confined to the southern part of the
Arabian peninsula, parts of east and south
Africa, and the Indian island-subcontinent.

South of the Saharan area, Africa was divided
into areas originally settled by prehistoric mi-
grants from the north and then conquered by the
North Africans, the Arabs, and the Tocharians.
And then by the Europeans.

As Two Hawks had suspected, the Negro race
had never evolved on Earth 2 because of the
multimillion-years separation of India from
Asia.

Africa was solely populated by Caucasians (if
Malayan Madagascar was discounted), though
the sub-Saharan aborigines were as dark as Negroes.

Kemet (Egypt) spoke a form of Greek. The
other North African states spoke New Cretan,
Berber, or Coptic dialects. As Two Hawks had

suspected, these nations had a very fertile soil
and large populations. At one time, for five centuries, they had been part of the empire of
Akhaivia. The Hellenic tribes had been diverted
on Earth 2 from invading the peninsula of
Greece by waves of Amerinds from Asia. Instead, they had ended up in Italy or Jugoslavia.
The Akhaiwoi people had come down from the
Danube region, conquered and finally absorbed
the Italics, and given their name to the land.
They had built up a civilization comparable in
some respects to Earth 1's Athenian culture but
lacking in others. Though they occupied Italy,
they had not been the Romans of this world.
They had kept the Etruscans, immigrants from
Asia Minor, from settling in western Italy. But,
unlike Rome, they had not been able to crush
the Semitic colonizers of northwest Africa.
In Two Hawks' world, these had been the
Carthaginians, descendants of Phoenicians.
Here the Cretans had beat out the Phoenicians
and established a nation comparable to
Carthage. They had conquered Iberia but were
prevented from doing the same to the country
north of the Pyrenees by a combination of Rasna
and Akhaivian city-states.

Some centuries later, the Greek equivalent of
Alexander the Great or Julius Caesar had appeared. Kassandras had united the Greeks and
then lead them on a conquest of all North Africa,
Hatti, and most of Asia Minor. For a while his
descendants had even ruled over Neftroia (Bul-
garia, inhabited by descendants of Trojan colonists) and had driven the Amerind nations into

Russia. One of his great-grandchildren had occupied south Rasna, but fifty years later the Akhaivians were run out.

Not until seventy-five years ago, though, had the Greeks lost their hold on Egypt.

Blodland (England) and Bamba (Ireland) had been inhabited by a meglith-building people when the Cretan traders came to the islands. Later, New Crete had colonized the southern part of these. Then the Celts invaded but had just become firmly established when the Germanic onslaughts began. These had happened in a much earlier time than on Earth 1. More waves came, sometimes Germanic, sometimes Celtic, and for a hundred years the Baltics had also landed on the shores of the larger island. So many were the wards that the Germanics had named it Blodland (Bloodland).

The Ingwine tribes had finally become the victors, and their speech developed into something like Old English of Earth 1.

But then the Danish and Norwegian and Swedish raids began, followed by mass invasions. In fact, half of Denmark, pushed by the Perkunishan tribes, migrated to Blodland over a period of a hundred years.

Danish and Norwegian kings ruled Blodland, Grettirsland (Normandy and Brittany), Northweg (Norway), Tyrsland (Sweden), Gotsland (Holland), and Frankland (Belgium). Then the Blodlanders had conquered Bamba (Ireland) and a hundred years later the Six Kingdoms union had been established. The languages of all had been closely related during the

conquests, and now Ingwinetalu was the domi-
nant tongue, used by the governments of all in
official documents and by the armed forces of all.
However, though the Shof (King) of Blodland
was the nominal head, the union was a loose
one.

Blodlander was a creolized English with an
enormous stock of Norse loanwords and a lesser
amount of Semitic Cretan, Etruscan Rasna, and
Greek-derived words. Perkunisha, however, had
contributed much to the scientific and
philosophical vocabulary.

The French and Latin words were missing,
and oh, what a difference! Learning Blodlander
was for Two Hawks learning a foreign tongue.

The Perkunishan empire consisted of Earth
1's Germany, Austria, Denmark, Poland, all
speaking the same tongue, the Algonquin speakers of Kinukkinuk (Czechoslovakia), and the
Celtic speakers of Trevetia (Switzerland).

The Perkunishans seemed to be the Germans
of Earth 2 as far as their industry, science,
philosophy, and aggressiveness were concerned.
Thirty years ago they had begun this planet's
first World War. They had seemed on their
way to the complete conquest of Europe and
North Africa when a plague (the Black
Plague?) had devasted Europe. Now, their armies powerful with a new generation and a mili-
tarily superior technology and a superman ideol-
ogy, the Perkunishans were trying again. This
time, it looked as if they might succeed.

Two Hawks saw what a difference the lack of
a United States of America made in this world.

Europe could not call upon it for aid against the Central European aggressors.

8

SERGEANT O'BRIEN, despite his convictions that he was going to die, got better. Soon he was on his feet and doing simple exercises. Two Hawks was working out with him in the gymnasium one day when an orderly told him he had a visitor. Two Hawks felt apprehensive, wondering if the secret police had come for him. He followed the orderly to the visitors' room. He was ready to kill if he had to and then to make an escape. If he was killed instead, so much the better. He was not going through that torture again.

On entering the room, his grimness dissolved into a smile. The Lady Ilmika Thorrsstein was waiting for him. She continued to sit in her chair, as befitted a member of the Blodland nobility in the presence of a commoner. However, she did reply to his smile with one of her own.

Two Hawks kissed her extended hand and said, *"Ur Huskarleship."* ("Your Ladyship.")

"Hu far't vi thi, lautni Tva Havoken?" she said. ("How goes it with you, freeman (or Mister) Two Hawks?")

"Ik ar farn be'er," he said. ("I am doing better.") *"Ur Huskarleship ar mest hunlich aeksen min*

haelth of." ("Your Ladyship is most gracious in asking about my health.")

She certainly gave no hint of having recently gone through an ordeal. She was no longer the dirty, hollow-cheeked, fatigue-eyed, and smelly woman he had known on the flight through the forest. She had put on some weight, rounded out nicely, and her eyes were clear, the dark circles gone. Her lips were rouged a dark red, her face was slightly powdered, and her cheeks lightly rouged. She wore one of the tall conical hats from which hung a thin blue gauze strip, the whole reminding him of the hats worn by the ladies of medieval times. Her dress was of some shiny pale white stuff, form fitting from the waist up, cut low and square at the bosom. A ruff of yellow lace circled her waist, and the skirt, held out by several stiff petticoats, fell to her ankles to shape a truncated cone. Her high-heeled shoes were of white leather and bore tiny blue puffballs on the toes.

She was very pretty. Two Hawks, looking at her, suddenly felt the thrust of desire that had been too long subdued by the rigors of the flight and then by the torture. Returning strength and long abstinence was making him extraordinarily horny, he thought. Or maybe not so extraordinarily. Just his usual state.

But this woman was not for him. He had learned of the strong class barriers that existed throughout most of Europe. They were as rigidly and harshly enforced, perhaps even more so, than they had been in, say, seventeenth-century France.

Only the country of the Hotinohsonih—"his people"—had anything approaching the American concept of democracy. This was the only nation which had given its women the right to vote. He was from a world and a time which regarded the social barriers of this world as of little importance, even ridiculous. So he could not help looking boldly at her. Some of his desire must have shown, for she lost her smile, and her eyes narrowed. He hastened to reassure her, since he did not wish to offend her and so lose his only personal contact with the outside world.

"*Foryi me, faeyer Huskarle,*" he said. "*Ik n'a seen swa bricht a faemme for maniy a daey. Yemiltsa.*" ("Forgive me, fair lady. I have not seen so bright a maiden for many a day. Show mercy.")

He added with a smile, "Besides, I am not responsible for my actions. Otherwise, I would not be here."

She smiled, though strainedly, and said, "You are forgiven. And I am happy that you brought up the subject of your . . . uh . . . staying here."

"Call it imprisonment," he said. "Although I can't complain about my treatment. They're very nice."

She leaned forward and said, face intent, "I don't think you're crazy."

He was a little startled and then it occurred to him that she had been left alone with him. That would not have been done unless she had requested it, since she was an important person. He had learned that she was the daughter of Huskarl, that is, Lord, Thorrsstein, the

Blodland ambassador to the nation of Dakota.
Thorrsstein and his daughter had fled towards
Iroquoia when the Perkunishans invaded Dakota. The Lord and his daughter had become separated, and later Ilmika had been taken by guerrillas through the Perkunishan lines.

"What makes you think I'm not mad?" he
said. He knew now that she was not here merely
to make a social call.

"I just cannot believe it," she replied. Making
an effort to hide her tension, she sat back in the
chair. She folded her hands on her lap and said,
"If you are not crazy, then what are you?"

He decided he could not lose by telling her the
truth. If she had been sent by the secret police to
see if he gave her a different story, she would
return with the same they had heard. However,
it was not likely that the Hotinoshsonih had
asked her to probe for them. They would have
gotten verification from Tarhe that Two Hawks
was sticking to his tale.

More probably, Ilmika represented her own
people, the Blodland secret agents. Perhaps they
had information which the Hotinohsonih lacked.
This information might have made them think
that Two Hawks could be from a "parallel" universe and so had knowledge of a superior technology. The wreck of the *Hiawatha* could have
been discovered. If it had been, it would present
the finders with a disturbing puzzle. The
Blodland agents, knowing of it and also of the
two strangers and their story, had contacted
Lady Thorrsstein. She was to question him to
determine if he could be useful.

If this were the true situation, the Blodlandish were not telling their Hotinohsonih allies what they knew. The Blodlandish wanted the information for themselves.

He smiled. Even in the desperate predicament in which both allies were, one was playing against the other. Power politics and national security were as paramount here as on his Earth

Still, the Blodlandish interest gave him a bargaining position. It might permit O'Brien and himself to escape not only from the asylum but from a country that seemed to be on its way to being defeated and occupied. So far, Blodland was not threatened by invasion.

Before starting his narrative, Two Hawks explained the concept of "parallel" universes as best he could. Ilmika listened attentively, and her questions showed that she was as intelligent as she was pretty. She had no difficulty in understanding him, but whether or not she believed him was another matter. Nevertheless, she encouraged him to go on, which meant she was willing to grant the possibility he might not be a lunatic. Or perhaps she had been told to get his entire story, even if it sounded to her like ravings.

Two Hawks followed his "theory" with a broad outline of how his Earth differed from her *Erthe,* as it was called in Blodlandish. Then he gave her the background of World War II and of his involvement. He ended with a description of the great American bombing raid on Ploesti and the passing of the *Hiawatha* through the "gate" and the parachuting into the peasant's field.

"Your Ploesti is *Tkanotaye'koowaah* or, as it's

called in Western Europe, Dares, after the original Trojan name," she said. "The Perkunishans wanted it for the same reason your Germans wanted its counterpart. Oil and gas. You were fortunate you arrived when you did. One day later, and you would have fallen into the enemy hands. They had the area under complete control by then."

Two Hawks walked to the huge picture window which gave a view of 'Estokwa. The asylum was on a high hill a few miles from the center of the capitol. The great white marble building of the *Teyotoedzayashohkwa'*, the Iroquoian version of Parliament or of Congress, dominated the metropolis. To one side was a smaller building, also in Greek style but of red granite. This was the residence of the *hakya'tanoh* (literally, *he watches over me*), the elected chief executive.

'Estokwa, once a seaport of the Trojan colonists, had been razed and its inhabitants massacred when the Iroquoians had taken it after a long siege. The longhouses of the barbarians had been built in the midst of the stone ruins. But now 'Estokwa was a modern city, indistinguishable at a distance from most West European metropolises. The government and business buildings were constructed of marble or granite and modeled after the classical Akhaivian architecture.

Two Hawks had seen closeup photos of the congressional building in Tarhe's office. The pillars of the great portico were carved to represent the seven tutelary animals of the seven major tribes that had comprised the original invaders. The exterior walls were covered with friezes depicting not only scenes from history but weird symbolic figures representing characters from religion and folklore. These were executed in the distinctive non-European style that the "red men" had developed after becoming civilized.

Two Hawks wanted it to be otherwise, but he had no genuine identification with these people. They were "Iroquois," but not the Iroquois he knew. Their past and present were too dissimilar, and the influences under which they had come were also too alien. He actually had less identification with them than he had with the white culture of his native United States of America.

Given time, he might have made a satisfactory adjustment. But this nation seemed destined to go down into defeat under the overwhelming might of Perkunisha. If it did, it would give him no home. It would be a hell. The official policy of Perkunisha towards conquered nations was the absolute destruction of all non-Perkunishan traits. First, genocide on a scale that not even the Germany of his world had been bold enough to proclaim publicly. Then colonization by Perkunishans and other Europeans thought sufficiently Nordic to be given Perkunishan citizenship.

Even now, a battle was raging some twenty miles to the west and north of 'Estokwa. Three enemy armies were battering steadily towards the gates of the capitol. Unless something unlikely happened, the invaders would be in 'Estokwa within a week. There would be house-to-house fighting then, but the government itself was making plans to evacuate.

As he looked over the city, he saw three dots appear in the blue sky. Presently, they were close enough to be seen as dirigibles. Three huge silvery cigar-shapes, they slid through the air while little black puffs of smoke arose beneath them. Serenely, they ignored the futile and primitive anti-aircraft fire and proceeded towards their targets, the congressional building and chief executive's residence. Many little objects fell from the mammoths' bellies as they passed one by one over the targets. Clouds of smoke with hearts of fire pillared up from the ground. A few seconds later, the picture window rattled, the asylum building trembled, and he heard the not-too-far-off boom, boom, boom.

Other great sausages appeared. More bombs. The hemispherical roof of the legislators' building was gone. Wooden houses began to blaze. A factory went up in smoke and flying beams.

Two Hawks heard a door open behind him in one of the brief recesses between the explosions of bombs. He turned to see Thorrsstein's slave stick her head inside the room. She was a pretty girl of Amerind-white ancestry, a descendant of the aboriginal whites enslaved by the Hotinohsonih. The Lady Thorrsstein had mentioned earlier that the girl had been loaned to her by the Hotinohsonih government because she could speak Blodlandish. Normally, she was stationed at the Blodland embassy in 'Estokwa. Probably, she was a spy for the Hotinohsonih.

Ilmika asked what she wanted. The girl timid-
ly replied that she wanted to make sure her mistress was all right, that she was not distressed by
the bombing. Ilmika did look pale, and her back
was even more rigid than usual. But she managed to smile and to say that she was quite all
right, thank you. The slave girl remained in the
room until ordered to leave. Not until the girl
had closed the door behind her did Ilmika speak
again. By that, Two Hawks knew that she too
suspected the girl. That must also be why Ilmika
had permitted herself to be alone in a room with
a man. Custom demanded that any unmarried
woman of noble birth always be chaperoned under such situations.

Ilmika spoke in a low voice. "My government
has reason to believe that your story could be
true."

"They know of the flying machine," he said.

"Yes. But there is more. Perkunisha knows of
it, also. Moreover, they have another flying machine. They also have the man who was flying it.
He is in Berlin now. The Perkunishans have
tried to keep both the machines and their captive secret, but we have our ways of getting
information."

Two Hawks swore. He had been so preoc-
cupied with his own affairs that he had not once
thought of the German plane that had appeared
at the same time the *Hiawatha* had gone through
the gate. Of course! The German aviator must
also have come into this world.

"You are in great danger," Ilmika said. "Just
as we know about this . . . this German . . . so
the Perkunishans know about you. And they be-

lieve that you are from another universe. You are a threat to them because you have knowledge of weapons and machines superior to those of Eorthe. Undoubtedly, the Perkunishans plan to use the German's knowledge and skill. But they don't want yours to be used by their enemies. So . . ."

"So they'll try to kill us the first chance they get," Two Hawks said. "I'm surprised they haven't already tried."

"Maybe they've hesitated because, if they failed, it would convince the Hotinohsonih government that your story is not a madman's. But now that the city will soon be under siege, they might try under cover of the confusion. They could try tonight. Or even now, during the bombing."

"In that case, you could be in danger, too," he said. "Your government must think me very valuable if it's willing to risk your life in an effort to get me on its side."

She waved a hand and said, "There are guards stationed around the house while I'm here. We'd like to leave them to protect you and O'Brien, but the Hotinohsonih might wonder why."

Two Hawks looked up through the window at the dirigibles. He thought that if the Perkunishans wanted to kill them, they could have ordered the asylum bombed. Yet the big airships were coming nowhere near the building. It was possible that the enemy would prefer taking them alive under the old proverb that two birds, in this case three, in the hand were better than one in the bush, or underground.

This might be true. However, he was sure that the Perkunishans would have no compunctions in killing the two otherworlders if they saw they could not be taken alive.

It was also probable that the Blodlandish were thinking along the same lines. Rather than allow the Perkunishans to capture the aliens and use their knowledge, the Blodlandish would kill the two.

Nobody loves us, Two Hawks thought. He laughed then. It was two against a hostile world. So be it. Whatever happened to him and O'Brien, the others would have to pay a price.

Two Hawks, grinning, turned away from the window to face the Lady Thorrsstein. He said, "So why doesn't your government tell the Hotinohsonih what they know? The Hotinohsonih could throw up a guard around the asylum or else hustle us off to a safe place."

He was surprised to see her blush. Evidently, she was not a professional agent. She had some sense of honor and was only being used because she had a legitimate reason to visit him.

"I don't know," she said. She hesitated, then blurted, "Yes, I do! I was told that the Hotinohsonih wouldn't let you go. They'd keep you for themselves, and that'd be stupid! They don't have time to develop anything you might give them. They'll be too busy fighting for their land, which they're going to lose in any case. Telling them about you would be throwing you away.

"You must get to Blodland. We have the brains and the materials and the engineers and the time to use them. The Hotinohsonih can't hold out for long."

"I don't know about that," he said. "They have lots of country to go yet. Losing 'Estokwa doesn't mean they're licked."

He thought of the great sectors of territory gobbled up by the Germans in Russia, the staggering loses of men and materiel suffered by the Russians. Yet, they were not only still fighting; they were driving the Germans back. Of course, the Russians could not have done this without American supplies, and this world had no America.

"All right," he said. "I'll go to England."

"Where?"

"Pardon me. Blodland. The question is, how do we get there?"

"You be ready," she said. "Tonight at midnight."

"You can't get me out of here without force," he said. "Are your men going to shoot their way in? Maybe kill citizens of your allies? Couldn't that create a serious diplomatic situation? And if it's unsuccessful, wouldn't the Hotinohsonih catch on to the fact that they might have something very valuable in their possession?"

"Never mind that. We know what might happen."

She rose to her feet. "This man O'Brien. Is he well enough to get out under his own power?"

"He isn't up to running very far or very fast," Two Hawks said. He frowned. It was obvious that the Blodlandish would not leave O'Brien behind to be used by the Hotinohsonih or Perkunishans. Not alive anyway.

"If you kill him," he said, "the deal's off. You'll have to kill me, too."

She looked shocked. He wondered if she were acting or if she really had not considered such a possibility.

"I . . . I'm sure my people wouldn't do such a thing. You don't know us. We're not savages. We are Blodlandish."

He grinned and said, "Secret agents are alike —German, Yankee, Russian, Perkunishan, Hotinohsonih, Blodlandish, you name them. National security is at stake, and murder means nothing to preserve it.

"All right. Come for us. But you damn well be sure to tell your people that I don't go unless O'Brien goes."

"Don't you dare talk to me like that!" she cried. Her face was red, and her eyes were narrowed. "You . . . you . . ."

"Commoner. Savage," he said. "Where I come from, we don't have royalty or nobility or any such parasitical and oppressive classes. It's true we have our parasites and oppressors, but they're not usually born to that condition. They achieve it through hard work or connivery. Everybody is born equal—in theory, anyway. The practice isn't perfect, but it's better than none.

"And don't forget I'm from a world more advanced than' yours. There you'd be the barbarian, the ignorant and not-too-clean savage, not me. And the fact that here you're a direct descendant of the great Dane Thorrsstein Blothaxe and of King Hrothgar doesn't mean an

ox-turd to me. I'd tell you to put that in your
pipe and smoke it, except it wouldn't mean anything to you."

Her face twisted and turned red; she spun on
her high heels so violently that she almost fell.
He was still chuckling after the door slammed
behind her. A moment later, he did not think
things so funny. O'Brien could not go far before
needing a rest. Then what?

He returned to his room. The sergeant was in
bed, on his back and one arm over his face.
Hearing Two Hawks enter, he lifted his arm and
turned his head. "One of the attendants told me
you had a visitor. The Ilmika broad. How come
you rate?"

In a low voice, Two Hawks described his conversation. O'Brien whistled and said, "I sure
hope they got a car. I just ain't up to much exertion. And how the hell they going to get us out of
the country?"

"Probably through the Black Sea and the
Dardanelles. The Perkunishan fleet is operating
in the Iginth, but a small boat could get through
them. After that, I don't know."

"I'm going to need all the strength I can get.
Tell you what. The food isn't bad here, though it
tastes kind of funny, the way they cook it. But I
been hungry for a big thick bowl of potato soup.
My mother used to make it for me all the time.
Hot, thick, creamy, with onions. Mmmmm. Do
you suppose you could talk the cook into putting
it on the menu?"

Two Hawks sighed and looked sad. O'Brien's
look of expectancy and rapture died. He groaned

and said, "Oh no. Go on now. Don't tell me the good old Irish potato . . ."

Two Hawks nodded. "It originated in the Andes of South America."

O'Brien cursed. "What a hell of a world! No tobacco. No turkey for Thanksgiving. And, oh, God, no potatoes!"

Two Hawks said, "Well, you can be thankful for one thing. There's no syphilis. But, knowing your recklessness and horniness, you better watch out for gonorrhea."

"In my condition, that's the least of my worries."

O'Brien closed his eyes and in a minute was snoring. Two Hawks wanted to discuss a plan for that night, but he decided it could wait. O'Brien needed all the sleep he could get. Besides, what could the two of them do but roll the dice and see how they came up?

9

MIDNIGHT ARRIVED with agonizing slowness. It was silent in the asylum except for a rumble of thunder from west and north. The room had only a small window placed two feet above his head. The door was thick oak, ribbed with iron, and locked on the outside. Although Doctor Tarhe gave his better patients plenty of freedom during the day, he made sure they were secure at night.

Faintly, the clang of the big clock down the hall came through the door. Two Hawks counted the strokes. Twenty-four. Midnight.

A panel in the door opened and made him start. Through half-closed eyes, he could see the light of a kerosene lamp shining through the narrow panel. He could also make out the broad-faced, big-nosed visage of Kaisehta', an attendant, making his rounds. The panel closed; Two

Hawks got out of bed. He shook O'Brien, who sat up, saying, "You didn't think I'd be sleeping at a time like this?"

Both were already fully dressed. They had nothing to do now but wait for developments. Two Hawks wished he had his weapons, the derringer and the automatic. Tarhe had told him that the secret police had kept the guns for a while, studying them, then had given them to Tarhe. The doctor kept them locked up in a big wall-safe in his study. At the time he was told about them, Two Hawks had wondered why the police did not consider the automatic as an evidence of the truth of his story. Nothing like it existed in this world. But the guns had been returned without comment to Tarhe, and Two Hawks could only deduce that the police considered the automatic to be one more testimonial to his madness. If so, they must be a singularly unimaginative group.

The two sat in silence on the edge of their beds. They did not have long to wait. There was a yell from down the hall. It was chopped off, and a moment later a clinking sound told them a key was being turned in the big padlock. A bolt shot back; the door swung open. Two Hawks stood up, not knowing whether he should expect rescue or death from a gun. Six men wearing hoods stood in the corridor. Their clothes were lower-class Hotinohsonih civilian wear. Two held six-shooters; two, single-shot rifles; two, long knives.

A thickset man spoke Hotinohsonih in a deep bass. He spoke it with a foreign accent. "Are you

Two Hawks and O'Brien?"

Two Hawks nodded and said, "Give us guns. Or knives, anyway."

"You have no need of them."

"I have two of my guns locked in the wall-safe," Two Hawks said. "One of them is an automatic pistol, a rapid-fire mechanism that would greatly improve the fire power of the Blodlandish. I need it for a model."

The thickset man hesitated, then said, "It'd take too long to get it from the safe. We don't have the time to drill and blow."

"I know the combination," Two Hawks said. "I've stood behind Doctor Tarhe and watched him enough. He's rather absent-minded."

"Very well. But hurry. We don't have much time."

Two men preceded the others down the hall. Deep Voice gestured with his pistol for the two Americans to go before him. At the end of the hall, the attendant who had cried out, Kaisehta', lay face up on the floor. The top of his head was bloody; his eyes and mouth were open. The skin beneath the dark pigment was a bluish-grey.

"The sons of bitches didn't have to kill him!" O'Brien said. "Poor fellow! I didn't understand a word he ever said to me, but he could make me laugh. He was a good Joe."

"No talking," Deep Voice said. They went down another hall, across the dining-room and into Tarhe's study. Two Hawks pulled up the painting that was supposed to hide the safe. By the light of a flashlight held by Deep Voice, he turned the dial, marked with the numbers of the

modified Akhaivian alphabet. The door swung
open, and he found his derringer and automatic
in a small cardboard box.

Deep Voice extended his hand for the weap-
ons. Reluctantly, Two Hawks gave them to him.
Evidently, they were as much prisoners of the
Blodlandish as of their former captors.

The party left the studio and went to the main
front door of the asylum. Two men with rifles
stepped out on the big verandah and a minute
later came back with an all-clear. Two Hawks
and O'Brien, followed by the other four Blodlandish, stepped through the door. The city down
below was dark except for fires here and there
that had not yet been put out. The moon was
behind thick dark clouds.

They started down the steps, their destination
two autos. These were parked behind shrubbery
along the curve of the driveway to their left. The
front ends of the cars were barely visible. Just as
the two riflemen reached the ground, the flash
and bang of guns came out of the shrubbery.
Two Hawks pushed O'Brien hard towards the
ground and then hurled himself down the steps
and out in a dive.

He hit the bare dirt with a force that almost
knocked the breath from him and rolled side-
ways. When he was in the shrubbery that grew
along the base of the verandah, he stopped.
More fire spurted from the small arms of the
men in the bushes. The two Blodlandish who
had been in front of him were on the ground at
the foot of the steps. One was wounded or dead.
The other fired at the Perkunishans from a prone

position. Two Hawks presumed that the attackers were Perkunishans and they had come
with the same idea as the Blodlandish but a little
later.

A man above Two Hawks screamed. A body
fell over the verandah railing just above him and
crashed down on his legs. By then the other
Blodlandish had scattered for cover behind posts
and the railing of the verandah. A Perkunishan
toppled from the bushes. The others took up a
new position behind the Blodlandish cars.
Lights were coming on in the house and outlining the men on the verandah. A Blodlandish
slumped over the railing, his gun falling into the
ground under the bushes near Two Hawks. The
man with the rifle grunted and quit firing.

Two Hawks crawled to the gun that the agent
had dropped. With this in his hand, he left the
relative safety of the steps and bushes and
snaked towards the dead or unconscious
rifleman. Using the body as cover, he searched
through its pockets. He found several small boxes, slid one open, and felt cylindrical shapes
packed within. They were linen cartridges with
brass percussion caps.

He examined the revolver with his fingers,
broke it open, and filled the six chambers. Behind him, O'Brien groaned and said, "I'm hit.
My arm's numb. Oh, Christ, I'm bleeding! I'm
going to die!"

"Shut up about dying," Two Hawks said.
"You sound too strong to be badly hurt."

He rolled over and felt O'Brien's upper left
arm. His fingers came away sticky. O'Brien said,

"I'm going fast. The life's pumping out of me with every beat of my heart."

"Quit crying," Two Hawks said. "You just think you're dying, maybe because you want to. It's only a flesh wound and not very deep at that."

"You ain't the one who's hit."

Two Hawks raised his head to look over the body. Two men on the verandah and two behind the cars were still shooting. Then one—he looked like Deep Voice—turned to shoot through the window behind him at the light bulbs outlining him. There was a sound as of a fist hitting flesh, and he flew forward. He pitched on his face and was lost from Two Hawks' view except for one foot. His revolver, however, launched from a nerveless hand, broke the window.

The survivor ran for the corner of the house. He bent over while he ran and fired at the Perkunishans. Their bullets smacked into the wooden walls. Just as he reached the corner, he sprawled out and slammed into the floor. Two Hawks supposed that, since he did not get up, he was either hit or playing possum. If he was acting, he had done a good job, since his gun had also clattered on the floor.

"Two Perkunishans left—that I know of," Two Hawks whispered to O'Brien. "And they must have orders to take us dead or alive. Maybe they don't care which, otherwise they'd not have cut loose at us in the dark."

He looked over the body again. He could see no men. They were probably crouching behind

the cars, reloading their revolvers and discussing
a plan of attack. They could not safely presume
that everybody was dead or incapacitated. They
would have to come out from behind the cars.

Nor would they have much time to check.
There was much noise in the house, voices shouting questions, a patient screaming, and the
sound of feet running back and forth. They
would have tried to phone the police, but the
wires would have been cut.

Nevertheless, the gunfire could attract the police patrols on the streets in the city below. They
could soon be coming up the winding hill, and,
if they did, the Perkunishans would find their car
blocked. Unless, that is, they had left their vehicle below and had come up on foot.

Two Hawks waited patiently, his revolver
cocked. O'Brien groaned, and Two Hawks told
him to shut up. He removed the long knife from
the scabbard of the fallen rifleman. With one
hand, he hefted it and tested its balance. It
would make a good throwing knife and would
give him a fair chance to demonstrate how effective his hundreds of hours of practice had been.

The Perkunishans had decided to proceed
cautiously. One ran out from behind the car and
towards the protection of the corner of the
verandah. Two Hawks let him go. It was too difficult in the dark and at this distance to make
sure of a hit with the revolver. Besides, if he re-
frained from firing, he might convince them they
had nothing to fear.

Slowly, he rolled over away from the body and
swiveled around to face the shrubbery at the oth-

er curve of the drive. As he had suspected, the second agent had gone through the bushes to approach the other end of the verandah. Two Hawks heard a twig cracking during a brief cessation of noise from the house. He crawled back to O'Brien and into the bushes at the base of the verandah. His back was soaked with the sweat of fear, and his skin felt as if it were bristling.

When he reached the point where the verandah abruptly curved to go along the side of the house, he stopped. He waited and then, as he had hoped, the Perkunishan dashed from the bushes toward the shrubbery behind which he crouched. Two Hawks shifted the knife to his right hand and the gun to his left. He arose, and, just as the man crashed into the bush, Two Hawks thrust the point of the knife into his throat.

The agent burbled and fell to his knees. Two Hawks pulled the knife out, stepping to one side to avoid the spurt of blood. The man fell over on his side.

The other Perkunishan called out. Two Hawks spoke softly in the only Perkunishan phrases he knew, deliberately making them indistinct. Satisfied with this, the other agent left the corner of the verandah. Two Hawks stepped out from the bushes and walked confidently towards him. In the darkness, the Perkunishan would not be able to recognize his silhouette until he got close, or so Two Hawks hoped. The agent, however, must have been able to see well enough by the light from the windows of the

house. He shouted and fired. His shout gave
Two Hawks enough warning to throw himself to
one side and into the bushes. The bullet
screamed by. There was the sound of shoes on
the crushed stone. Two Hawks, looking out, saw
him disappear around the car. He leaped up,
heedless of noise, and ran across the driveway
into the tall shrubbery. When he was several
yards from the vehicle, he slowed down and
walked silently.

A dim bulk was moving soundlessly except for
the crunching of steel-rimmed wooden wheels on
the broken stones. For a minute, Two Hawks
thought that the car was being pushed. Then the
absurdity of such an act became apparent, and
he knew the car was steam-operated. He ran forward. Again, he traded weapons with his hands,
placing the knife in his right. Why waste a bullet
he might need later? Besides, if he should miss,
the Perkunishan would have no lance of flame
from a gun muzzle to show him where his enemy was.

He burst out of the shrubbery just alongside
the car. The driver sat on the right side, since
traffic went on the left lane in this country. But
the left window was down and so offered no ob-
stacle. The knife struck true, going through the
open window and into the side of the neck of the
driver. The driver slumped forward. Two Hawks
ran around in front of the car, which continued
its slow backing up.

He jerked the door open, reached in, and
pulled the corpse out by its arm. He did not have
time to retrieve his knife. Once in the driver's

seat, he frantically tried to locate the proper controls. Fortunately, he had seen illustrations of operating apparatus of steamers in Tarhe's library and had studied them for just such an occasion.

Two short sticks on a horizontal table projecting from the instrument panel regulated direction and speed. The left one moved right or left to steer. The right one, when pushed forward, resulted in forward acceleration. Before discovering this, Two Hawks had stopped the car with the foot pedal on the floor, although it protested at the strain between brakes and engine. Two Hawks placed the speed stick in neutral, pushed it forward, learned that the car went forward, and then pulled the stick towards him. The vehicle went backward.

He drove the car forward and around the curve. With an almost inaudible chuff of steam escaping and wheels crunching on the stones, the car moved up to where O'Brien lay. Two Hawks stopped it and then tried to determine which knobs on the panel controlled the lights. The first one he turned operated the single windshield wiper, placed in the center of the shield. To do its job, it had to describe a 180-degree arc. Two Hawks thought that Hotinohsinih cars had a long way to go before they could compete with those of his Earth

But he was happy that he had at least this much.

He turned another knob. A small panel light and the two front head lights, set on top of the fenders, came on. These were not very powerful, but they were good enough for his purposes. The beams lit up the front of the asylum, the bodies on the verandah and the bodies on the steps and on the driveway. He yelled at O'Brien, who rose slowly and walked to the car.

"You're doing all right, lieutenant," he said in a low voice. "But where do we go from here?"

Two Hawks did not answer. He was studying the indicators on the panel. These were glass cylinders set in the middle of the instrument panel. There were six, illuminated by lights behind them. Each had a lighted symbol above it, the symbols being derived from the ideographic writing the Hotinohsonih had used before abandoning it for the Greek alphabet. At various levels, a pale red fluid was rising in each tube, across which were white gradations. The tubes apparently indicated the level of water supply, temperature of steam, amount of fuel, the speed, the battery condition, and the mileage. Two Hawks knew what the degree marks were supposed to mean, but since the Hotinohsonih had a peculiar measuring system, he had trouble converting them into English units.

The water and fuel indicators showed full. As for the speed, he would judge by the seat of his pants. He waited until O'Brien got into the seat beside him, then started down the steep and winding road that led to the city below. Behind them, men emboldened by the absence of gunfire, burst out of the house. At that moment, the moon broke clear of the clouds. He turned off his lights and drove more swiftly by the illumination of the moon. On reaching the bottom of the hill,

he stopped the car and got out to look at a street
sign. The fact that there was one there showed
that he was near a main highway, since very few
streets had signs. In the residential districts, a
stranger either had to have a map or ask questions if he wanted to find his way around.

His study of the map of 'Estokwa in the library had familiarized him with the main arter-
ies of exit. He was only a few blocks from the
great highway which led east. Actually, he had
known this, but he wanted to confirm the accuracy of the map.

They rounded a corner and there, at the end
of the street, was the highway. Now they could
hear the noise of traffic, the murmur of voices,
and the creak of axles. The highway was
jammed with refugees, men, women, and children carrying big bundles or pushing wheel-
barrows or drawing two-wheeled carts loaded
with all they could take.

The appearance of confusion was misleading.
After Two Hawks had edged the car between
two groups, he found that soldiers, stationed every few blocks, were directing traffic. These carried kerosene lamps or large flashlights. The first
trooper did not stop their car, but Two Hawks
wondered how far they would get before being
asked for identity papers. Without these, they
could be arrested, perhaps even shot on the spot.
So, at the first chance, he swung the car back
onto a sidestreet.

"We'll have to take a chance, hope we don't
get lost," he said. "And when we're forced back
onto the big highway, we may have to make a

break for it, ram through a guard post."

"That's all right," O'Brien said, "but where are we going?"

"How's your arm?" Two Hawks said.

O'Brien groaned and said, "I'm bleeding to death. I ain't going to make it lieutenant."

"I don't think it's that bad," Two Hawks said. He stopped the car and examined the wound in the brightness of a flashlight he had found in a box under the panel. As he had thought, the wound was shallow. There was still a little flow of blood, which was, however, easily stanched with a handkerchief. He bound it around the arm and resumed driving.

O'Brien's reactions had puzzled him until recently. The sergeant had been a good soldier, very competent, cheerful, and courageous. But ever since he had realized that they were out of their native universe, he had changed. He felt as if he were going to die. And this, Two Hawks thought, came from a sense of utter dislocation. He was cut off forever from the world in which he had been born and lived. He was an alien in a place he did not understand. He was suffering from a homesickness the like of which no man had ever experienced. It was literally killing him.

Two Hawks knew how he felt, although he was sure he did not suffer to the same degree. In the first place, he had learned to live with a similar feeling on his native Earth. A child of two cultures, never wholly in phase with either and not believing fully in the values and mores of either, he, too, had been a stranger. In the second place, he was basically more flexible than

O'Brien. He could survive the shock of transplantation, rally, and even thrive if things went right. But he was worried about O'Brien.

10

TWO HOURS LATER, after being lost a dozen times, they came out on the main highway, the *kadziiwa'* road. A half-mile away was a large number of soldiers. Even as Two Hawks watched them, they took a man from a car and marched him off to a tent at one side of the road.

"Checking for spies and deserters," Two Hawks said. "All right; we'll go around them."

That was not so easy. They had to cut across a shallow creek a mile away. They drove through slowly without getting stuck only to be stopped five minutes later by a stone fence which seemed to run to both horizons. By then, dawn had come. The car paralleled the fence for a mile and a half, which finally ran out. However, a dense grove of trees and a broad creek further barred them.

Two Hawks drove the vehicle into the stream, which was about thirty yards wide. They plowed ahead for ten yards with the water beginning to seep from under the doors. Then the car stopped, its wheels spinning. Nothing after that could get it out of the mud.

"We'll hoof it," Two Hawks said. "Maybe it's just as well the car got stuck. If we'd gone on, and the water got too deep, the boiler might've blown up."

"Now you tell me! Let's get to hell out of here!"

They traveled over the farm country paralleling the highway. Four days later, the paved portion ran out. From there on, the road was dirt.

The two ate from food stolen from the peasants. Two days passed. They had a chance to steal a car, an internal-combustion type, and they took it. They made thirty miles that day, cutting along the side of the road, blowing their horn at the refugees in their path. Then, hearing of a check station ahead, they turned onto a narrow dirt rural road. When they had run out of gas, they continued on foot.

"The nation of Itskapintik is to the north," he told O'Brien. "The last I heard, it was neutral. We'll cross the border and throw ourselves on whatever mercy they have."

"I don't like the way you said that," O'Brien said. "What kind of people are they?"

"Basically, Indians with a lot of white genes. They speak a language belonging to the Nahuatl family, something like the Aztec speech of Mexico. They're much like the Aztecs, in fact. They came out of Asia about the same time as the Iroquois, both pushed out by a powerful Amerind nation that later conquered half of northern Asia.

"The Itskapintik defeated another tribe, half-white, half-Amerind, that had just finished terrorizing eastern Europe. The Itskapintik slaughtered half of them and enslaved the rest."

"They're pretty rough, huh?"

"I got that impression. For instance, it was only fifty years ago that they quit sacrificing people at religious ceremonies. And their slaves are not only treated as sub-humans but have no chance of becoming freemen, as they do among the Hotinohsonih."

"Then why are we going there?"

"Not really with the idea of throwing ourselves on their mercy. We'll try to cut across the country, hide from them, travel at night. Our goal will be Tyrsland, Earth 1's Sweden. Perkunisha has declared war against Tyrsland, but it's not made any belligerent moves against it. If we could get there, we could arrange to be transported to Blodland. We'd be important men there; we'd really have something to live for."

"Sweet Mother of Christ! I'd give my right eye to live in a place where they speak English."

"I don't want to discourage you," Two Hawks said. "But you'd have to learn it all over again. However, it would be easier for you than Iroquoian."

They had been cutting across the back-country, using rural roads as guides but keeping parallel with them. Only at night, when the roads were deserted, did they take to them. Even then, Two Hawks did so reluctantly. But walking on fields of wheat or meadows or through the woods slowed them down so much that they had to chance the swifter means of travel now and then. Fifteen days after leaving 'Estokwa, they came across a main highway, going north. From the hilltop, he could see that the great river of refugees had not diminished. At this point there were no soldiers evident, so he decided that it would be safe to mingle with the traffic.

For two days they trudged along on the fringe of the column, finding that they could make better time this way. The dawn of the third day, they heard cannonfire to the west. By nightfall, the rattle of small firearms came from a distance. The next day, Hotinohsonih troops appeared. They were reinforcements from the south, headed for the northwest where a battle raged. Two Hawks and O'Brien went back into the middle of the refugee column to make themselves inconspicuous. Besides, the reckless speed of the military vehicles on the side of the road made travel there dangerous.

The fourth day, at noon, the refugees were diverted eastward at a crossroads. Two Hawks said, "The Perkunishans must have taken the road up ahead. They're really advancing."

"I always thought the Iroquois were mighty warriors," O'Brien said. "But they don't seem to be doing any better than the Russians."

Two Hawks was a little irritated, as if criticism of the Hotinohsonih was, in a way, a criticism of him. He knew that O'Brien always thought of him as an Indian and that, although never outwardly disrespectful, he had his private opinions.

"I'll tell you one thing," Two Hawks said.

"The Perkunishans may be winning, but they're paying a hell of a higher price for it than the Germans did. War's a little different here. There aren't any Geneva Conventions, you know. What a nation does with its prisoners of war is strictly its own business. The Perkunishans have found out from previous experience that the Iroquois don't make good slaves. They either keep on trying to escape or get killed trying.

"So Perkunisha has declared a no-quarters war. No prisoners except when one is needed for information. And they torture to get that information. The Hotinohsonih know this; they fight to the death. And when they retreat, they kill their own wounded if they aren't able to carry them out. As a result, the invaders are getting a much stiffer resistance than they otherwise would. But their superior technology and their strategy of bypassing pockets of defenders to be mopped up later accounts for their present speed. Plus the fact they're willing to suffer high casualties.

"You see, Perkunisha wants to conquer as much territory as possible before winter comes. This land occupies the same area as Rumania and southwest Russia of Earth 1, without the relatively mild climate. Europe is near-subarctic cold in winter. That's another reason why we have to get to Tyrsland before the snows come. We don't want to get caught in the open country then; we'd freeze to death in short order."

O'Brien shivered and said, "Brother, what a world! If we had to go through a "gate," why couldn't we have been lucky and found a nice warm and peaceful world?"

Two Hawks smiled and shrugged. There might be such a "parallel" Earth, but if so, they were not in it. They had to live in the one luck had dealt them.

A few minutes later, they passed a car stuck in the soft earth on the side of the road. Three men were trying to push it out. Two Hawks said, "Did you notice the woman at the wheel? She had a scarf around her hair, and the face was pretty dirty. But I'll swear it was Ilmika Thorrs-stein."

He hesitated for several minutes, then decided that her presence might be a lucky break. Maybe she was heading for Itskapintik because her position as daughter of the Blodland ambassador would ensure her good treatment and even a return to her country. She would want to take Two Hawks and O'Brien with her. After all, that had been her original intent, and he could think of no reason why she should have changed her mind.

He walked boldly up to her. For a minute, she seemed puzzled. Then she recognized him. Incredulity was succeeded by a smile of joy. "Can we go with you?" he said.

She nodded and said, "This seems too good to be true."

He did not waste any more time. The two Americans went to the rear of the car and helped the other three men. After the vehicle had regained the harder dirt, Two Hawks and O'Brien got into the front seat beside Ilmika. The others, who turned out to be members of the Six Kingdoms embassy at 'Estokwa, rode in the rear. Il-

mika drove the steamer as fast as she could
without endangering the pedestrians. She used
her horn frequently to warn them out of the way,
and if they did not dodge quickly enough, swung
onto the shoulder. It was just such a maneuver
that had trapped her in the mud ten minutes
before Two Hawks came along.

While they rode, he told Ilmika what had happened. She knew, of course, that the Blodland
agents had been killed, but she had supposed
that the Perkunishans had succeeded in abduct-
ing the two otherworlders. She was now on this
road because her original avenue of escape had
been cut off. The Perkunishan fleet had broken
into the Black Sea, defeated the Hotinohsonih
navy and the small contingent of Blodland ships.
They controlled the waters and the air of the
Black Sea. The small dirigible on which she had
planned to take the two to Dassa (Turkey) had
been destroyed. So she had fled towards
Itskapintik.

They drove all day and night, and dawn found
them much further northward but also out of
fuel. They had no luck trying to get more from
the army vehicles that passed them. Of the twenty, not one stopped in response to their signals.

"It's a long way, but we'll have to walk," Ilmika said. "If I can get into contact with an officer, I might be able to get another car."

She did not sound hopeful. It was evident that
the Hotinohsonih were too occupied with the
battle to the northwest to spare time or materiel,
even for the Lady Ilmika Thorrsstein. And they
had walked no more than four miles, when they

got evidence that the soldiers were too busy taking care of themselves to bother with them.

A score of troopers a half-mile ahead ran from a woods and cut across the road. The refugees near them abandoned their carts and ran after them. Word passed back along the column and with it panic. The road suddenly became a litter of vehicles and no people.

Forty yards ahead of them, the earth blossomed into a pillar of upflung dirt and smoke. The people who had just deserted the highway were unhurt, but the next shell exploded near a group who had not heard the news in time. They were tossed in every direction.

Two Hawks and the others had flung themselves in a small ditch when the first shell landed. They hugged the earth while a second, third, and fourth, running down the road, deafened them and covered them with dirt. A severed foot landed by Two Hawks' head. He took one look and then drove his face into the grass. The fifth shell stunned and half-buried them, but no one was hit. The sixth exploded a little further down; the seventh struck the ditch and killed a number of men, women, and children.

Then the cannonade ceased. Two Hawks raised his head. Across the road was a burnt-out wheat field and beyond it a sloping hill. Over the top of the hill came five armored cars. Two carried long-snouted cannons; the others were armed with weapons that looked from this distance like the barrels of machine guns. Two Hawks knew that machine guns had not been invented yet. In fact, this was one of the items he

had intended to explain to the Blodlandish. But
he did not like their looks, although the cannons
would have been enough for him to decide on
flight. He rose with the others and dashed across
the blackened stubble of the wheat field on his
side of the road. He had seen the Iroquois troops
take cover in a copse of trees about a quarter-
mile to the northwest. They would be the object
of attack by the armored cars, so there was no
use trying to hide there. He led the others south-
east across the field towards a distant line of
half-burned trees that probably hid a stream. By
the time the refugees had reached the middle of
the field, the Perkunishans had crossed the road.
They fired a few rounds at the group, which kept
on running. Glancing behind him, Two Hawks
could see the bullets throw up fragments of
earth. The rate of fire amazed him. He was sure
that the cars had some sort of rapid-fire weapon.
His reading had not indicated the existence of
such a gun, but it was evident that it must have
been developed secretly and only now revealed.
Gatlings?

One more reason for the Perkunishans' rapid
advances. Their firepower must be overwhelming.

The cars swung towards the woods, and soon
the racket of battle was hideous. It lasted for perhaps ten minutes. After that, a silence. By then
the refugees had passed through the tree-lined
creek and had entered a relatively thick and ex-
tensive woods. They walked until nightfall, slept
several hours, then resumed their flight. Two
days afterwards, they came upon a group of dead

soldiers. A gully near them concealed a small car —equivalent of a jeep—which was undamaged and had a half-tank of gas. They drove it northward until the fuel ran out and began walking again. A week later, they were somewhere near the Itskapintik border.

They had heard light rifle fire ahead of them. While Ilmika and a man who had been sick hid behind some trees, the others crawled up the slope of a hill. They were armed with rifles and revolvers taken from the dead who had also provided them with the jeep. Nevertheless, they did not intend to take any aggressive action. They just wanted to determine what the situation ahead was and if they would have to take a wide detour.

He got to the top of the hill and inspected the fight through binoculars. The skirmish was almost at an end. There were a number of bodies on the ground at various distances outside a stone rampart, all that was left of a farmhouse which had burned. The bodies wore the black and orange uniforms of the Perkunishan infantry. There were seven attackers left, and they were working in closer to the defense behind the wall. Two Hawks watched for a while and saw that only three were still firing from the wall. Then a Perkunishan, crouching behind an overturned wagon near the ruins, threw a grenade. It landed over the wall and in a corner.

After the explosion, there was no return fire. Still cautious, the Perkunishans continued to hug the ground until they were several yards away. One exposed himself briefly but drew no fire. There was a signal from one, and all rose and dashed towards the wall. Suddenly, smoke from a gun behind the wall rose, and seconds later Two Hawks heard the crack. A Perkunishan fell. Another shot; another crumpled.

The others were too near the wall to turn to run. They kept on charging but fired as they did so to force their enemy to keep his head down. He, however, paid no attention to the bullets which were bouncing off the stone near his head. He kept on shooting and with deadly effectiveness. Two more staggered; one fell backward and the other ran forward again a few steps after stopping before he too slumped.

Two Hawks was surprised. He could see the helmet and upper part of the defender's uniform. Both were the same type as the Perkunishans'. There was one difference. He wore two broad red stripes on his chest.

Then the survivors were through a break in the wall. They fired pointblank at him, but if he was struck he gave no indication. He reversed his rifle, swung the stock like a club, and felled the closest man. He disappeared momentarily from Two Hawks' view, then came up with the body of the man he had struck down held above his head. He hurled the body at the other two and knocked them both down. What he might have done after that, however, was matter for speculation. He seemed to have the upper hand all of a sudden, but one of the men who had been shot down came to life. He rose and fired at the man with the red stripes. The helmet flew off his head, and he dropped.

A minute later, the three survivors had
dragged their enemy out onto the ground. The
wounded Perkunishan did not help them but
busied himself shedding his coat and tearing off
his shirtsleeve. He then bandaged his upper
right arm. The other two hauled the body of the
enemy to a place beneath a maple tree. From
somewhere they had gotten a rope, a section of
which they used to tie his hands. They removed the man's boots and bound his feet
together.

One end of the rope was tied to the man's
wrists and the other thrown over a branch. Two
men hauled on the rope, and the captive was
borne upright until his bare feet were about
eight inches from the ground. His position must
have been painful, since all the strain of weight
was on his arms, tied behind him, and forced
back and up. Despite this, the face of the hanging man was expressionless. He spun slowly at
the end of the rope and did not even open his
mouth to protest when the soldiers piled wood
for a fire below his feet.

Two Hawks decided to interfere. He admired
the big man's magnificent fight, although this
alone would not have been enough to make him
attack the soldiers. He was curious about the
reasons for the fighting between two groups of
Perkunishans.

He told the others in his party what he wanted
to do. They agreed to follow him, especially after
he said he thought the captive might give them
valuable information. They spread out, taking
some time to go around the hill and crawl along

a depression. Entering the woods from the depression, they cautiously approached the Perkunishans. Ten minutes elapsed before they were crouching behind trees, close enough to hear the conversation. Since this was in Perkunishan, Two Hawks did not understand much of it, but it was obvious they were cursing and taunting the hanging man.

By then, the fire was blazing high enough to lick at his bare feet. He had to be suffering intense agony, yet he said nothing. Two Hawks did not wait any longer for a more advantageous time. He did not want the captive to be crippled. He drew a bead on the stomach of the soldier nearest him; the others also sighted in. Two Hawks lifted one hand, held it, then chopped down. An almost simultaneous crash of gunfire smashed the three Perkunishans backwards. None of them moved again.

Two Hawks rushed out, kicked the burning sticks to one side, and then cut the rope where it was tied to the tree-trunk. Two Blodlandish lowered the hanging man.

Two Hawks removed his knife from his scabbard, but he did not offer to cut the giant's bonds. He looked too dangerous. He was at least six feet seven high and three across the shoulders. His arms, chest, and legs were gorilloid in bulk. His face was broad and highcheekboned; his nose, aquiline; his hair, straight and black. However, his skin was not especially dark, and his brown eyes had large green flecks.

One of the Blodlandish, Aelfred Herot, questioned the man in Perkunishan. There was some rapid conversation, and Herot said, "He's a Kinukkinuk."

Two Hawks nodded. Kinukkinuk was the Algonquian nation which occupied the area of Czechoslovakia of Earth 1. For over a hundred years, it had been part of Perkunisha.

"He says his name is Kwasind, that is, The Strong One. He was in a Kinukkinuk regiment under the command of Perkunishan officers. He and other Kinukkinuk decided to desert and join the Hotinohsonih. But they were tracked down and cornered in the farmhouse. You saw the rest. I've explained who we are. He says he would like to throw in with us. He also speaks Hotinohsonih, since his mother was a slave from that country. He says she was freed by his father before he married her, so Kwasind is not the son of a slave. The Kinukkinuk are very proud, even if they are treated as subhuman by the Perkunishans."

Without a word, Two Hawks cut the ropes from Kwasind. The giant rubbed his wrists while he walked around to restore his circulation. The skin of his feet was very red but not burned. He sat down on a corpse to put his boots back on. Two Hawks handed him a rifle and a belt of ammunition and a knife.

In Hotinohsonih, Kwasind said, "Thank you."

"You can walk all right?"

"I can walk. But if you had been ten seconds later . . ."

Two Hawks sent Herot back to bring up Ilmika and her guard. The casualties were checked. Three Perkunishans were still living, seriously wounded. Kwasind and the Blodland-ish put them out or their pain with knives in the solar plexus. Kwasind took a sword from a dead officer and hacked off the heads of the Perk-unishans. He arranged them in a little pyramid and then stood back a distance to admire the arrangement.

O'Brien vomited. Two Hawks felt sick.

Herot explained. "By severing the heads of his enemies, he's keeping their souls from going to Michilimakinak, the Kinukkinuk heaven."

"Very interesting," Two Hawks said. "I hope he doesn't have any more customs which will de-lay us."

Ilmika and Elhson joined them. Ilmika turned pale on seeing the heads, but she did not say anything.

Kwasind chanted over the bodies of his fellow countrymen, then opened their jackets and shirts. The left breast of each was tattooed with a swastika in a circle. These Kwasind removed by cutting a circle around them and stripping off the skin. He restored the fire that Two Hawks had kicked apart and threw the tattooed skins into the flames.

Herot said, "The tattooed symbols contain the 'souls'. If they're burned, the souls are free to fly up to Michilimakinak. But if they're taken by enemies, they could be dried or preserved in al-cohol. The souls would then never get to Michilimakinak."

Two Hawks waited until Kwasind was fin-ished. If the delay had been caused by anything but a religious custom, he would have insisted on leaving at once. In this case, it was important not to offend. To strike at a man's religion was to strike at his basic identity.

11

THE PARTY WALKED northwards across the country all that day and the next. The dawn of the third, they were startled out of their sleep by the roar of many motors. Two Hawks crawled to the edge of the hollow in which they were hidden and looked down the slope of the hill at the road a quarter-mile below. It was crowded with a column of armored cars and trucks pulling cannon on caissons. All the vehicles were painted scarlet with blue bars. The doors bore the image of a black bear, rampant.

"Itskapintik," Ilmika said behind him. "They must finally be invading Hotinohsonih. We've known for some time that Perkunisha was trying to persuade the Itskapintik to join them. They've promised half of Hotinohsonih to them."

Two Hawks watched the stream of men, weapons, supplies, and vehicles roar by. The features of the soldiers under the round steel helmets somewhat resembled those of the Mexican Indians of Earth 1, although the skin was lighter.

All day, the column rode by. The watchers from the hill dozed and took turns guarding. They did not dare to venture out in the light, even in the woods, because there were patrols in the countryside. When dusk came, they resumed their march. The next day, Aelwin Graenfield, the sick Blodlandish, could not get up. Weakly, he urged the others to leave him behind. They would not hear of it. He continued to get worse and by dawn was dead.

They placed his body in a shallow grave scooped out with knives. Herot conducted the services, which consisted of a prayer by the Blodlandish as they circled sunwise around the open grave and dropped a fistful of dirt on the body at the bottom. Two Hawks stood with bowed head but watched the proceedings. The Blodlandish, like all west Europeans, subscribed to the same religion. This had been founded only a thousand years ago by a man named Hemilka. Inspired by a revelation, he had renounced the worship of the old gods and proposed to replace it with a monotheism. He had been martyred— suspended from a rope by one leg and both legs broken and then left to hang until he died from pain, thirst, and exposure. This was a form of execution for heretics, a form which had died out only seventy-five years ago.

After Hemilka's death, his disciples had scattered to escape the same punishment and also to spread his message. Eventually, Hemilkism triumphed, as the Christianity of Earth 1 had won after a long period of persecution.

There were many parallels to Christianity in Hemilkism: salvation for all who believed in Hemilka, his virgin birth, a heaven, a hell, and a limbo for virtuous pre-Hemilka pagans. There was also a doctrine much like that which the Mormons held, baptism of the dead.

Two Hawks explained the history and tenets of the religion to O'Brien. The sergeant was especially interested and proud that Earth 2's Christ had been an Irishman.

"It's quite a coincidence," Two Hawks said, "that the great western religions of our Earth were founded by Semites. Judaism and Christianity by the Jews and Islam by an Arab who took much of his religion from the previous faiths. But here . . ."

"A mick is God's only son, not a hebe," O'Brien said. "Didn't you say he was born in Ireland! And who was his mother? Surely, she was Irish, too."

"Curiously enough, she was named Meryam," Two Hawks said. "As for Hemilka not being Jewish, well, he must have been at least part Semitic. His name is Cretan. As I've told you, the Kerdezh were in southern Ireland, or Bamba, for many centuries. Meryam is also a Cretan name. Also, it's obvious that Hemilka borrowed a lot from both the Neshirite religion of the North Africans and the Mithraic religion of Asia Minor and much of Asia."

"One thing," O'Brien said. "Why in hell is Ireland called Bamba? Is that a Semitic name?"

"No. It's Celtic. In ancient days on our Earth, Banba was a sort of pet name for Ireland. Banba was the chief goddess of the pagan Irish. The name, by the way, means "pig". I assume that here the pet name became the official name. In time the "n" became the labial "m" because of its close proximity to the labial "b". Or maybe it was Bamba from the beginning. None of the languages are exactly like their Earth 1 parallels."

Graenfield's body was covered with dirt, and they got ready to resume the march. It was then that the Itskapintik police rose from behind the trees from which they'd been observing. There were six, clothed in blue uniforms and wearing steel helmets covered with scarlet cloth. Their badges were in the form of eagles clutching writhing snakes. All were armed with single-shot rifles, short swords in scabbards, and large billy clubs.

While four aimed the rifles, two bound the captives' hands behind them. A small boy, a farmer's son who must have reported the strangers to the police, stood proudly to one side.

The chief officer, a short dark man with a big mouth full of very large protruding teeth, walked leering up to Ilmika. He reached out, felt her breasts, and then began stripping her. Finding that this was difficult while her hands were tied, he removed the binds. Ilmika did not protest; she knew that it would be useless. As the daughter of a Blodlander noble, she would not give the men the satisfaction of hearing her plead or cry out.

There was nothing the prisoners could do but stand as passive witnesses. Or so, at least, that was what Two Hawks thought. He closed his eyes when Ilmika was thrown down on the ground. But, O'Brien, who was by his side and breathing like a winded horse, suddenly gave a whoop. Two Hawks opened his eyes. The

Irishman had run towards the woman and the chief, who was covering her. One of the policemen swung the butt of his rifle at him but missed him. O'Brien crossed the few yards between the prisoners and the police before the latter were aware of what was happening. He leaped into the air, bent his knees, and then kicked straight out. The policeman, bending over Ilmika, heard the warning shouts of the others and turned. His chin took the impact of both of O'Brien's hard-driven boots. There was a crack as of a stick breaking, and he flipped onto his back.

O'Brien slammed hard onto his back. His arms, tied behind him, took the brunt of the fall. He cried out with pain and rolled over and tried to struggle to his feet. A rifle butt cracked against the back of his head; he pitched forward on his face. The man who had struck O'Brien reversed his rifle and shot him in the back of his neck. O'Brien straightened out, quivered, and was still.

The Itskapintik whom O'Brien had kicked was also dead, his jaw shattered and neck broken. Furious, the police began to beat the prisoners. Two Hawks was knocked to the ground by a rifle butt slammed into his shoulder. He was then kicked in the ribs twice. Another boot-toe driven into the side of his head stunned him.

Their fury finally vented, the police quit. They talked violently among themselves for a while. The prisoners groaned or moaned or lay mute and motionless. The most brutally beaten, Herot, vomited through lips torn by a gun butt.

Blood and teeth poured out on the ground.

Two Hawks could not think straight for a
while. His head felt as if a hot spike had been
driven into it, and his shoulder ached like a rot-
ten tooth. Later, he figured out why O'Brien had
acted so suicidally. The sergeant had been slowly dying ever since he had learned that he was
cut off forever from his native world. A deep grief
had possessed him, one so piercing that his will
to live poured out through the skin of his soul.
And so he had deliberately caused his own
death. It was an act of bravery and gallantry and
thus did not look to the others as self-murder.
And he had struck back at this world.

Another blow to him, perhaps the most wound-
ing of all, had been the knowledge that his religion did not exist here. He could not attend
mass or confess. He would die with no chance of
last unction or of being buried in holy ground.

O'Brien's act was not entirely in vain. It had
taken the interest away from Ilmika. The chief
growled an order. Dazedly, Ilmika struggled to
her feet and submitted to having her hands retied.

Herot quit vomiting. He got to his feet and
resumed talking to the chief. The Itskapintik
told him to shut up, and when Herot continued,
the chief placed the muzzle of his revolver
against Herot's stomach. The Blodlandish was
either out of his mind with grief and pain or else
a very brave man who was not going to back
down for anybody. From Herot's tone, Two
Hawks was sure that a good part of his talking
was invective. He expected the chief to blow
Herot's guts out. The chief only grinned, shoved

Herot away, and ordered the captives aboard a
truck which had driven up. They were on the
truck ten hours without food or water. The truck
finally drove into a military camp. Here the prisoners were marched into a high-walled com-
pound. A little water, some stinking stew and
hard dry black bread was given them. Those
whose lips and jaws were not too painful from
the beatings ate.

Night fell, and with it came a horde of mosquitoes. Morning brought some relief. An officer
who could speak both Blodlandish and Hotinohsonih questioned them. Their stories
seemed to alarm the officer. Guards came an
hour later and took Ilmika away, treating her
with courtesy.

Two Hawks asked Herot if he had any idea of
what was going on. Herot mumbled through
swollen lips and broken teeth, "If Itskapintik
was still neutral, we'd be set free with an
apology. But not now. The best we can hope for
is a life of slavery. The Lady Thorrsstein will
probably be chosen by some high-ranking officer
to be his whore. After he's tired of her, she'll go
to a lesser officer. God knows what after that.
But she's a Blodlandish noble; she'll kill herself
at the first chance."

Two Hawks was not so sure. He suspected
that something unusual was happening. The following day, he and Kwasind were taken to a
building and into an office. Ilmika Thorrsstein,
an Itskapintik officer, and a Perkunishan official
were also there. The latter was splendid in a
scarlet-and-white uniform, many medals, and

huge gold epaulets. Ilmika looked much better. She had bathed, her hair was in a Psyche knot, and she was wearing a lady's jacket and long skirt. However, she seemed withdrawn. The Perkunishan had to repeat questions several times before she would respond.

Two Hawks caught on quickly. The very efficient espionage system of Perkunisha had learned about the capture of Ilmika shortly after it had taken place. Its government had immediately "requested" that Ilmika, Two Hawks, and Kwasind be turned over to it. The Itskapintik government may have wondered what was behind the "request," but it had no way of finding out. If it had suspected the truth about Two Hawks, it probably would have denied having him.

It was not until later that Two Hawks found out why Ilmika and Kwasind were also wanted by Perkunisha. Ilmika was a grandniece of its ruler, the Kassandrash. She was the daughter of his niece, who had married a younger brother of the king of Blodland. After the king's brother died, the Kassandrash's niece had married Lord Thorrsstein, himself a cousin of the king. Ilmika was born of this marriage. The Kassandrash did not want his grandniece to fall into the barbarous hands of the Itskapintik.

As for Kwasind, he had been mistaken for O'Brien. That error would soon be detected, but it would last long enough for him to be taken to Berlin with the other two. The Blodlandish were never heard of again. Two Hawks supposed that they were swallowed up in the maw of a labor camp.

Before the three boarded the steam train that was to take them to Berlin, they witnessed the execution of the men who had raped Ilmika and his aides. These were marched naked into the courtyard of the prison and halted before pillars topped by horizontal beams. The charges and the sentences were read to them by an official wearing a blue uniform and a long-feathered headdress. Two Hawks didn't understand the Nahuatl, but the official read the document again in badly pronounced Blodlander.

Then the executioners, all clad in black, their faces hidden by demons' masks, threw thin wires over the ends of five beams. One end of each wire was rolled around a large heavy drum held by two tall supports affixed to the cement by bolts. The other end was pulled down from the beam and looped tightly around the testicles of a prisoner.

The executioners began turning the cranks of the drums. In a short time the wires had begun lifting the scrotums of the condemned. Though the flesh continued to stretch, its owner was lifted off his feet. All five were presently horizontal and rising slowly. With their hands tied behind them, they could do nothing but submit. Two did so gracefully, the chief and another. The rest struggled. None cried out. They were made of tough stuff; Two Hawks had to give them that.

When the condemned had been lifted four feet above the ground, the drums were locked. After that it was only a matter of time until the flesh of the scrotum separated at the root, and, one by one, in swift succession, the still voiceless men

dropped flat on their backs. After they had recovered their winds and their wits, they were
lifted up. The wires were straightened out at the
ends and then rewound around the penises.
Once more, the lifting began.

Two Hawks did not feel sorry for them. They
were getting what they deserved, though he
would have preferred that they just be shot. Nevertheless, he felt sick, and he was glad when the
organs finally parted. This time, only one survived, the chief. Though he was bleeding so
heavily that he could not have lasted more than
a minute, his throat was cut.

The official then asked Ilmika if she was satisfied.

She said loudly and firmly, "I will tell my
father that the Itskapintik are a just people. I
thank you for avenging my honor."

Two Hawks did not think he was going to like
what lay ahead of him in Berlin, yet he felt relieved when they crossed the Itskapintik border.
Not until then did the uneasiness in his mind go
away.

The car in which they rode was, in many
ways, luxurious. Two Hawks and Kwasind had
a compartment for themselves. The food was ex-
cellent, and they could drink as much beer,
wine, or whiskey as they wished. They could
even take a bath. Nevertheless, there were iron
bars over every window, and armed guards stood
on both sides of the doors at each end of the car.
The officer in charge, a Khiliarkhosh (Captain)
Wilkish, was never far away. He took his meals
with the two men and helped Two Hawks with

his lessons in Perkunishan.

Ilmika stayed in her compartment. The few
times she came out, she seemed constrained. He
supposed that it was because he had witnessed
her disgrace. Not only did she feel embarrassment that he had seen her suffering an outrage,
she probably felt contempt because he had not
tried to defend her. In her code, any gentleman
would have died rather than permit a
noblewoman to be dishonored. Two Hawks did
not try to defend himself. She had seen what had
happened to O'Brien. Moreover, her own people, Herot and the others, had not fought for her.
They had chosen the realistic path—and wisely,
he thought.

Ilmika said nothing about this. She answered
Two Hawks' greetings with a cold nod. He
shrugged and sometimes smiled. What did he
care? He had been attracted to her, but they
were abysses apart. He was neither Blodlandish
nor noble. Even if she were in love with him—
and she had not given the slightest sign she was
—she would have to forget about him.

Two Hawks occupied himself in learning the
language and also studying the country he saw
through the car windows. Its topography, he
supposed, would be much like that of Poland
and Germany of Earth 1. The dwellings were not
too different in structure, although there was a
tendency to decorate with what he called
"curlicue" architecture. The peasants were
dressed simply, were shaggy-haired and not too
clean. The absence of horses gave him a strange
feeling. There was no plowing at this time, but

Wilkish told him that oxen were used, although
the beasts were being replaced by steam or gas
tractors on the big estates. Wilkish boasted that
his country had more farm tractors than any
other nation in the world.

At the city of Gervvoge, another officer joined
them. Vyautash wore an all-black uniform with
silver epaulets and a silver boar's head on his tall
red shako. His face was gaunt and thin-lipped,
yet he turned out to be affable and quick-witted.
He was liable to pun at the slightest or no excuse. Two Hawks was not deceived. Vyautash
was there for preliminary questioning of the two
prisoners.

Two Hawks had decided he might as well tell
everything. If he refused to cooperate, he would
end up by spilling his guts anyway, and be in
very bad health in the bargain. Besides, he had
no definite loyalties to any country of this world.
Fate had originally thrown him in with the
Blodlandish and Hotinohsonih, yet the latter
had tortured him and then locked him up and
the former had betrayed their own allies to get
their hands on him. There did not seem to be
much difference between the practices of Perkunisha and Blodland. Yet he did not feel right in
becoming an ally of a German. Working for the
same nation with which the German flier was
working was, in some undefinable way, betray-
ing his own country, his own world.

But—here there was no United States of
America, just as there was no Germany.

After a half-hour of interrogation by
Vyautash, Two Hawks understood the reasons

for the type of questions. Vyautash was checking the answers against those in a large bound volume of typewritten sheets. The book undoubtedly contained information given by the German.

Two Hawks said, "How do you know that the fellow—whatever his name is—has given you a true story?"

Vyautash was startled. Then he smiled and said, "So you know about him? The Blodlandish told you? His name, by the way, is Horst Raske."

"And what do you think of our tales?"

"There's enough evidence to convince those who matter. To me, though, there are very puzzling aspects. Let's say that there is a universe occupying the same 'space' as ours but not intersecting. I can understand why the same type of animals, including human beings, might develop on both planets. After all, the size and distance of the Earths from the sun are identical, and the geophysical factors are similar.

"But I cannot understand why almost identical languages are found on both worlds. Do you realize how mathematically improbable such a coincidence is? About several billion billions to one, I would say. Yet, I am asked to believe that not one, but many languages, have their near-counterparts on your Earth."

Vyautash shook his head and said, "No! No! No!"

"Raske and my men passed through a 'gate,' " Two Hawks said. "Perhaps there have been many gates. During the hundred thousand years or so that man has existed, there may have been much traffic between the two Earths. Perhaps mankind did not originate on this planet. He may have come here from my Earth. The fossil evidence in my world indicates that man originated there. However, it's not proved beyond all doubt. No fossils have been found that are undeniably a direct link between modern man and subman."

Vyautash said, "Until fifty years ago, speculation about the evolution of man was forbidden. Even now, there's much resistance to the idea that man may not have been created in one day and that day only 5,000 years ago. However, there is strong evidence that man has existed much more than five millenia. Not only man but several types of subhumans."

"I would maintain that the people of this planet originated on my Earth," Two Hawks said. "Only . ..."

"Only what?"

"If the original men came through gates to this world, then their horses and camels should have come through with them. But say that various tribes of Earthmen did come through in enough numbers to establish themselves here but came at a time *before* the horse and camel were domesticated. That could account for the fact that Earth 2 has any number of ethnic types and languages which are similar enough to certain Terrestrial groups to be descended from them. It might also account for the complete absence of other Earth 1-type peoples here: the Slavs, the Hebrews, the Italics, the Australian aborigine, and so forth.

"Yet, if human beings could come through the 'gates,' why not animals? Why not the horse, the camel?

"Also, it seems peculiar that immigrants from Earth 1, who must have passed over only in small numbers, could have come to dominate the same general regions, as on Earth 1. Why were the people who already occupied those regions, and who must have been more numerous, defeated by the newcomers? I just don't know."

Vyautash said, "I don't know either. But the hard and indissoluble facts are that Perkunishans and Rasna and so forth are here. And we have to live here, and you are here and also have to live here. So, let's get on with our discussion."

Two Hawks was with Vyautash almost every waking moment of the trip. However, Two Hawks managed to get in some questions of his own. Vyautash did not mind answering, and his manner was such that Two Hawks was convinced his interrogator believed his story. One of the things Two Hawks found interesting was that the concept of zero had originated only three centuries before and had come to Europe only two hundred years ago. As on Earth 1, the concept had come from the East to Europe.

Vyautash gave this information, but he was more interested in Two Hawks' disclosure that the Arabia of Earth 1 was rich in oil. Apparently this Arabia was so little explored that oil had not been discovered there. Moreover, the German had not told the Perkunishans about it.

"Arabia will have to come under our rule," Vyautash said. "At the moment, the southern coasts are held by Blodland. But we will take their bases away from them. You know, this one item of information makes the whole interrogation worthwhile."

"You would have found out sooner or later from Raske, anyway," Two Hawks said. "What I'd like to know is, what does your government plan on doing with us?"

"Since you are cooperating so well and seem to be a mine of vital information, you'll be treated very well. In fact, we can offer you citizenship. It'll only be a second-class citizenship, of course, because you're not all-white."

Vyautash was silent for a while, then said, "I think it can be arranged to give you a special category. It's been done before. We could make you a first-class citizen by edict of the Kassandrash."

12

THE TRAIN PULLED into Berlin late at night, and Two Hawks did not have much opportunity to examine the city. Ilmika, Kwasind, and he were taken in a car which drove swiftly. An armored car preceded it; another followed it. He did get a chance to see the houses and large buildings, all of which had a medieval appearance. The streets were narrow and winding, and the houses abutted directly on the streets. There were gas streetlights but only on the corners of crossroads. Occasionally, a civilian rode by on a bicycle. The riding must have been bumpy because of the lack of rubber tires.

Then they were in the heart of the city. Here, the old buildings had been torn down to make way for wide paved streets and huge buildings with immense pillars in front. They passed a square in the center of which was a stone monument depicting the conquests of the great-grandfather of the present Kassandrash or Emporor. A half-mile beyond it was the palace of the Kassandrash himself.

The car stopped in front of the palace. Ilmika was conducted from the car to the palace. Before leaving, she looked once at Two Hawks from under the shadow of her hood. She was frightened and she was signalling him for help. He could do nothing, however, except to grin at her and to hold up his two fingers in the sign of the V. She could not know what that meant, but she did manage to smile faintly at him. Then she was gone.

Two Hawks and Kwasind were escorted to another building near the palace. They went through some huge and magnificently decorated rooms, up two flights of stairs, down a thickly carpeted hall, and into a suite of four rooms. This was theirs until further notice. They were told, however, that the windows had bars over them and that six soldiers were stationed outside their doors. Vyautash then said, "It's very late, but Raske wants to talk to you. I will wait here until he has left you."

A few minutes later, a challenge came from the noncom officer of the guard outside the main door. There was a mumble; the door swung open. A tall, very handsome youth entered. He wore the blue-and-scarlet uniform of an officer in the Imperial Guard. He removed his shako, covered with polar bear fur, to reveal a blond crewcut. He was smiling, and his eyes, a deep blue, reflected the warmth of his smile. He had very long and dark eyelashes.

Two Hawks could understand some of Vyautash's remarks about the influence this man was having over the daughter of the Kassandrash. He was one of the most handsome men Two Hawks had ever seen, yet he had enough masculinity to escape being called pretty.

The officer clicked his heels, bowed slightly, and said in a rich baritone, "Lieutenant Horst Raske at your service." He spoke in an English which had only a trace of German accent.

"Lieutenant Roger Two Hawks."

Two Hawks then introduced Kwasind. Raske barely nodded at him; he knew that Kwasind was one of the inferior races and a man who could not help him in any way. He also knew that Kwasind was there only because Two Hawks had insisted that he be kept with him. When the Perkunishans had discovered that Kwasind was not O'Brien, they had intended to take him off to a labor battalion. They did not know that he was a Kinukkinuk and a deserter, otherwise they would have shot him within the hour. But Two Hawks had told Vyautash that Kwasind was a Hotinohsinoh who had escaped with him from the asylum. He demanded that Kwasind be left in his care; he needed a servant. Vyautash had consented.

Raske told Kwasind to bring them some beer. He sat down on a huge sofa covered with wolf-skins, started to put his hand inside his jacket, then stopped. He smiled and said, "I still reach for a cigarette. Well, that's one of the things I'll have to learn to get along without. A small price to pay in a world which offers me—us—so much more than our native planet. I tell you, Lieutenant, we have it made. These people will give us anything for our knowledge. Anything!"

He was watching Two Hawks to observe the effect of his words. Two Hawks sat down on a chair facing the sofa and said, "You seem to have done very well, considering the short time you've been here."

Horst Raske laughed and said, "I'm not one to let the grass grow under my feet. I am a superb linguist; I've already mastered this barbarous language, at least enough for my purposes. Of course, I was lucky in being half-Lithuanian; Perkunishan is remarkably close to my mother's tongue, you know. But don't you think that coincidence is a sign of my lucky star?"

He took the glass of beer offered by Kwasind and raised it to Two Hawks.

"A toast, my friend! To our success! Two Earthmen in a strange but not necessarily unhospitable world! Long may we live and thrive! Thrive as we never could back there!"

"I'll drink to that," Two Hawks said. "And let me congratulate you on your remarkable adaptability. Most men would be in a state of shock from which they would never entirely recover."

"You seem to be doing all right," Raske said.

"I'm tough. I eat whatever is placed before me. But that doesn't mean I won't be looking for tastier food."

Raske laughed again. "I like you! You're a man after my own heart. I was hoping you would be."

"Why?" Two Hawks said.

"I'll be frank with you. I'm not quite as self-sufficient as I seem. I am a little lonely, only a little, you must understand, but a little lonely for the companionship of sombody from my Earth."

He laughed and said, "I would have preferred a woman, of course, but I can't always get what I want. Besides . . ." He raised his glass and winked at Two Hawks over it. "Besides, I have all the female company I want. The best, too. I have managed to gain the interest, more than interest, I might say, of the daughter of the Kassandrash. She wields great influence."

"You need me for more than companionship," Two Hawks said. "What other reason is there for this red-carpet treatment?"

"I'm glad you're not stupid. If you were, you wouldn't be of much use to me. Yes, I need you. In fact, you owe your presence here to the fact that I arranged for you to get here. I have a friend who's high in the espionage service; he told me about the two otherworlders who had been put in the insane asylum. I suggested the kidnapping and . . ."

"Were you also the one who suggested we be killed if we couldn't be captured alive?"

Raske was taken by surprise, but he rallied swiftly. Smiling, he said, "Yes, I did. I couldn't have you giving information to the Hotinohsinoh that would put them on a technological level with the Perkunishans—my adopted people— could I? Wouldn't you have done the same if you had been in my shoes?"

"Probably."

"Of course, you would. But you weren't killed. And you owe your escape from a terrible death in an Itskapintik labor camp to me. It was I who insisted that the Perkunishan government demand your release. Of course, the Kassan-

drash was furious when he heard about how his
niece had been violated. He was the one who insisted that the policemen be executed."

"And what will happen to her now?" Two
Hawks said.

"She'll be offered citizenship. If she takes the
oath, she'll be treated well, very well, as befits
the Kassandrash's niece. If she refuses, and she's
likely to do so, being a stubborn Blodlander,
she'll be imprisoned. But she'll be in a nice prison, probably have private rooms and servants in
some castle."

Two Hawks sipped at his beer and looked at
the German. German? Raske had already forgotten about the war on his native world. He was
interested only in what he could get for himself
here and was delighted that he had something
valuable to trade. His attitude, Two Hawks had
to admit, was realistic. Why continue the war
here? Deutschland and America and Russia
might as well be on a planet in another galaxy.
The oaths of allegiance he and Raske had taken
were as nullified as if both had been killed over
Ploesti.

This, of course, did not mean that he trusted
Raske. The man was an opportunist. Once he
found Two Hawks no longer useful, he would get
rid of him. But that attitude could work two
ways. Raske could be used by Two Hawks.

"I can be of great value to Perkunisha," Raske
said, "because I am an aeronautical engineer. I
also know something of chemistry and electronics. But I do not know what your academic
background is."

Two Hawks said, "My field isn't going to be of much help, I'm afraid. I have a Master's in Indo-European Linguistics. But I did take a number of courses in mathematics and electronics because I knew that linguistics was eventually going to use these as tools in language analysis. I have a first-class radio operator's license, and I know a lot about automobiles. I worked part-time as a mechanic to put myself through school."

"That's not so bad," Raske said. "I need somebody qualified to be my assistant in developing our radio equipment and airplanes. I've been drawing up plans for a fighter plane; it'll be equipped with radio and machine guns. However, it won't be very advanced. It'll be about the same as a late World War I plane. But it will sweep the skies, send every Blodland *lyftship* flaming to the ground, and it'll be tremendously useful for observation and for strafing ground-troops."

Two Hawks was not surprised that Perkunisha was not building a modern aircraft. After all, they were of materials derived from an advanced technology. To make superior steel and aluminum (not even known here), to build the factories which could manufacture such metal and machine them, could be done. But it would take a very long time, and the Perkunishan government would not want such a delay. It desired something that could be used in the near future, not after the war was over.

So Raske would have offered them a craft which would seem obsolete and very inefficient to him, but would be daring, even futuristic, to this world.

Raske continued to talk. He was overburdened with work; he was getting very little sleep. His schedule interfered with his other activities, namely, entrenching himself socially and politically and wooing the daughter of the Kassandrash. Fortunately, he needed little sleep and had managed to operate effectively. But he could use a man who would take over the burden of overseeing all the little details and making the daily scores of decisions. Yes, Two Hawks would be a great help.

He pointed at the silver two-headed wolf symbol on his left breast. "I have a military title which is the equivalent of Colonel in the Luftwaffe. I can arrange to make you a Major as soon as we can get you a special citizenship. Normally, that would take weeks, but we'll get it done by tomorrow. Then you become a full-fledged Perkunishan, by grace of the Kassandrash. You couldn't do any better. This country is destined to become the ruler of all Europe and probably of Africa and much of Asia, too."

"Just as Deutschland was?" Two Hawks said.

Raske smiled. "I am not a stupid or unrealistic person," he said. "I could see the handwriting on the wall the moment the United States entered the war. But here, you see, there is no America. Moreover, Perkunisha is relatively more powerful than Germany. Its citizens occupy a much larger area to begin with. Its technology and military tactics are superior to all other nations. And with us two, it will soon have

an invincible technology. But there is much work
to be done, much work. It takes time to build
mills to make a better steel and to make
aluminum. We might have to take Greenland
before we can get our hands on bauxite. And
then the bauxite has to be mined and transported here. And synthetic rubber has to be
made. And factories have to be built and new
tooling machines made, and these cannot be
done without blueprints and a big adminis-
tration. Thousands have to be trained.

"It's a Herculean task. But it can be done, and
what do you think the position of the men who
make it possible will be? I ask you, but you need
not reply. Oh, we're going to be very very important, Roger Two Hawks. You'll be a great man;
you could never have dreamed of such power
and wealth when you were a young man on the
reservation."

"I never lived on a reservation," Two Hawks
said.

Raske stood up, walked over, and put his
hand on Two Hawks' shoulder. "I did not mean
to hurt your feelings. Do not be so touchy. I do
not know what offends you and what pleases
you. I will find out some day, when we have
time. Meanwhile, let's work together as best we
can. And let's not forget what the future holds
for both of us."

He walked toward the door but stopped before
opening it. "You get some sleep, Roger. In the
morning, you can take a bath and then be fitted
for new clothes. Then, to work. Work, work,
work! And if you get tired, think of what all the

drudgery will bring you some day. *Auf wiedersehen!*"

"So long!" Two Hawks said. After the door was closed, he rose and went into the bedroom. The bed was a huge four-poster with velvet curtains on which were depicted scenes from events in Perkunishan history. There was one that showed the torture of a Viking king captured during a raid on Perkunishan territory. Two Hawks did not find it conducive to sleep, but it did make him think. He must use caution in whatever plans he made to escape. That is, if he did try to escape. He had to admit that he was tempted by Raske's offer.

Well, why not? On Earth 2, one country was as good as another, as far as he was concerend. He owed no one anything. Even those people closest to him, the Hotinohsinoh people he could easily have identified with, had tortured him and then shut him away in an insane asylum.

At that moment, Kwasind stuck his broad dark face into the room. He asked if he could talk with Two Hawks before he slept. Two Hawks gestured at him to sit down on the bed beside him, but the Kinukkinuk remained standing.

"I didn't understand that language you and Raske were using," he said. "Is it permitted that you tell me what it was all about?"

"Don't talk like a humble slave," Two Hawks said. "You have to be my servant if you want to survive, but that doesn't mean we can't talk man to man when we're alone." He had thoroughly searched the room for listening devices and found nothing. He did not think that electronics was advanced enough to make "bugs" anyway. Still, there was the possibility that eavesdroppers could be hidden behind the wall. He said, "Come on, Kwasind, sit close to me and talk in a low voice."

Two Hawks gave him the meat of his talk with the German.

Kwasind was silent for a while, his thick black brows lowered in thought. Then he said, "What this man says is true. You could become a great man, although you would always know that you were a stranger and you would see the contempt behind the smiling and the bowing and great houses and beautiful women they would give you. To the Wapiti (whites), you would always be the upstart barbarian. And when the war is over and they no longer need you, then what? It will be easy to find some reason to disgrace you, to strip you of your title and honors, perhaps even make a slave of you, perhaps even kill you."

"You're trying to tell me something," Two Hawks said. "So far, you're telling me nothing I haven't already thought of."

"They plan to make all Europe into one Perkunisha," Kwasind said. "They are evil. They mean to exterminate the Dakota, the Kinukkinuk, the Hotinohsinoh, and their own allies, the Itskapintik. And the white peoples of Europe will be made to speak the language of Perkunisha; their own languages will be forbidden. Someday, only Perkunishan will be known. The flags of others will be burned; their history books, burned. Some day, every white child in Europe will think of himself as a Perkunishan, not a Rasna, a Blodlandish, an Aikhavian."

"So what's new?" Two Hawks said. "Maybe that'll be the best thing. No more national hates, no more wars."

"You sound like one of them."

"I'm not. But their goals sound fine. Only I don't like the means. But what's the alternative? Are the Blodlandish any better; wouldn't the Kinukkinuk wipe out their hereditary enemies, the Itskapintik and the Hotinohsinoh, if they got a chance? Doesn't Blodland want to extend its dominion over the world? Wouldn't Aikhavia like to resurrect the empire it had under Kassandras the Great?"

Kwasind said, "You told me that you thought slavery was wrong. You said that the white man of Europe of your world had abolished slavery as a great evil, and that the whites of this . . . this America . . . had done the same. You said that the black men and the brown of America were still treated like slaves, but that some day they would be accepted as equals. You said . . ."

"You're leading up to something besides a lecture on ethics," Two Hawks said. "You're sounding me out because you're not sure you should tell me something. Right?"

"You see into my liver and read all that is therein."

"Not quite. But I'll bet ten to one that someone's contacted you about an escape. A Blodlandish has talked to you."

Kwasind nodded and said, "I have to trust you. If I don't, there's no escape. They want you, not me. Now, I talked to you about the evils of

Perkunisha because I wanted to get your reaction. I wanted to know how you *felt* about them, not what you thought about them. In your liver, do you *feel* that Perkunisha is wrong? You know that its enemies have their faults but you also know they have a right to work out their own destinies. How do you *feel?*"

Two Hawks rose from his chair and walked over to Kwasind. He put his hand on Kwasind's huge shoulder. "I don't really know about Blodland or the other countries. But I feel that Perkunisha has too many similarities to the Germany of my world. Maybe I could learn to stomach the Perkunishans. I don't really think so."

"That is what I hoped to hear you say."

Two Hawks said, "If I'd said I was sticking with Perkunisha, you would have killed me, wouldn't you? The Blodlandish want me alive, but if they can't get me, they'll try to make sure their enemy won't have me either. Isn't that so?"

"I won't lie," Kwasind said. "You are my friend; you saved my life. Yet, for my country, I would have killed you with these hands. Then I would have killed as many Perkunishans as I could before they killed me!"

"O. K. So, what's the plan?"

"I'll be told when the time is right. Meanwhile, you're to cooperate with the enemy."

Kwasind went to his bedroom. Two Hawks lay awake for a while on his own bed. He thought of Horst Raske. The German thought this world was his toy. But if the Blodlandish meant to kill Two Hawks if he did side with the Perkunishans, then they must be planning to assassinate Raske. Only by killing him could they deprive the Perkunishans of the superior weapons and technology Raske could provide.

13

THE FOLLOWING WEEK was busy. Each morning, Two Hawks spent three hours with language lessons. After these, he worked until midnight or later in his office. This was in a huge factory on the outskirts of Berlin. He rode to work in a car which was preceded and followed by armored cars. He knew they were there not only to bar his escape but to guard him against assassination.

Raske gave him the task of building a device to synchronize machine-gun fire with the revolutions of an airplane propeller. Two Hawks knew the basic principles. Even so, it took him four days to construct a prototype. His first job done, he then supervised a group working on rockets to be fired from an airplane. This took him a week. After that, he was made head engineer of a group that was designing machines, tools, and techniques for building aircraft on a mass basis.

Two Hawks had only gotten started on this when Raske removed him. The German said, "I have a much more interesting job. You and I are going to train pilots. These will be the nucleus of the Imperial Perkunishan Air Force. How does it feel to be cofounder of an air force?"

Raske glowed with joy. He was always en-

thusiastic, happy, and optimistic. Two Hawks
knew that Raske would have him shot if he
thought Two Hawks was a traitor, but he could
not help liking Raske. The feeling certainly
made it easier to work with, and for, him.

Three weeks passed. Fall came swiftly; winter
would soon be here. Two Hawks asked Kwasind
if he had received any more messages from the
Blodland agents. Kwasind replied, "No. I was
told I would not be contacted again until they're
ready to act."

Two Hawks did not tell Kwasind that he was
not, at the moment, concerned about escape.
Despite himself, he was getting enthusiastic
about the pilot-training. By then, there were four
two-seater monoplanes ready, all hand-built.
Each had a rotary, water-cooled, 12-cylinder engine, dual controls, and a range of 150 miles.
They could cruise at 100 mph.

They were far from being what Raske could
have built if he had had more time and better
materials. Aluminum was lacking, and the steel
was not even up to the 1918 A. D. standards of
Earth 1. The gasoline was low grade. Thus, the
airplane had to be of utmost simplicity and confined in speed and range. Still, they were ade-
quate for the present purposes of the Perkunishan Air Force, which were scouting and
strafing and bombing of near-front ammunition
dumps. And the destruction of dirigibles.

Raske planned on building more rugged and
faster pursuit planes later and also hoped to have
a force of two-motored bombers. The Perkunishan High Command said that this would

have to be much later. It expected to have finished the conquest of Europe before these were
needed. When the time came to tackle the
Ikhwani of South Africa and the Saariset (the
Finnic speakers of the Japanese islands of Earth
1), then better and more varied aircraft could be
designed.

The day that Raske flew the first one, the
Kassandrash himself came out with the High
Command to observe.

The Perkunishan ruler was a tall, heavily
bearded man in his early fifties. He had lost his
right arm in the last war when he led an infantry
charge against the only Blodlandish fort holding
out on the European mainland. During the face-
to-face combat that followed, a Blodlandish officer had severed the young officer's arm during
a sword-fight. The outraged Perkunishan troops
had massacred all the defenders.

Two Hawks was introduced to the Kassandrash. Having been drilled for an hour on the
ritual phrases and gestures used during the occasion, he got through it without disgracing
himself. The Kassandrash had Two Hawks
stand by him since he wanted his technical questions answered while Raske was aloft. Raske
swaggered out of the hangar. He wore a red,
black, and blue uniform he had designed himself
as the dress of the new air force. On his head was
a helmet with a spike on top, a long yellow scarf
was tied around his neck, and he carried a pair
of goggles with hexagonal rims.

The Kassandrash's daughter, Persinai, went
to him, and he put his arm around her waist and

kissed her lightly on the cheek. Her father did not seem to mind what they were doing, but some of the noblemen scowled. They belonged to a faction that did not like the princess being in love with a foreigner even if he was to be ennobled. Nor did they like the power he had in military affairs. It was no secret that the head of Internal Security, himself only a lesser nobleman, half-Rasnan, was a very good friend of Raske's.

Raske climbed into the plane and started the engine. This made the High Command gasp, since internal-combustion ground vehicles so far had to be cranked and the dirigible motors had to be turned over by auxiliary steam-engines before starting. The silvery low-wing monoplane took off, climbed to 3,000 feet, and then went through a series of spins, loops, and Immelmans. It came in for a three-point landing. Two Hawks winced at the impact on the rubberless rims of the wheels. While the others clustered around Raske to congratulate him, Two Hawks examined the landing gear. The spokes of the wheels were bent a little. After a few more landings, the wheels would have to be replaced. It would be two or more years before synthetic rubber would be available. The chemists were experimenting on the basis of information from Raske, but he had only a vague idea about the making of neoprene from chloroprene.

The next five days, the German and the American tested out all four prototypes. They also made machine-gun strafing attacks on dummies on the ground, shot rockets, and dropped

bombs. Two Hawks noticed that, when he took
a plane up, its tank was always only a quarter-
full. Raske was taking no chances that his col-
league might cut and run for the seacoast, only
90 miles away.

The aircraft factory was working in three
shifts at top speed. Despite this, the first mass-
produced planes would not be turned out for at
least a month. Raske and Two Hawks were up
in the air every daylight hour training pilots.
When ten had enough skill (not in Two Hawks'
estimation), they began to instruct others. The
inevitable happened. One plane spun in with
both instructor and student. Another stalled
during takeoff and was completely demolished,
although the pilot suffered only minor injuries.

Raske was furious. "We've only two left. And
we're losing time on those, what with repairs
and changing wheels!"

Two Hawks shrugged, but he was more concerned than he appeared. He had a plan which
required one of the planes. If the accidents continued, he would be grounded for a long time.

One evening, while he was working on a design for auxiliary detachable fuel tanks, Kwasind
came into his study.

"Day after tomorrow," he said. "The
Blodlandish agent says we must be ready when
dusk comes. Just before we leave the airfield to
come here."

"What's the plan?"

Kwasind said that the two armored cars
which usually accompanied them would be ordered off to deal with a fake emergency. The or-

der would be given by a Blodlandish agent in the
uniform of a Kreion (general). After the guards
had driven off, Kwasind would kill the soldier
that rode with them, and Two Hawks would dis-
pose of the chauffeur. Should the commander of
the armored cars refuse to obey the pseudo-
Kreion's orders, both cars would be bombed and
the survivors shot by agents hidden near the
field. However, the Blodlandish hoped this
would not be necessary.

"Where are they taking us?"

"They'll drive us through the country at night
and we'll hide out during the day at various sta-
tions. When we get to the coast, a boat will take
us to Tyrsland (Sweden). Perkunisha hasn't invaded Tyrsland yet, it isn't strong enough to
worry about. In Tyrsland, we'll be flown out by
a dirigible to Norway. From there, a ship will
take us to Blodland."

"Sounds risky to me," Two Hawks said. "But
I guess they know what they are doing."

Raske greeted him as he came into the hangar
just after the second of the morning's instruction
flights. The German had a peculiar smile. Two
Hawks wondered if the escape plot had somehow been exposed. He looked around for arrest-
ing officers, but everything seemed normal. The
workers were putting together two new planes,
the parts for which had been rushed through factories and shipped to the field. A group of students was listening to a lecture by one of the recently graduated aviators. The only soldiers in
sight were the usual guards. Nevertheless, he
patted the derringer stuck inside his belt to re-

assure himself that it was there. The Itskapintik
police had missed it when they had searched
him, they were so eager to get to Ilmika. And the
Perkunishans had never searched him because
they presumed the Itskapintik had done so.

Raske said, "You once told me you admired
the Lady Ilmika. How would you like to have
her?"

"What do you mean?" Two Hawks said. He
was not sure that Raske was not trying to trap
him, although he did not know how an interest
in her could do it.

"Don't you know what's happened to her?"

Two Hawks shook his head.

"I don't suppose anybody told you. She's in
disgrace; she's in prison. The Kassandrash
himself offered her her freedom if she would re-
nounce Blodland for allegiance to Perkunisha.
The stupid bitch slapped his face! Can you im-
agine that? Struck the Kassandrash in the face
and before the entire court! It's a wonder she
wasn't executed on the spot! Believe me, His
Majesty was angry enough to do it.

"But his wife pleaded for the girl, and the
Kassandrash merely had her imprisoned. He
couldn't stand being humiliated, however, so
he's been thinking of some suitable punishment
for her."

Raske grinned and continued, "I remembered
how you said she was so beautiful, but you'd
never be able to touch her. So, my red-skinned
friend, just to show what a high regard I have for
you, and also how I take care of my own, I've
arranged for you to have your heart's desire. I

spoke to the Kassandrash this morning, and he
was delighted. He believes my plan will provide
the abasement and the hurt she deserves. And
you'll be benefited. I wish I were in your shoes.
I'd love to have her for myself. Only I wouldn't
dare. The Kassandrash's daughter isn't very lib-
eral minded."

"Are you serious?" Two Hawks said.

Raske laughed and said, "The Lady Ilmika,
niece to the Shof (king) of Blodland and grandniece to the Kassandrash, is yours! She's to be
your slave! You have carte blanche with her.
I . . . What's the matter, *Zwei Habichten?* I
thought you'd be delighted. Or are you . . . ?"

"Overwhelmed is the word," Two Hawks
said. "Only . . . Never mind. What happens to
her if I don't accept her?"

"Not accept? You must be out of your mind!
Selig! If you are so insane to reject my offer—
well, I don't know. I heard that Ilmika could be
placed in solitary until she dies. Or perhaps sent
to a military brothel, although I don't really
think the Kassandrash would do that to his
grandniece. Who knows? Who cares?"

Two Hawks should not have cared. But he
did. Without considering the realities and logic
of his situation, he knew he had to take Ilmika in
as his slave. This was the only way to save her.
Her presence would complicate the escape plan.
The Blodlandish agents would be furious. Or
would they? She was the daughter of a noble and
niece to the ruler of their country. Why wouldn't
they be glad to include her?

He said, "O. K. Send her over."

Raske clapped him on the shoulder and winked. "Tell me how it works out, heh?"

Two Hawks wanted to hit him but forced himself to unclench his fists and to smile.

"I might do that."

Raske said that they had had enough fun; they must get back to work. Two Hawks would have to handle the aviation school today. Raske had to attend a conference with the head of Ordnance.

"He's the most reactionary and stupid man I ever met," Raske said. "I designed a clip-loaded carbine which will give the infantryman ten times the firepower he now has. Do you think that pighead will accept it? No, he says the common soldier will misuse it; he'll spray the bullets instead of taking careful aim. The carbine will waste ammunition.

"However, that isn't his only reason for not wanting my carbine! Did you know that the gatling gun crews are all officers? No noncoms or privates are allowed to handle a gatling except in extreme emergencies. This ridiculous rule is based on what happened 30 years ago. When Perkunisha was defeated, part of the army and a great number of workers, serfs, and slaves revolted. The uprising was stamped out, but ever since then the aristocracy has made sure the commoner doesn't get his hands on powerful weapons. The rule might have been necessary at one time, but now it's absurd! The swine!"

Two Hawks waited until an hour before dusk to begin the initial stage of his plan. Raske was not likely to come to the field at this late hour, so

Two Hawks felt safe. On the pretext that one of
the planes had a motor that sounded peculiar, he
grounded the plane. Then, as if the thought had
suddenly come to him, he announced that he
wanted to try an experiment. While some me-
chanics were trying to locate the source of the
"funny noise," others were welding attachments
to two gasoline tanks. These, Two Hawks explained, were to be installed on the underside of
the wings. The tanks were fitted to the mounting
apparatus for the rockets. Hoses were connected
to the tanks and run up to the motor's gasoline
intake. He supervised the installation of necessary valves. By then, those working on the motor
said that they could not locate the supposed
trouble. Two Hawks told them to forget about it;
he might have been mistaken. He climbed into
the cockpit and restarted the motor. The main
gas tanks had been drained until they were
almost empty. Two Hawks let the motor run for
several minutes before turning on the valve to the
auxiliary tanks. The motor continued to turn
over without a single miss during the switchover.

It was midnight by then. Two Hawks ordered
the auxiliaries disconnected and removed. He
had the tanks carried back to the hangar rear,
where they would be out of Raske's sight. On the
way back to the apartment in Berlin, he explained to Kwasind what he had done.

"I want you to get hold of your contact and
find out what he intends to do. Tell him the
plans have been changed. No, better still, have
him talk directly to me. I have to explain in detail what's needed."

Kwasind protested that the Blodlandish would refuse. It was too dangerous to contact Two Hawks personally.

"Tell him if he doesn't, the whole thing's off. Now, when can I meet him?"

"Early tomorrow morning. Before you leave for the airfield," Kwasind said.

When they walked into their suite, they found two soldiers with Ilmika Thorrsstein. She sat on a sofa, her hands folded on her lap, her back straight, her face haughty. Despite her dignity, she looked washed out. The coil of long blonde hair on top of her head was loose, with strands of straying hair, and she wore no makeup. Moreover, she wore a loose-fitting blouse and skirt of cheap dyed cotton, a slave girl's garments.

When she saw Two Hawks enter, her eyes widened and her lips parted. Evidently she had not been told whose apartment this was. Perhaps, she did not know what her lot was to be.

Two Hawks dismissed the soldiers.

She spoke first. "What am I doing here?"

Two Hawks told her bluntly. She took the news without flinching.

"You must be tired and hungry," Two Hawks said. "Kwasind, bring her some food and wine."

"And then?" she said. She gazed steadily at him. He grinned at her until she flushed.

"Not what you think," he said. "I don't want a woman who doesn't desire me. I won't force you."

She looked at the two Kinnukinuk girls, who had just come out of the kitchen.

"What about them?"

"They're slaves. They won't be staying to-night. You can sleep in their room. What's more, you can lock the door on the inside."

Suddenly, tears ran down her cheeks. Her lips quivered. She rose to her feet and then began to sob loudly. He put his arm around her shoulders and pressed her face against his chest. She cried violently for a few minutes before drawing away from him. He gave her a handkerchief to dry her tears. Kwasind appeared and said that her supper was ready in her room. Ilmika, without a word, followed Kwasind.

When the giant had returned, Two Hawks said, "I'll talk to her before she goes to sleep. She has to know what's going on."

"Why are you doing this for her?"

"Maybe I'm in love with her. Or maybe I'm hopelessly chivalric—a red-skinned Gawain. I don't know. I do know I can't just let her be locked up for the rest of her life or be sent to an army whorehouse."

Kwasind shrugged to indicate that he did not understand. But if Two Hawks wanted it that way, so be it.

After a short and refreshing sleep, Two Hawks left the bedroom to go to the kitchen. He stopped when he saw a man in the recreation room talking to Kwasind. The stranger wore the blue-and-grey of a servant and carried a bundle of linen. He had long brown hair, a thick brown moustache, and a hawk nose. His name—his real name—was Rulf Andersson.

Two Hawks ordered the two into his room.

While Andersson busied himself changing the bedclothes, he talked in a low voice.

"Kwasind told me your plan. You're insane!"

"Would Blodland like to have a brand-new flying machine?" Two Hawks said. "A readymade model the possession of which would cut months off of the designing and building of others? My plan isn't impossible. In fact, it's the very daring, the very unexpectedness of it, that will aid its success."

"I don't know," Andersson said. "It's fantastic."

"Can you get in touch with your compatriots in Tyrsland?"

"Yes. But to set up what you want, we need a few days."

"No extra time," Two Hawks said. "Raske is bound to notice the auxiliaries sooner or later. Or somebody will tell him about them. We have to move fast. Day after tomorrow, the latest."

"All right, we'll do it. I'll see Kwasind later, and he'll tell you if we'll be able to make it."

Two Hawks explained his plan in detail and made sure that Andersson knew exactly what was required. The agent left. Two Hawks tried the door to Ilmika's room. It was locked.

"Kwasind, you stay here today. We have to pretend we are going along with the idea she's my slave. So you make her do some work here, dust, cook, and so on. Get her some makeup and pretty clothes. I wouldn't want my slave mistress to be unattractive, would I?"

He left for the airfield. He was busy that day, since he also had to do Raske's work. The German was at a conference with the High Command. This was fine with Two Hawks. He did more work on the auxiliary tanks and then took the plane up for a flight test of the apparatus. After landing, he was met by the officer in charge of assembling two planes in the rear of the hangar. The officer told him that the planes were ready for installation of their gas tanks. The auxiliaries would have to be removed from the plane and the attachments cut off. He was sorry, but there were no other tanks on hand to use.

"Very well," Two Hawks said. "Do it tomorrow."

"But Raske ordered that the planes be assembled without delay. The second and third shifts can install the tanks tonight."

Scowling, Two Hawks spoke harshly.

"I want Raske to see my auxiliaries. They'll extend the range of our planes by a hundred miles. No, this is far more important than a day's holdup on those machines. I order you to leave those gas tanks alone."

"My men won't have anything to do! Raske will hold me responsible for the delay!"

"I'll take full responsibility," Two Hawks said. "You and your men take the night off. You've been working too hard. I'll sign the order for a night's leave."

The officer seemed reluctant, but he saluted and then walked off to tell the others the new orders. Two Hawks watched him. There was a chance the officer might phone Raske to get verification of the change. If Raske heard of this, he would guess at once what the American meant to do.

Two Hawks went after the officer.

"You seem to be worrying that you may get into trouble," he said. "I suggest you call Raske now. If he orders you to continue work, then do so. I will still be responsible for any delay up to the moment you get into contact with him."

The officer brightened. He hastened away, only to return in ten minutes with a frustrated expression. "He is in conference. He refused to talk to me but did send word that if I had any problems, I was to go to you."

"So, you see, you have no more responsibility."

Two Hawks breathed easier; his gamble had paid off.

Kwasind met Two Hawks the moment he walked into the suite.

"Andersson says that the agents in Tyrsland have been informed about the change in plans. And the agents at the emergency field are ready, just in case. Andersson can't tell us any more until tomorrow morning. But he's very worried. If the winds along the coast are too strong, the plane can't be gotten out."

"In that case, we'll have to forget about the plane and take the fishing boat," Two Hawks said. "Where's Ilmika?"

"She just went into her room."

Two Hawks knocked at her door. It swung open to reveal a different woman—on the outside, anyway. Her Psyche knot was flawless, her eyes were made up, and her lips rouged. She was wearing a Neo-Cretan gown, cut low in front, a golden belt tight around her waist, and a hoop skirt with a broad V in front which showed a rich silk petticoat.

"Your Ladyship looks beautiful," he said. "However, you'll have to change into something less attractive but more durable and unrestraining. Can you look like a Perkunishan soldier?"

She laughed and said, "I've been cutting and sewing all day to refit one of your uniforms."

Seeing him raise his eyebrows, she said, "Blodlandish ladies have slaves or servants to do the work, but they're still taught all the domestic arts. How can we properly educate and supervise our slaves if we know nothing ourselves?"

"That seems sensible," he replied. He had much to say about slavery, most of it condemnation. This was, however, no time for discussion.

"We'll leave early enough to get to the airfield before daybreak. I've purposely not held to a rigid schedule, so there'll be no suspicions about variations in departure."

She looked so fresh and beautiful that he wanted to kiss her. He restrained the impulse, knowing that she would be offended. Even if she were attracted to him, she could show no more affection towards him than towards any faithful servant or devoted commoner.

He said goodnight to her and went to bed. He fell asleep at once and, it seemed a minute later, was being shaken by Kwasind.

"It can't be time yet?"

"No. You're wanted on the phone. It's Raske."

"At this hour?" By the dim light of the gas jet, he looked at the clock on the bedside table. It was 2 a.m.

"What the hell can he want?"

Kwasind said, "I don't know. I hope nothing's wrong."

Two Hawks lurched into the next room and picked up the phone. There was a hiss and crackle on the line, and Raske's voice sounded a little blurred. The Perkunishan system of reproducing voice left much to be desired.

"Raske?"

"Two Hawks!" Raske exploded. "What're you trying to pull? As if I didn't know! You ought to be smarter than that, my Indian friend!"

Two Hawks said, "What are you talking about?"

Raske told him. It was as Two Hawks had feared. The worrywart in charge of assembly had not been reassured enough. After agonizing for a long time, he had tried again to get hold of Raske. This time, he succeeded in reaching the German, who was at a party given by the Kassandrash's wife. As soon as Raske was told about the auxiliaries, he had guessed Two Hawks' purpose.

"I'm not going to say anything to anybody about this," Raske said. "I like you. What's more important, I need you. So you're getting off easily. But you're going to have less freedom. You'll follow a schedule to the minute; I'll know where you are and what you're doing every second of the day and night."

Raske paused. Two Hawks did not reply.
With a slightly plaintive tone, the German resumed.

"Why do you want to run off? You've got it
made here. Blodland can't give you a thing.
Besides, Blodland is doomed. It'll be conquered
by this time next year."

"I'm just not sympatico with the Perkunishans," Two Hawks said. "They remind me
of the Germans too much."

"You red-skinned swine!"

Raske stopped again. Two Hawks could hear
him breathing heavily. Then, "One more trick
and you go to the firing squad! Or to the torture
chamber! Do you understand me?"

"I get you," Two Hawks said. "Anything
else? I want to get back to bed."

Surprisingly, Raske laughed. "You're a cool
one. I like that. Very well. You will leave your
suite at exactly 6 a.m. and will report to the airfield commander as soon as you arrive.
Moreover, your slave, Kwasind, is to be restrict-
ed to the suite. I'll notify your guards at once.
Another thing. If you don't behave, your little
blonde playmate will be taken away. Got it?"

"Got it," Two Hawks said. He hung up.

14

HE REPEATED RASKE'S conversation to Kwasind. The giant listened without change of expression. He said, "What now?"

"It's now or never. We can't go out the front way, so we'll use the back."

Kwasind looked puzzled. Two Hawks said, "Out the window. You try playing Hercules with the steel bars of my bedroom window. I'll wake Ilmika."

Five minutes later, he and Ilmika entered his bedroom. She was in the uniform of an officer of the Perkunishan Imperial Air Force. Her cap sat snugly on her head, since she had cut off her long hair.

Kwasind had torn one bar out of its stone socket and was bending another. The two watched him in awe. Slowly, the inch-thick steel curved. Kwasind, face impassive and free of strain, feet braced against the wall, pulled. Just before the separation of the bar ends from the stone, he lowered his feet to the floor. Now the lower part of his body was against the wall, and the upper part bowed outwards. Screeching, the steel tore loose. Kwasind caught himself, bent his knees, half-turned. He placed the bar on the carpet and grinned.

"We can squeeze through now."

They cut strips from the bedsheets and knotted the ends together. They had just enough material to make a strong, double-thick rope which reached from the third-story window to about five feet from the ground. Two Hawks scanned the broad street and sidewalk below. There was no one in sight. However, he knew that a sentinel was stationed at the north exit, to their right. He was on the other side of a massive pillar. Unless he stepped out onto the great portico, he would not see the white ribbon hanging along the outer wall.

"Stick that bar in your belt," Two Hawks said to Kwasind. "I'll take the other. We might need them."

He went through the window first. He slid out without hesitation, having tested the security of the knot at the upper end. This was tied to a bedpost. Hand under hand, he descended swiftly. When he dropped to the ground, he looked around. No one had appeared on the street yet. Ilmika followed him a minute later, then, Kwasind.

Two Hawks led them down the street, away from the guard at the north door. He wanted a car, but they walked four long blocks—over a mile—before they found one. Rather, it almost found them. A glare of headlights from a side-street warned them just in time. They ran into a deep doorway and pressed against the door to be as far as possible in the shadow. Two Hawks decided he would have to risk a peek. The car sounded as if it were traveling slowly enough for him to run up to it and jump upon the running board.

He looked and saw the white body of a topless car and the image of a knight in armor with raised sword on its hood. It was a police car with three men in it. He told Kwasind what to do. Both had the bars in their hands. The hood of the vehicle drew even with the doorway. Two Hawks said, "Now!" He ran out with the bar held slantwise in front of him, Kwasind even with him.

The patrolmen had been talking. They stopped, rigid and speechless for a second with surprise. Then the driver slammed on the brakes when he should have stepped on the accelerator. Two Hawks leaped up into the top of the rear door and hurled himself at the man sitting in the rear seat. He swung the steel bar as he did so. The patrolman stood up and raised his rifle to parry the blow. There was a clang as the bar drove against the gun barrel. Both fell on the seat with Two Hawks on top.

Two Hawks, using the bar as a sword, jammed its end into the man's mouth. A rifle exploded, almost in his ear, but if it had been aimed at him it had missed.

The patrolman's teeth broke. Two Hawks got to a kneeling position on the man's chest and leaned his weight on the bar. It entered the throat, and, despite the frenzied efforts of the patrolman to push it out, remained there. His eyes bulged; his face darkened. Suddenly, he quit struggling.

Two Hawks held the bar until he was certain

the man was dead. He rose, took the bar out, and turned his attention to the others. Kwasind had no need of him. The driver was lying on his side on the seat, his neck was broken by a blow from Kwasind's bar. The other, the man who had fired the rifle, had been knocked out of the car. He, too, was dead, strangled by Kwasind.

"You hit?" Two Hawks said.

"His rifle went off as I knocked it downwards," Kwasind said. "I'm all right."

Two Hawks looked up and down the street. If anyone had heard the gunfire, they were making no outcry about it. He dragged the corpse off the back seat and onto the pavement. While he restarted the motor and became acquainted with the controls, Kwasind dragged all three bodies into the doorway. A few minutes later, armed with revolvers and single-shot rifles, they drove off. Two Hawks followed the route taken to the airfield every morning. Twice, they passed patrol cars going the other way. The drivers tooted at them, Two Hawks tooted back, and that was all. Two Hawks asked Kwasind if he knew where the Blodlandish agents were located. He had some hope that they could be used to make a diversion, as originally planned. Kwasind replied that his contact had refused to give him that information.

"Then we'll have to do this by ourselves—The Lonesome Threesome. The only trouble is, we're way ahead of schedule. I'll bet that worrywart officer went back to the hangar and had the auxiliary tanks removed. That means we'll have to land once to refuel before we get to the coast. If the Blodlandish don't have the gas ready, we're screwed."

"Maybe we ought to worry about getting into the air first," Kwasind said. Two Hawks glanced at him. The panel light showed him the giant's usual stolid expression. However, his face gleamed with sweat. Two Hawks smiled. He doubted that the perspiration was caused by exertions or nervousness from the fight with the patrolmen. Kwasind had been more than uneasy when told how they would escape. Brave and cool in combat on the ground, he was terrified at the idea of flying. He had not said so, but his questions and a rigidity whenever the subject came up betrayed him.

There was, however, more to his nervous state than just the concept of leaving the ground. The ancient European religions had been heavy with stories of flying demons. The new religion of Hemilkism discredited these as mere superstitions. Old horrors die hard; at least half of the population firmly believed in the demons. And Kwasind was a member of one of the old religions which had not died. It thrived in underground form in his oppressed country. Even now, thinking of the winged monsters, Kwasind must be hearing the beat of their wings.

Leaving Berlin proper, they drove on a broad highway through the suburbs. A ten minutes' traffic-free drive through these and five minutes of speeding through farmland brought them to the airfield. This was completely encircled by a thirty-foot high barbed wire fence. Dogs much like German shepherds patrolled the fence at

night. There was no way of entrance except
through the main gate. They would have to
brazen through.

Two Hawks stopped the car in response to a
guard's order. The other guard remained by the
sentinel box, his rifle ready, while the first
walked up to the car.

"Pulkininkash (Colonel) Two Hawks and
party," Two Hawks said. He spoke as if he had
great authority.

The soldier was hesitant. Finally, he said,
"Where is your bodyguard, Colonel?"

He looked at the car and his eyes widened.
"This is a police car!"

Two Hawks raised his revolver and shot the
guard in the solar plexus. The guard fell
backwards, and Two Hawks shot him again.
Kwasind had raised his rifle at the same time.
He fired just above Two Hawks' head, deafening
him. The guard by the box had lifted his rifle to
fire at them, but he was too slow. Kwasind's first
bullet turned him 180 degrees around. Kwasind
dropped the rifle and pulled his revolver from its
holster. By then, Ilmika had hit the guard with a
bullet from her revolver.

Kwasind jumped out of the car and removed
from the dead sergeant's belt a ring full of keys.
He tried four keys before he found the proper
one to unlock the big padlock on the wire gate.
Ilmika collected the sentries' rifles and cartridge
belts and put them in the back seat.

Kwasind opened the gates. Two Hawks eased
the car through to give the giant a chance to get
back into the car. Shouts rose from the barracks

near the rear of the hangar. A man with a revolver ran out of the officers' quarters. Two
Hawks pressed down on the accelerator. The officer ran after them, shouting. His revolver
cracked. Half-dressed soldiers with rifles ran out
of the barracks.

The car hurtled around the corner of the
hangar, then skidded as Two Hawks tapped on
the brakes. He straightened it out, made a sharp
right turn, and wheeled it through the doorless
front of the hangar. He stopped the car with a
squeal of brakes and tires by the airplane titled
Raske II. Kwasind jumped out and ran back to
the corner of the building, where he began firing
at those who had been chasing them.

The workers assembling the two planes in the
rear had stopped work when the car had roared
in. Two Hawks shot once over their heads. They
did not wait for a second bullet but fled to the
exit in the rear. Ilmika took a position behind an
empty barrel to shoot at the first soldier to enter
the rear door.

Two Hawks swore when he looked at the
Raske II. The auxiliaries and their attachments
had been removed. He shrugged and said, *"C'est
la guerre,"* put on his helmet and climbed into the
monoplane. He turned on the valves and
switches. At least, the tanks were full, and the
machine guns had a full supply of ammunition.

He pressed on the starter. There was a whin-
ing noise. The wooden propeller turned over
slowly at first, then more swiftly as the motor
coughed as if speed were stuck in its throat.

Kwasind and Ilmika left their posts to run for

the plane. She climbed into the rear cockpit.
Kwasind stopped at a signal from Two Hawks
and stepped up onto the wing so he could hear
Two Hawks. He grinned, climbed back down,
and removed the chocks from the wheels.

Two Hawks gave the motor more gas and
turned the rudder a hard right. The plane described a half-circle to face the *Raske I*. Kwasind
got under the tail of the *Raske II* and lifted. When
the fuselage was parallel to the floor, Two
Hawks began firing the twin machine guns. The
other plane shivered under the impact as big
holes appeared in its fabric in a line that sped
towards the gas tanks as Kwasind continued to
move the fuselage.

The *Raske I* exploded. Dense smoke spread
through the hangar and set Two Hawks and Ilmika to coughing. He felt the heat from the
blaze. Fortunately, the *Raske I* had been at the
other wall of the hangar, some hundred yards
away. Even so, Two Hawks had not been sure
that the flaming gas would not spread out to his
own plane. He had to take the chance, because
he did not want anybody pursuing him. Overloaded with three people, he would be too slow
and awkward to dogfight the *Raske I*. And he did
not have time to destroy the plane any other
way.

The plane continued to pivot as the giant
moved its tail. Two Hawks fired again while the
nose described a horizontal arc. The smoke was
so thick that he could not see whether or not the
soldiers had left the protection of the other side
of the hangar wall. If they had tried to rush

through the smoke, they would have been caught in the fire from the machine guns. Similarly, any troops entering the rear door should have been discouraged by the hail of lead.

Kwasind continued to carry the tail around until the plane was facing the entrance.

Two Hawks held the brakes until Kwasind had squeezed in beside Ilmika. The giant's face was rigid. Two Hawks looked back, grinned at him, released the brakes, and pulled the throttle out. The plane jumped like a frightened rabbit; his head was driven back into the headrest. The *Raske II* roared out into the firelit night. Soldiers ran out from behind the hangar walls and shot at the plane. A bullet tore a hole in the fabric of the cockpit.

The tail lifted, but the wheels clung to the ground. There was more weight than the craft was designed to normally carry. For what seeemed like a deadly long time, the plane refused to rise. The end of the paved strip shot up; beyond was a hundred yards of earth and then a thirty-foot high fence.

Two Hawks waited until the plane had bumped over fifty yards of grass. By then, the wheels were a few inches off the ground. He pulled back on the stick, and they left the earth and passed over the fence with six inches to spare. Past the fence was a copse of trees, the tips of which brushed agains the wheels. Two Hawks breathed out relief and continued the climb. Now he would head northward until dawn gave him enough visibility to get his bearings. He wished there had been enough time to attach the auxiliary tanks. This would have made the emergency landing at the halfway point unnecessary.

Then it occurred to him that the extra weight of the auxiliary tanks would have sent them into the fence. He could have tried taking off to the north, where the field was longer, but he would have been in a crosswind. Moreover, taxiing down to the south end would have given the Perkunishans a chance to go after him in cars. No, things had worked out much better this way. The whole crazy way.

Improvisation is my forte, Two Hawks said to himself. He sang a Seneca warchant his mother had taught him and then some lines from The Vagabond King. Kwasind was rigid, head bent down. Daylight came. Two Hawks talked to him through the earphones. Kwasind said he felt sick. Looking at anything but the cockpit floor made him want to vomit. His knees were turned to water, and he was curling inside like a pillar of smoke.

Ilmika, however, was thrilled. She exclaimed with joy as they passed over houses and barns a thousand feet below, and she pointed like a delighted child at the tiny people and cows. Two Hawks, as the sun climbed, lost his exultation. The fuel indicator was dropping faster than he had expected. He was also worried about the earliness of their arrival at the refueling point— if they got there. Should the Blodland agents in Berlin not find out about the escape soon enough, they would not notify the agents at the farm near Gervuoge. And then there was the possibility that the agents at Gervuoge had been discovered, and that Perkunishans would be waiting for the plane when it landed.

Two Hawks groaned, but a little while later laughed at himself. O, God! The mighty Iroquois warrior one minute and the next a big worrywart. So something goes wrong. I've been doing all right so far by playing it by ear.

Their second landing, the last to be made in Perkunishan territory, was to be on the Baltic Sea coast. This stretch of shoreline was the northernmost reach of a peninsula that was on Earth 1, if Two Hawks remembered his geography correctly, the island of Rugen. Since the glacial conditions of this world had locked up so much water in ice, the Baltic Sea was smaller than on Earth 1. Thus, the island had become a peninsula, and the southern Baltic coastline extended further north.

After landing on this coast, the refugees were supposed to be picked up by a Blodlandish dirigible from the island of Aabryg. On Earth 1, this island was Bornholm and was Danish territory. Here, Aabryg belonged to Tyrsland, Earth 2's equivalent of Sweden. The dirigible was to transport Two Hawks and party and the plane, if it could be managed, to Aabryg, then to Tyrsland, then to Norway and thence to Blodland.

By the time he had reached the southern shore of the large lake of Ramumas, the gas indicator had just reached empty. This meant he had one gallon left. Not much to fly around on while he looked for the farm. For one thing, he was too far to the east, or thought he was. Going west, he had to beat against a strong headwind, which was eating up his precious gallon just that much faster.

Come on, you limeys, he prayed. He passed over a crossroads in the form of a Celtic cross and knew he was three miles from the assignation point. There should be another dirt road two miles westward, then a little peninsula in the form of a question mark. A half mile past it should be a farm isolated from two others by a quarter-mile stretch of woods. The roof of the barn would be painted with two interlocking triskelions, the three-limbed symbols that were on the national flag of the six kingdoms that originally comprised the empire of Blodland. If it was all right for him to land, he would see two rocket flares. If not, he would see nothing, except maybe a troop of Perkunishans waiting for him. In either case, he would have to land, he was so low on gas.

The farm came into sight as they passed over a high hill. Ilmika jabbed her forefinger below and smiled. Just ahead was a large white barn with two red interlocking triskelions on one side of its sloping roof. He circled over the farm, searching the ground and also waiting to hear the sputter of motor. Three times he went around, coming lower each time. If the signals did not come, he would try to get past the woods to the farm on its other side. At least, they would have a headstart on their pursuers, although a successful escape seemed unlikely. But the Perkunishans would get a run for their bloodmoney.

Three men came out of the barn. Two held up

tubes which glittered in the sun. Each tube spat a dark object up to a height of thirty feet, at which the flares burst into a red and a green.

The landing could have been easy, since a long and broad meadow with a flat surface offered itself. However, a split-log fence bisected the meadow. Two Hawks had to sideslip to lose altitude fast enough and then gauge his glide path so he barely cleared the fence. The plane stopped with its nose not a foot from the edge of the woods. After taxiing back to the fence, he cut the motor and climbed out. Six men and a woman, all dressed in the coarse brown homespun of peasants, were waiting for him.

The introductions were short. Aelfred Hennend, the leader, said, "We got word by wireless just in time." He gave an order, and the other men left to get the gas and oil. Two Hawks said, "The fence has to be broken down if we're to have enough runway." Hennend replied that that would be done. He invited them into the house for some food and coffee. On the way he said, "Our neighbors may come nosing around. Your flying machine is bound to make them excited. There may even be troops on the way. We'll have to disappear just as soon as your machine is fueled. Too bad, too. Hate to give up this place, it's a good station for our underground. But if you can deliver that contraption to Blodland, the sacrifice will be worth it."

Two Hawks did not apologize. While he ate, he asked Hennend about the next landing. He went over a map with him. A radio operator came in to say that the weather on the Baltic

coast was all right. There was an overcast but no
promise of rain, and the wind was moderate.
Also, the *lyftship*, the dirigible, was on its way
from Tyrsland.

Two Hawks returned to the plane to supervise
the refueling. The fence had been taken apart in
the middle for a distance of fifty feet. The oxen
and the cart that had brought barrels of gas were
by the plane. The tanks were filled in twenty
minutes, even though the fuel had to be poured
in by hand.

He considered removing the machine guns
from the plane. The loss of weight would aid
their takeoff and also cut down on fuel consump-
tion. But he had enough leeway in fuel; it would
be better to keep the weapons. The Blodlandish
would not only have an aircraft as a model but
would also have the guns as prototypes.

The two male fliers shook the agents' hands;
Ilmika extended her hand to be kissed. They
bade the agents godspeed and got into the
cockpits. Two Hawks grinned when he saw
Kwasind's reluctance. Kwasind had made no attempt to hide his great joy at returning to earth
safely. Two Hawks felt sure that Kwasind would
stay behind and try to get to Tyrsland via the
underground if Two Hawks were to suggest the
idea. Perhaps this was a good idea. Without
Kwasind, the range and speed of the plane
would be much improved.

No, let him suffer now. The sooner he got out
of the country, the better. He was so obviously
an Indian, he would have a difficult time traveling by day. If he were to be caught, he would

be on Two Hawks' conscience. Besides, he was fond of Kwasind.

The takeoff was easy, although Kwasind might not think so, since the iron-rimmed wheels cleared the treetops by ten feet. To Two Hawks, ten feet was as good as a hundred. He climbed to 500 and leveled off. Their destination was an isolated but reasonably smooth beach on the Perkunishan (Baltic) Sea. Two Hawks located the highway Hennend had marked in red on the map and followed it northward. When he saw the seaport of Saldus at its end, he turned east. Saldus was a city of about 40,000 civilians and 10,000 sailors. There were warships in the harbor and an airship field at the outskirts, but he saw no dirigibles.

Ten miles to the east of Saldus, the land sloped upwards to become a series of rocky cliffs. After two miles of these, he saw the beach. A group of men was standing at one end, and a quarter-mile out was a two-masted fishing boat. Two Hawks made the landing, which was bumpier than he liked, with a hundred feet to spare before the cliffs began again. Even so, he had to sideslip to drop altitude swiftly just as he had done on the previous landing. As soon as he got out of the plane, he checked the landing gear. The wire spokes of the wheels were bent but not enough to worry about. Besides, if the plan went well, neither they nor the cliffs would be a problem.

He talked with agents, who enlightened him on the progress of the war. From the Perkunishan viewpoint, it was progress. From the

Blodlandish viewpoint, it was disaster. Perkunisha had completely overrun Dakota, Gotsland, Neftroia, and the eastern half of Hotinohsonih. They had occupied the northern part of Rasna (Earth 1's France) but had bogged down in the conquest of the southern half. The Perkunishan armies had overrun Akhaivia (Italy of Earth 1) as far as Vespros (Florence). It was expected, from the way things were going, that Akhaivia, Doria (Jugoslavia), and Hatti (Greece) would be occupied within a month or two. The Perkunishan fleet dominated the Mediterranean, since the Shofet of New Crete (the Iberian peninsula) had permitted the fleet to steam through the straits of Khasdrubal (Gibraltar).

A large fleet of Perkunishan airships had defeated a Blodlandish fleet over the Narwe Lagu (English Channel). Another fleet had bombed the city of Bammu (London). So far, the surface navies of the two nations had not had a full-scale battle. However, the Perkunishan navy was somewhat larger than the Blodlandish. There would be a showdown soon, an invasion army was being assembled on the Rasnan coast. The present air superiority of Perkunisha could tip the balance in a naval clash. A dirigible had already sunk a Blodlandish dreadnaught.

Stunning news had come in just that morning. The Shofet of New Crete had decided to jump into the war on the winning side. New Crete had long had a claim on southeastern Bamba and Cornwall, taken from them by the Blodlandish several hundred years ago. Espionage reported that the Shofet and Kassandrash had met and agreed that New Crete would get their ancient possessions back. But first, the isles had to be invaded.

The withdrawal of the Blodlandish fleet from the Mardakan (Indian) bases to aid in the defense of the homeland had been an invitation to the Saariset. The semi-caucasoid Finnic-speakers of Saariset (Earth 1's Japanese islands) had launched their navies towards Mardaka. This would make Perkunisha angry, of course, because they intended to add the rich subcontinent to their empire. At the moment, Perkunisha could do nothing about it.

"What about the Ikhwan?" Two Hawks said, referring to the Arabic nation of southern Africa.

"They're not declaring war, just making war. Their armies are marching into both Perkunishan and our African colonies. Moreover, part of their fleet and a host of troop ships are hastening to western Mardaka to reclaim it. We took it away from them, you know."

"Both Earths are in a mess," Two Hawks said. "As usual. Have you heard of any reaction from our escape in Berlin?"

Erik Shop, the chief, said that he had heard nothing. A man interrupted them to report that the dirigible from Tyrsland was sighted. Two Hawks turned to see a small object on the horizon to the seawards. A second later, a shadow fell on them, and the hum of faroff propellers came to them. They looked up. Another airship, its silvery side marked with a black boar's head, was above them. It was going northward at a speed of forty miles an hour and at an altitude of 500 feet.

Shop swore. "Perkunishan, Mammoth class!"

Two Hawks said, "What chance does your ship have against that monster?"

"The *Guthhavok* is only a light cruiser," Shop replied. He was pale. "Can you fly across the Baltic to Tyrsland?"

"I'd never make it." He looked at the huge airship, shrugged, and said, "There's only one thing to do, like it or not."

15

HE STRODE TO the plane, the tank of which had been refilled in case just such an emergency happened. He asked Shop some questions about airships and then got into the cockpit. He started the motor and taxied down to the extreme end of the beach. The men, who had run after him, held onto the wings while he put his brakes on and then revved the motor up as far as it would go and still not move the plane.

The others had run after him, so he was able to call Ilmika to his side. Above the roar of the motor, he shouted, "If I don't get back, you and Kwasind leave on the fishing boat with the others! They'll get you home!"

Ilmika reached up and pulled his head down and kissed him.

"You're a brave man. Two Hawks! I haven't told you that because I was too proud! After all . . . !"

"I don't have blue blood, and I'm a red-skinned Hotinohsonih," he said. "Thanks, anyway! I know what it took for you to bend your stiff Blodlandish neck!"

She must not have heard his final words, since she smiled at him. Then she was busy hanging

onto the wing, working with the others to hold
the plane down while he held his brakes and
sped up the motor. He chopped his hand down,
the men let loose of the wings, he released the
brakes, and the *Raske II* shot forward. It sped
down the beach, bumping, lifted and climbed as
steeply upwards as he dared direct it. The black
cliffs rushed towards him. He could not clear
them if he continued straight ahead, but he
could make a sharp bank to the left. He was on
his side, the waves directly below him. Then the
plane righted, and he began to climb. The throttle was all the way out, since it did not matter
how much gas he used.

The long sinister shape of the dirigible, small
at first, grew larger. Even though it had a headstart, its top speed was forty mph; his, 100. The
Blodlandish airship had not turned tail. It was
continuing straight towards its larger and more
heavily armed foe.

Brave but foolhardy. Yet he had to admire its
officers and crew. They had their duty, and, if it
involved battling an enemy that almost hopelessly outclassed them, they would not turn tail. The
Blodlandish, despite many dissimilarities to
their Earth 1 counterparts, resembled them in
courage and stubbornness.

Both airships reminded him of the early German rigid airships of his world, the quaint-look-
ing vessels which had charmed him so when he
saw their illustrations in various books on aviation. Both their sterns and bows were fitted with
a vertical series of elevators, four each. The open
control gondolas and the motor gondolas hung

from wires attached to the framework. The sides of the gondolas only came up to the waists of the crew; they would be freezing at high altitudes. Wooden ladders gave access from the cars to openings above in the cigar-shaped body.

Since aluminum was unknown here and other metals were too heavy, the framework was of spruce, a light, tough, and flexible wood. Balsa wood would be lighter, but it was lacking in this world, since it was indigenous to South America. He had a vague memory that wooden rigids had been built by a German company during World War I. If so, they would have been much like the two he was now seeing. The cross-frames and longitudinal sections were wooden, and the skeleton was covered by goldbeaters' skin. The difference would be that the internal bracing wires here would be steel, not aluminum. These would make this world's airships heavier, of course.

He'd been told that the dirigibles had to stay in their hangars if the wind was over twelve miles an hour. Fortunately, the wind today was only an estimated five mph, unusually low for this area. If it had been over the limit, a surface vessel was to pick up the refugees. If time permitted, the airplane would be disassembled and taken to the rescue ship.

He could see it now, a two-master about a mile off-shore. But six miles from it to the west was a small object from which black smoke poured and behind which was a white wake. It was a Perkunishan gunboat racing towards them.

The captain of the rescue ship would be wise to turn and run right now. He didn't have a chance to carry out his mission if the Blodlandish dirigible failed.

The situation was grim. Unless Two Hawks managed to shoot the enemy airship down, he and his party were doomed.

The two aircraft were a half-mile apart when Two Hawks caught up with the larger one. He began climbing to get above it, noting as he did so the huge black letters painted on its side. *Pilkash Tigrash*. Perkunishan for *Grey Tiger*. It was huge, and there were only five of its size built so far. But twenty more of the Mammoth Three Class were being built and more would come.

Above the letters were square ports. From them barrels poked, and from the barrels shot needles of flame. The fabric on his right wing ripped as bullets tore through it. He pulled away, seeing at the same time a rocket flashing towards him. It passed fifty feet in front of his plane and exploded. The shock wave rocked the craft; some fragments tore some more fabric, this time in the left wing.

Two Hawks continued to climb while four more rockets exploded around him. Shrapnel or case fragments stitched the side of his cockpit, but the energy was spent and they did not get to him. He attained his desired height of three hundred feet above the dirigible and turned. He dived, his angle of descent 45 degrees, then 60. Black squares in the forward upper skin of the airship flicked out little red tongues. Two rockets

raced each other to get to him first. Both passed
above him and blew up behind him.

When he was five hundred feet away, he fired
his twin machine-guns. He kept firing the incen-
diary bullets until he was so close he had to veer
away or crash into the airship. As he turned, he
felt, then heard, the explosion. He looked back
and up, since he was now past and below the
ship. The center part was wrapped in flames.
Quickly, the fire spread throughout the great
craft. It settled slowly towards the sea while blue
dolls—men—fell from it. They preferred a swift
fall and a quick painless death against the hard
waters to burning.

Two Hawks leveled off and watched while the
Grey Tiger sank past him, its stern high, its nose
down. It crashed into the sea, and, still flaming,
broke up, the light wooden skeleton shattering
on impact.

Four minutes later, the *Grey Tiger* was gone.
Only some large spiral pieces of wood, a few sections of fabric, and little islands of burning oil
were left. He returned to the beach and landed.
Ilmika embraced him while the others danced
and laughed. He should have felt exultant. He
was the victor of a historic event, the first battle
in this world between an airship and an airplane. But the sight of the men leaping from the
doomed *Grey Tiger,* some with their uniforms
blazing, had dampened him. He had too much
imagination, or too much empathy, not to feel
some of their terror. He had been close to that
time of not-to-be-avoided and utter end too
many times himself.

The *Guthhavok*, the Blodlandish cruiser, approached the airplane upwind and at a height of fifty feet. The wind was about eight mph and steady, and the big craft did not bob enough to cause Two Hawks concern. When the dirigible was directly above, it lowered a net on the end of a cable from an opening in its belly. The net was spread out on the beach, and the plane was pushed over it. After the net had been lifted up and wrapped around the plane, Two Hawks signalled the airship to start hauling up the cable. The dirigible, tempering the thrust of its propellers to the wind, hovered in one spot. There was an unavoidable jerk when the cable first lifted. Then the plane was rising smoothly, its nose pointing downward because of the weight of the motor, yet so securely wrapped in the net that it did not slip through. The pressure of the net might crush the plane a little, but Two Hawks did not worry about that. It could be repaired when it got to Blodland.

The plane disappeared into the belly of the aerial whale. A few minutes later, the cable was let down again. A large basket, probably taken from an observation balloon for this trip, was at the end of the cable. Ilmika, Kwasind, and Two Hawks climbed into it, grabbed the supporting ropes, and the basket was lifted. The dirigible began rising and at the same time turning northwards. Before the three were inside the airship, it had begun its journey across the sea to Tyrsland.

The basket went up through the hole and was swung to one side, away from the port and onto a small platform. They climbed out with a feeling of relief. An officer conducted them down a catwalk which ran above the longitudinal axis of the *lyftship*. Two Hawks stared at the perforated spiraling wooden frames and the huge spherical cells containing hydrogen. The officer, answering his questions, said that the cell coverings were made of goldbeater's skin. Two Hawks had thought that they would be made of this material, since a rubberized fabric in a world without rubber would be impossible. And so far no one had invented synthetic rubber. He was no chemist, but he could give the scientists enough hints for them to begin research. This world needed him far more than his native world, he thought. The only trouble was, he needed his native world far more than he needed this one. There was no winning. Just fighting.

With which unhappy but not unendurable thought he went down through the port and down a slidepole into the gondola, the bridge. There the *heretoga* (captain) and his chief officers were introduced to the new passengers. Two Hawks was congratulated on his victory over the Perkunishan airship. The *heretoga* went up with Two Hawks to look at the plane, the exit being made on a very steep and narrow staircase and two handropes. Aethelstan, the captain, was not as jubilant about the plane as he should have been. Two Hawks was puzzled at first, then began to understand. Aethelstan loved his command; he loved the great gas-borne ships. And in this fragile little machine nestling inside the airship like a baby bird in its nest, he saw doom. When enough heavier-than-air machines were

built, they would sweep the dirigibles out of the
sky. His career would soon be over. He could
either go back to surface ships or learn to fly a
dangerous and unfamiliar machine, and for the
latter, he was too old.

There would be many like him. The war
would bring on changes, like all wars, and men
would find themselves deprived of that for which
they were fitted and which they loved. And the
introduction of Raske and Two Hawks into this
world was a catalyst to precipitate change even
faster than it would normally have occurred and
in a far stranger fashion.

Three days later, the three were in Bammu,
the capital city of the empire of Blodland. Bammu was on the same site as the London of Earth
1. It had been founded by New Cretan traders
who had renamed the Celtic village Bab Mu—
the gate of the river. The city was not as large as
its Earth 1 counterpart, having only a population of 750,000, including suburbs. The
architecture of buildings was more like the city
of the 12th century of Earth 1, in Two Hawks'
eyes, anyway. The business and government
buildings had an alien flavor, a vaguely Levan-
tine impression. Indeed, the west Semitic influence of the New Cretan colonizers was very
strong. Many street names were of Cretan origin. The Blodlandish equivalent of Earth 1's parliament, the Witenayemot, was a mixture of Semitic and Germanic elements. Even the king was
not called by the old Germanic title; he was the
Shof, derived from Shofet, the Cretan word for
ruler.

Two Hawks went through a period of interrogation, one very different from that in Hotinohsonih because the Blodlandish knew his value. It was only a week after he had begun making plans for an aircraft plant that he was given
a rank of minor nobility. At an evening ceremo-
ny, the Shof made him a lord of the realm, the
Aetheling of Fenhop. He became the owner of a
castle and a number of farms in the west country. In Bammu itself, he had a small mansion
and a number of slaves and servants.

Two Hawks asked Ilmika about the former
owners. "The Huskarl of Fenhop was a heretic,"
she said. "He was hanged about thirty years
ago, not for heresy but for murdering one of his
slaves. If he had not been a heretic, he would
have gotten only a large fine and a small jail sentence. His sons migrated to Rasna, and the
property reverted to the crown."

"And now that I am a nobleman," he said,
"does that mean I can marry a woman of the
nobility?"

Her face reddened. She said, "Oh, no, your
patent is to be held by you while you live and is
cancelled when you die. Your property goes
back to the crown. Your children will be commoners. And you can't marry a noblewoman."

"So my blood isn't good enough to mingle
with Blodlandish blood?" he said. "And my
children, after being accustomed to the high life,
can go begging. From castle to cabin for them,
right?"

Ilmika was indignant. "Would you have us be
adulterated? Why, the purity of the ancient

Blodlandish nobles would be sullied! Our children would be mongrels. Isn't it enough for you that you're a peer of the realm, even if . . . ?"

"Say it, Ilmika Thorrsstein! Even if I'm an outlander and a red-skinned savage, that's what you didn't have enough guts to say, right?"

He spoke two words of ancient Germanic lineage and walked away. He felt an anger that had carried him to the point of striking her. Almost. It was anger that had deeper roots than reaction to being regarded as a mongrel. He knew that he had had some hope—however slight—that Ilmika might be his wife. Damn it! He was in love with a cold-hearted, superstitious, bigoted, illiterate, emotionally stupid, patrician snob! Damn it and damn her! He would do what he should have done at the very beginning! He would forget her.

Yet, she was the one who had praised his courage, valor, and high worth to the Shof and the Witanayemot. She had suggested that he be given a patent of nobility.

She would do the same for any man, no matter how baseborn, he thought, who had saved her twice from the life of a slave-whore. Her gratitude went that far but no further, and she certainly was not in love with him.

He hurled himself into the labors of creating airplanes. Day and night, he worked. In addition to the airplane factory and organizing the Blodland Shoflich Lyftwaepon (Blodland Royal Air Force), he designed a carbine and a tank for the ground forces. He also spent some time in trying to educate the military medical branch in

cleanliness and treatment of wounds. After a
short and fierce struggle, he had to give up. This
world had no Pasteur as yet, and it was not
about to accept Two Hawks as one. In the meantime, soldiers would die unnecessarily of infec-
tions, typhoid and smallpox, and women would
die of puerperal fever. Two Hawks cursed the
forces of darkness and prejudice and went back
furiously to the business of building better tools
for killing.

A month after he had arrived at Bammu, the
Perkunishans invaded the island. The Perkunishan and New Cretan fleets slugged it out
with the Blodlandish navy in the Narwe Lagu.
The defenders inflicted heavy damage and made
the enemy pay with two ships for every one of
their own. But it lost two-thirds of its own
strength, including all but two dreadnoughts,
and had to run for it. The Blodlandish air fleet
had engaged the Perkunishan at the same time
as the surface battle. It was a disaster for both
sides; it ended in a draw with exactly forty airships on both sides going down in flames.

Nature seemed to be allied with the invaders.
The channel was unnaturally smooth and the
winds were slight the day the enemy landed. For
five days, the weather conditions held. At the
end of that time, the enemy had established a
beach-head five miles wide and five miles deep.
To accomplish this, they had sacrificed 20,000
men.

A New Cretan army landed on the southern
Bamba shore and advanced rapidly, again with
disproportionate casualties.

Then, winter struck. It was such a winter as
Two Hawks had never known. Within a month,
the two islands were covered with great drifts of
snow. The arctic winds howled down from the
north; the temperature dropped to 30 below.
Two Hawks shivered and dressed in polar bear
furs. Yet this was only the beginning. Before
winter was finished with its icy rage, the ther-
mometer would be the equivalent of minus 40
degrees Fahrenheit.

He thought that surely the fighting would stop
now. Nobody could carry on efficiently—if at all
—in this frozen hell. But the invaded and in-
vader alike were used to the severity. They
fought on, and where armored cars and trucks
bogged down, men on skis or snowshoes pulled
toboggans of supplies. Men fell and were buried
in the snow. Mile by bloody mile, the Perkunishans claimed Blodlandish territory, and
near winter's end were holding the white lands
which corresponded to the Kent, Sussex, Surrey,
and Hampshire of Earth 1's England.

By then, Two Hawks had twenty monoplanes,
all armed with machine guns and with skis for
landing gear. He had trained four young men to
fly, although in this cold it was difficult even to
get the motors to start. The four then became
instructors. By the spring thaw, the Lyftwaepon
had a hundred fighter planes, a hundred and fifty pilots, and two hundred students.

Espionage informed Two Hawks that Raske
had 500 first-line craft and 800 qualified pilots.

It was then that he got the idea for his self-
propelled icesleds. Why not build a vehicle that

moved on runners and was propelled by an airplane motor? A fleet of such could operate on the frozen surface of the straits and channel. It could cut up the lines supplying materiel to the invading forces. If enough supplies could be destroyed, the Perkunishans on the island would find themselves short of food and ammunition when the spring thaw came. The waters between mainland and island would be unnavigable at that time. Before the waters were fit for renewal of supply, a big push by the Blodlandish could destroy the food-short, ammunition-short, personnel-short enemy.

His suggestion was rejected. The High Command thought the idea was too radical. Two Hawks told the Command he did not understand their pig-headed blindness. His only answer was a savage lecture on keeping his place. Old Lord Raedaesh, a stiff old man with bushy white whiskers and eyes pale and cold as sea-ice, delivered the lecture. Raedaesh had made it plain from the start that he regarded Two Hawks as an upstart who was not quite sane. He had opposed the use of the newfangled flying machines for anything other than observation purposes. If it had not been for the orders of the Shof, Raedaesh would never have permitted this wasting of men and materials for such nonsense.

Two Hawks listened until he could control himself no more. Interrupting Lord Raedaesh, he pleaded with the others to listen to him. The iceboats could do more than cut off the enemy supply lines. They could destroy the entire Perk-

unishan navy. The ships were all in icelocked
harbors, and the Blodlandish knew where each
was. A fleet of iceboats could cross the ice, even
into the North Sea and Baltic, and could torpedo
every immobile dreadnaught and cruiser, destroyer, troop ship, supply ship.

Now was the time to act, this day, before the
spring thaw started. The propellers and motors
of his planes could be mounted on the iceboats.
These would carry a crew, machine guns, torpe-
does, even small cannon. Iceboats to carry com-
mando troops could be built. If the idea sounded
fantastic, a desperate situation demanded desperate action.

Lord Raedaesh, his face scarlet, thundered at
him to get out of the council room. He was to get
back to his flying toys and his unsportsmanlike
rapid-fire weapons. Let him not dare to annoy
the High Command any more with his madman
schemes.

Trembling, inwardly raging, Two Hawks
obeyed. He could do nothing else. Returning to
his house, he told Kwasind, "I'll adopt a what-
the-hell attitude. Laugh at Raedaesh and his fellow asses. After all, they're just being human,
that is, living fossils, stupid tradition-shelled
turtles. They are no different from their counterparts on my Earth, past and present.
Kwasind, I could tell you the history of man's
stupidity on Earth, especially the stupidity of the
typical military mind. You'd be shocked."

"The Blodlandish don't have a monopoly on
stupidity, arrogance, or rigidity," Kwasind said.
"Have you heard the latest?"

New Crete and Perkunisha were at war. The New Cretan forces in Bamba had depended largely upon their ally to supply them during the winter. But the Perkunishans had been very tight-fisted with the supplies. They gave the excuse that they were having enough trouble providing for their own troops. The Shofet of New Crete had seen the real reason behind his ally's actions. Although Perkunisha had pledged Bamba as a prize of war, it wanted the island for itself. If the New Cretans were defeated and Perkunisha had to take over, Perkunisha could claim Bamba by right of conquest.

The Shofet had accused his ally of betrayal. The arrogant Perkunishans reacted violently and swiftly. Even now their Mediterranean fleet and troops in south Rasna were fighting their former allies.

"They think they can take on the whole world," Kwasind said. "Now, they go too far— I hope. That's not all, you know. Perkunisha has demanded that Ikhwan hand back the African colonies it's occupied. And it's also told Ikhwan to stay out of western Madraka. If Ikhwan doesn't obey, Perkunisha will declare war on them."

"What's the Blodlandish government doing about this? Ikhwan has a powerful navy, probably the most powerful, now that Perkunisha has lost so many ships. If the Ikhwan would become allied to us . . ."

"They won't. Obviously, they plan to let Europe tear itself apart. Then they'll move in. You watch."

"It's Fimbulwinter," Two Hawks said. "Got-
terdammerung. The Twilight of the Gods."

But the winter passed without the end of the
world. The snows melted; mud had its fun with
the armies that tried to slog through it. The
Blodlandish were well entrenched in strategic
positions, their cannons in place. The Perkunishans had to haul their big artillery wherever
they were needed. Since the few paved roads on
the island had been blown up and the railroads
removed by the retreating Blodlandish, the invaders had to build new ones. This took time,
and their armies bogged down.

The Blodlandish Air Force had its first big
engagement with the enemy planes, 20 miles
south of Bammu. Although outnumbered by ten
craft, the Blodlandish fought fiercely. They lost
six planes and sent twelve enemy down in
flames. Two Hawks was flying that day because
he believed his men needed an experienced combat man with them.

The fliers, based on the northern side of the
capital city, flew ten sorties that day. Two
Hawks went up a second time, leading fifty
planes in an attack on the enemy field closest to
the front lines. The twenty planes on the ground,
all hangars, a bomb dump, and four anti-aircraft
posts were destroyed. For two weeks, the
Blodlandish flew from dusk to dawn. They lost
heavily in the many dogfights over Bammu,
since the Perkunishans were intent on destroying
the islanders' air effectiveness. Fortunately, the
full weight of their enemy's air arm was not
brought to bear against them. Espionage said

that Raske had wanted to use every plane he had in the campaign, but the High Command had vetoed this. Half went to fight against the New Cretans; only a fourth were being used on the island.

Raske was in Berlin, probably afraid to leave it because of politics. He had many enemies among the nobility, who would take advantage of his absence to dislodge him if they could. The commander of the Perkunishan Air Force in Blodland was an ex-dirigible man who had not even learned to fly heavier-than-air craft. He did not understand the effective use of his craft. The officers who led their men into aerial combat were as inexperienced as those they led. Since the flight leader's planes were always marked with a scarlet plumed helmet, they got a concentrated attack from the Blodlandish. Two Hawks had given the orders that the flight commanders should be dealt with first, if possible. It became almost certain death for a commander to engage in combat, yet, if he did not, he would have been regarded as a coward by the men under him. The rate of promotion in the invading air force became rapid.

This was very satisfying to Two Hawks, but his successes seemed to have little effect upon the battling on the ground. The enemy took one fort after another, one town after another, losing three-to-one in the process but seemingly not caring. Suddenly, the capital was invaded. A fleet bombarded the forts at the mouth of the Harbash river for a week, then landed troops. The Perkunishan air force provided a cover that day. Two Hawks led his complete force against them, and in one day the Perkunishan fliers were almost wiped out.

It made no difference to the men on the ground. In seven days, the invaders were hammering at the gates of Bammu.

Two days later, fifty of Raske's new twin-engined bombers landed on a Perkunishan field. They refueled and took off to bomb Bammu, escorted by a hundred new fighter planes. Only half the bombers returned and 60 fighters. Two Hawks shot down ten enemy that day, bringing his score up to fifty-one. He returned with only thirty Blodlandish, all that remained of his pilots.

16

DESPITE THE staggering losses, the bombing raid was a success. Four bombs struck the Witenayemot while the lords were in final session, before evacuating to the north. Old Lord Raedaesh was killed. Two Hawks thought that this was the best thing that could happen for the Blodlandish. But the bomb had also killed the Shofet, his two younger brothers, the queen, and the Shofet's children. The entire royal family was wiped out, except for the Shofet's uncle, who had been in a madhouse for twenty years. In the confusion that followed the announcement of the disaster, a young Kreion (General) named Erik Leonitha, a bastard son of the mad uncle, declared himself the protector of Blodland. He ordered the army out of Bammu to take a position to the north. He freed the slaves in a proclamation that declared that slavery was at an end forever in Blodland. This was not done out of democratic principle but to keep the slaves from revolting. The Perkunishan agents had been spreading disaffection among them since before the war.

Erik Leonitha also promised that after the enemy had been driven out, more rights would be

given the common people and they would have a
chance to advance themselves in the military and
in the big businesses. The nobility were strongly
opposed to him, so he needed as much support
as he could get from the masses.

Two Hawks, acting on his own, had given orders to dismantle the aircraft factory and move
the machinery to the north. He stayed in Bammu until the last piece of equipment had been
loaded on a freight train. He and Kwasind
boarded the final train out of the city. Even as he
stepped onto his car, shells burst not more than
a quarter-mile away. He went through several
cars crowded with officers and high-born refugees. While going through an aisle, he heard his
name called. He turned to look down into the
blue eyes of Ilmika Thorrsstein.

"It's been a long time, Milady," he said. "I
heard about your mother and brothers. I sent a
letter of condolence. Did you get it?"

"No," she said. "The mails are so bad now.
But I thank you for your sympathy."

He tried to continue the conversation without
much success. She seemed withdrawn. Perhaps,
he thought, she was just too tired. Her face was
pale, and she had large dark circles under her
eyes. He excused himself, saying he hoped to be
able to talk with her again before they reached
their destination. After passing through two
more jammed aisles, he found his compartment.
It was a tiny room, but he was fortunate to get it.
The army had reserved it for him and for another important man, a Kreion. The officer rose
when Two Hawks entered and returned the

salute. Then, to Two Hawks' surprise, he held
out his hand to be shaken.

"I am Lord Humphrey Gilbert," he said.
"The fates have been good to me. I've been
wanting to meet you for a long time."

Two Hawks looked curiously at him. Gilbert
was a name of French origin, or so he had always
believed until now. There was neither a French
nation nor language in this world, so he must
have been mistaken. Yet he felt a warmth at
coming across something that reminded him of
his lost world, coincidence or not.

Gilbert was a short and husky man, about fifty. His thick greying hair was curly, and he had
thick black eyebrows, grey eyes, a broad face,
and a double chin. His moustache was dark and
long and pointed. Gilbert invited Two Hawks to
sit down, which Two Hawks would have done
anyway, since he had no intention of standing.
Gilbert began to talk to Two Hawks as if he had
known him a long time. Two Hawks warmed up
to him even more, since most of the aristocracy
he had met had treated him somewhat coldly or
over-politely. As it turned out, Gilbert had, in a
way, known Two Hawks for a long time. He had
been learning as much as he could about him.

"I inherited my title from my father," Gilbert
said. "He came from a middle-class but very
wealthy merchant family, most of whose riches
came from a large fleet of merchant ships. Now,
I have lost all my lands, most of my ships, well,
this is not relevant to my story, except that I
want you to know my background. You see, my
family was founded by my great-great-great, I

forget how many greats, grandfather. He came
to Blodland in the Year of Hemilka 560."

Two Hawks calculated the date, comparing it
to the equivalent date of Earth 1. Hemilka 560
would be 1583 A. D.

"My ancestor, also named Humphrey Gilbert, did not come from the mainland. He came
out of the western ocean, the Okeanos, in a ship
such as no man had ever seen before."

Gilbert paused as if waiting for a reaction of
some sort. Two Hawks looked blank. Gilbert
continued, "The ship was *The Squirrel,* sister ship
to *The Golden Hind.*"

Gilbert looked disappointed when Two
Hawks merely looked politely interested. He
said, "It's apparent to me that the disap-
pearance of my ancestor from your world made
no more than a ripple in your history, if that. I
had thought he might have been a man of note.
Well, no matter. Humphrey Gilbert was an Eng-
lishman—ah, I see your eyes light up now! He
was one of the early sailors to the continent of
America . . ."

"How do you know all this, I mean, about
Englishmen and America?" Two Hawks said.

Gilbert raised a fat hand. "Patience! I'll get to
that presently. As I was saying, his ship had
been in a storm which separated it from its sister
ship. When the storm disappeared, Gilbert
could not locate the other ship, so he sailed on
back until he came to what he thought was England and home. He sailed into the port of Ent
(Earth 1's Bristol). There he and his men were
regarded as madmen. But to Gilbert and his

crew, the others were mad. What had happened? Here was a people who looked something like the English but were speaking a tongue that only distantly resembled it. Nothing that they had known was familiar. Where were they?

"The Blodlandish locked up the whole crew in an insane asylum. Some of the sailors did go insane, but my ancestor must have been a very adaptable man. He finally convinced the authorities he was harmless. After he was released, he became a sailor and eventually a captain of a ship. He went into African slave-trading—Africa was just being opened up then—and became wealthy. He married well and died rich and highly respected.

"He was intelligent enough not to insist on the truth of the story he had told when he'd first sailed into Ent. In fact, he never again mentioned it. But he did write down his story, plus a history of his native world. He titled it *An Unpublished Romance, or Through the Ivory Gates of the Sea*. The manuscript has been in the family library since his death. Most of his descendants have not read it, and those who did thought their ancestor had a rather feverish imagination."

Gilbert paused, then said, "I never thought so. There were too many consistent details in his history. He had tried to put down the whole of his world on paper. He even wrote an English-Blodlandish comparative grammar and dictionary. I became fascinated by the manuscript —which has more than 5,000 pages—and made the study of it my hobby. I investigated the tales of other strange appearances and became convinced that another Erthe existed. And that, from time to time, men somehow passed from one world to another.

"Are you sure you've never heard of Sir Humphrey Gilbert?"

Two Hawks shook his head. "If I read anything about him, I've forgotten it. And I'm an omnivorous reader, too. I graze in all fields."

"Perhaps he was only one of many who perished during their explorations. It doesn't matter. What does is that your presence here verifies his story. It is more than a fantasy. And my research has convinced me of one thing. The 'gates' are certain weak spots in the forces that separate the two universes. They only open at infrequent intervals, perhaps most of them never more than once."

He leaned towards Two Hawks, his eyes bright. "But I believe that I've located one gate that is more or less permanent. At least, it is in one place, and it has opened up more than once and may again."

Two Hawks became excited. "You know of such a place? Where?"

"I've never actually seen it," Gilbert replied. "I was planning to take a trip there to investigate, but the war stopped me. However, I came across a reference to something that sounds like a gate while I was reading a book on the sorcerers of Hivika."

Hivika, Two Hawks thought. That was the name of the chain of islands that was the only prominent feature of the sunken North American continent. He had seen their name on maps.

From their location, they should be the upper part of the Rockies. The largest island was approximately where the state of Colorado was on Earth 1.

Polynesians, immigrants from Hawaii, inhabited the mountainous islands. And, so far, Hivika had remained neutral and independent. The Hivikan inhabitants, like the Maori of Earth 1, had learned early how to make guns and gunpowder on their own and how to use them effectively. The first Old Worlders to make contact with the Hivikans had not been Europeans but the Arabic Ikhwani of South Africa. These had carried on trade with Hivika for a hundred years before the first Blodlandish ship had accidentally discovered the islands. The Europeans found a handsome and intelligent brown people who mined iron and gold, sailed ships armed with cannon, and were not awed by the white man's technology. Moreover, the Hivikans had gone through several plagues brought to them by the Ikhwan. The descendants of the survivors were fairly resistant to European diseases.

Gilbert said, "The Hivika still practice the old religion, you know. Their priests, who claim to be sorcerers, keep constant vigilance over certain tabu places. One of these is a cave high up on the loftiest mountain of the largest island. Not much is known about the cave, but a Perkunishan scholar found out some things. The priests call the cave The Hole Between The Worlds. Terrible sounds sometimes come from the rear of the cave, where the Hole sometimes appears. The back wall of the cave seems to dissolve, and the priests get glimpses into another world. Perhaps *world* is not the right translation for the word they use. It could mean the Place of the Gods. The priests dare not go near the 'gate,' because they believe that the chief god, Ke Aku'a, lives in this world."

Two Hawks said, "This is too good to be true. I'm afraid to get too excited about it. It'll probably turn out to be some natural phenomenon."

"The gates are natural phenomena," Gilbert said. It's certainly worth investigating, don't you agree?"

"I intend to investigate," Two Hawks said. "In fact, I'd like to leave for Hivika right now. Only, it's impossible."

"When the war's over, we might go together. If there is a gate through which we could pass, I'd like very much to see the Earth of my ancestor."

Two Hawks did not reply, but he was thinking that, for Gilbert, Earth 1 might be an interesting place to visit but not to live in. Gilbert would have the same sense of dislocation, of utter severance, that Two Hawks and O'Brien had had. Even now, despite an increasing familiarity with this planet, Two Hawks never felt quite at ease. He just did not *belong*.

However, it was a feeling he could endure with no more than a little bit of discomfort and out-of-jointedness most of the time. The nights were the worst, when he was alone.

Somebody knocked on the compartment door. Two Hawks opened it, a young officer saluted and said, "Beg your pardon, Koiran. The Lady

Thorrsstein has taken ill, and she's asked for you."

Two Hawks followed the officer into Ilmika's car. He found her lying on the seat, surrounded by solicitous men. She was very pale but had recovered from her faint. A doctor standing over her said to Two Hawks, "She'll be all right as soon as she gets something to eat."

Two Hawks said, "Ilmika, why didn't you ask . . . ?" He stopped, then said, "No, you'd be too proud."

"Hers is not an uncommon story in these unhappy times," the doctor said. "There are many high-born who have lost their lands—money, everything but their titles. And . . ."

The doctor closed his mouth as if he had said too much. Two Hawks looked sharply at him. He seemed to be deriving some sort of satisfaction from Ilmika's condition. Probably, he was a commoner, and, like many, shared the repressed but very keen resentment of the lower classes towards the privileged. Two Hawks understood their feeling, since the majority suffered hardships and injustices exceeding those of the lower classes of the early 18th century of his own planet. Nevertheless, he was angry at the doctor. Ilmika was a human being who had also gone through many privations and griefs. Her family was dead; her home and possessions were in the hands of the enemy. And, as he talked to her while he fed her hot soup, he discovered she did not have a coin to her name.

She wept while she drank the soup. "I couldn't help fainting. Now, everybody knows

how destitute I am. I am a charity case. The
name of Thorrsstein is disgraced."

"Disgraced?" he said quietly. "If you are, so is
three-fourths of the nobility of Blodland. Why
should you be so proud? It's the fault of the war,
not you. Besides, now is the time to show that
nobility is made of stronger stuff than a mere
name. You have to act noble to be noble."

She smiled weakly. He got a slice of ham from
one officer and a piece of bread from another and
fed them to her. When she had finished eating,
she whispered to him, "If only I could get away
from their stares."

"There's room in my compartment for you,"
he said. He lifted her up, and, supporting her,
got her to his compartment. She lay down on one
of the seats and was quickly asleep. When she
awoke late that evening, he had supper with her
in the compartment. Gilbert had gone to the din-
ing car, and Kwasind was outside the door, so
they were alone. Two Hawks waited until they
had eaten the cold and coarse food. Then he
asked her if she would work for him. He needed
a secretary, he said. She turned so red that he
thought he had angered her. But when he heard
her stammer, he understood that she had mistaken the intent of the offer.

He laughed, although he was not amused, and
said, "No, Milady, I am not asking you to be my
mistress. You will have to do nothing beyond the
requirements of your secretarial duties."

She said, "Why shouldn't I be your whore? I
owe you so much."

"You don't owe me that much! Even if you

did, I'd never ask you to pay up. I want a woman who loves me—or at least desires me."

She was still red in the face, but she looked steadily into his eyes.

"If I did not desire you, do you think I'd accept your food and lodging now? Do you think me so empty of pride?"

He stood up and then leaned over her. She raised her face and closed her eyes for his kiss. Her arms came up around his neck, and she rose. She worked her mouth against his and pressed her body against him.

He pushed her away. "You're trying too hard. You don't really want to kiss me."

"I'm sorry," she said. Turning away, she began to weep. "Does no one want me? Do you reject me because I have been dishonored by those beasts in Itskapintik?"

Two Hawks turned her to face him. He said, "Ilmika, I don't understand you. Are you doing this because you feel that your virtue was taken away by an act of force?"

"Don't you know? There's not a nobleman in Blodland who'd have me now, since my story is known."

"So you'll take me because I'm of commoner origin, and commoners don't care about virtue in their women? Or a commoner should be delirious with joy to get a noblewoman, no matter what her state of virtue? I'm the last refuge, right?"

She slapped him hard. Then she came at him with her fingernails. He caught her wrists and held her away from him.

"You dumb bitch! I love you! I don't give a damn about your virginity! I love you and want you to love me! But I'll be go-to-hell if I'll have a woman who thinks of me as being so low I can't refuse even her! You're not going to punish yourself by punishing me!"

He shoved her so hard she fell on the seat, and he said, "The offer is still good. Give me your decision when we reach Tolkinham. Meanwhile, I'm getting out."

He slammed the door behind him. The rest of the night, he slept sitting on the floor of the aisle, propped against the side of a seat. He did not sleep well. When the train pulled into Tolkinham, he returned to the compartment. Gilbert was the only one in it.

"Where did Thorrsstein go?" Two Hawks said.

"I don't know. I thought she went to say good-bye to you."

Two Hawks pushed through the crowd on the aisle, drawing some black looks and muttered rebukes. Once outside, he looked through the station. She was gone. He thought of sending Kwasind to look for her, but an officer stopped him. He was handed his latest orders, which were to report to the Kreion Grettirsson. Two Hawks wondered why an infantry general wanted him. He hitchhiked a ride on an army car to the big camp outside Tolkinham and went to the Kreion's camp. Grettirsson informed him that the Blodlandish Lyftwaepon was no more. The shortage of gas and oil was so acute that fuel supplies would be reserved for military ground vehicles only. Two Hawks was to serve as commander of a regiment of armored cars. That is, he would until the gas ran completely out. Then he would be an infantryman.

Two Hawks left the tent knowing that the island was doomed. Within a month or two, the Perkunishans would own Blodland.

During the four weeks of fighting that followed, Two Hawks heard about developments in Perkunisha. Despite triumphs abroad, all had not gone well in Berlin. The two sons of the Kassandrash had been killed in a train wreck. The Blodlandish agents reported their doubts about the wreck being an accident. On hearing of his sons' deaths, the Kassandrash was paralyzed by a stroke. Six days later, he died of pneumonia. His male heir, a nephew, was assassinated on his way to Berlin. The Perkunishans accused Blodland of the killing and soon after accused it of having caused the train wreck. Blodland denied any connection with the deaths. The Blodlandish agents had their own suspicions, all of which pointed at Raske.

The German's ambitions were well known. He wanted to marry the Kassandrash's daughter. If he did, he would become Prince Consort— provided that the Grand Council made her queen. The Council was convening now, debating whether to crown her or to choose a Kassandrash from a list of male nobles.

Meanwhile, the armies in the field conducted business as usual. The Protector of Blodland, Erik Leonitha, proved to be a brilliant tactician. Three times he defeated the invaders in large-scale battles. Each time, he had to retreat, unable to hold the ground he had won. The Perkunishans brought up new armies, strong with fresh troops and superior weapons. The enemy air force, no longer having Two Hawks' planes to fear, made northern Blodland hideous with strafing and bombing attacks.

Then, the Blodlandish fuel supply was gone. The army retreated on foot to their last stand. The enemy planes harassed them, and the enemy armor bit at their heels. Two Hawks and Kwasind, riflemen now, made it to Ulfstal. Two Hawks was handed a note from Humphrey Gilbert. He read it, then said, "Kwasind, Ilmika is a nurse in the army hospital here. And before that she was working in an ammunition factory. She has guts. I knew I wasn't in love with just a pretty face."

Kwasind was not tactful. "She may have guts. But does she love you?"

"I don't know. I'm still hoping. Maybe she's supporting herself just to show me she can be independent. Maybe she'll come to me as an equal after she's proved she doesn't have to take me because I'm the only one who'll have her."

"A woman is not the equal of a man," Kwasind said. "You should have taken her and taught her to love you. What is all this talk about independence? A woman should be dependent upon a man."

Two Hawks went looking for Ilmika that evening. He found the hospital, but it had been bombed and was no longer used. The wounded were in tents around the gutted building. It took him an hour to locate her in a large tent on the edge of the camp.

Seeing him enter, she was so startled she dropped a roll of bandages. She picked the roll up off the dirt floor, evidently intending to use it without sterilizing it. He said nothing about the bandages, since he had long ago learned that it was useless to protest. These people knew nothing of germs and did not want to hear about them.

"Greetings, my lord," she said.

"Health to you, Milady. Dammit, Ilmika, don't be so formal! We've been through too much for this my-lord-my-lady crap!"

She smiled and said, "You are right—as usual. What are you doing here?"

"I could say I came to visit with a sick friend."

"Do you mean me?"

He nodded and said, "Will you marry me?"

She gasped and almost dropped the bandages again.

"Surely, you're . . . You shouldn't joke about a thing like that."

He put his hands on her shoulders and said, "Why should I be joking? You know I love you. I couldn't ask you to be my wife before because . . . well, you know all the reasons too well. But things have changed. Blueblood, class barriers don't mean much any more. And if Blodland wins or loses the war, things will never be the same again. And if you can ever quit thinking like an aristocrat, look at me as a woman looks at a man, we can be happy.

"Can you do that?"

She did not reply. He waited until he could stand the silence no more.

"Say yes or say no!"

"Yes!"

He took her in his arms and kissed her. She did not seem to be trying to imitate passion this time.

A doctor interrupted them and ordered her to get back to work. Two Hawks said, "Ilmika, if things go badly tomorrow, I'll try to meet you in Lefswik. I'll be shipping out to Karbashan (Dublin) from there if we're defeated here—and I expect we will be. I have plans for us, but there's no time to talk about them. Meanwhile, I love you!"

Tears in her eyes, she whispered, "I love you. But, Roger, I'm afraid of tomorrow. What if I don't ever see you again?"

"Then you won't. But it'll only be because I'll be dead."

She shivered.

"Don't say that!"

"Everything should be said."

He gave her a final kiss and walked away, returning the doctor's glare with a smile. On the way back to his quarters, he was stopped by a noncom, who told him he was to report to the Protector. Wondering what Leonitha wanted of him, Two Hawks followed the noncom to the pavilion-tent. He had to identify himself to two officer-guards before he was admitted. This security precaution was necessary, since assassination of high-ranking officers was normal procedure in war. In fact, the Protector had narrowly escaped being killed two days before. One of the unsuccessful Perkunishans had shot himself in the head before he could be taken. The other was too seriously wounded to kill himself. When he regained consciousness, he was hung upside down over a bonfire.

17

IN THE TENT, Two Hawks snapped to a salute before the Protector, seated behind a desk. His arm, however, did not fall back to his hip with the prescribed swiftness. Two Hawks was too astounded at sight of the man on a chair at the rear of the tent.

"Raske!"

The German grinned and waved airily.

"My old friend—and enemy—the red-skinned Two Hawks!" he said.

A beautiful blonde woman sat on another chair by Raske. She was richly dressed, and her neck, fingers, and arms glittered with gems. Two Hawks guessed at once that she was Persinai, daughter of the Kassandrash.

The Protector explained their presence. A new Kassandrash had been elected by the Grand Council. One of his first acts had been to order the arrest of Raske. The German was charged with the assassination of the heirs to the throne.

Raske had been one step ahead of him. He had talked the Kassandrash's daughter into run-

ning away with him. The two had fled from
Perkunisha in one of the new two-engined fighter
planes. Raske landed at a field in Rasna (Earth
1's France) and brazened his way through. He
got his plane refueled, after which he got as far
as a meadow on the eastern coast of northern
Blodland.

He and his bride were asking for sanctuary.

"I don't know whether I should shoot him or
listen to him," the Protector said. "He's worth
nothing as a hostage, and it's too late to use his
technical knowledge."

Raske said, "If you can scrape up enough gas,
I'll fly Two Hawks to Bamba. Blodland will
need both of us, since you will have to make a
last stand there."

Two Hawks said, "Bamba doesn't have any
gas, either. So what good could we do
there?"

"I'll tell you something the Perkunishans have
been keeping very secret. There won't be any invasion of Bamba until next year. Perkunisha has
overextended itself. It's committed so deeply on
the mainland and here that it can't launch another major campaign. Of course, Perkunisha
will try to bluff. It'll demand that the Blodlandish forces in Bamba unconditionally surrender.
But if you refuse, if you hold out, you'll have a
year to make preparations. By then, you may
have supplies, gas, oil, ammunition. I've been in
touch with the Ikhwani. They're willing to provide all Bamba needs. And they've no fear of the
Perkunishan navy. They figure it's been too
weakened by its losses."

Raske started to rise but was restrained by the guard behind him.

"If Two Hawks and I will give the Ikhwani all the information they need to build an air force, they'll aid Blodland!"

The Protector spoke to Two Hawks. "Can we believe him?"

"Oh, yes, you can. I don't doubt that he's been dealing with Ikhwan, just in case he did have to run for his life. But all this about Ikhwan rearming and resupplying us in Bamba is hogwash. Even if the Ikhwan dared to run battleships and freight ships to Bamba, they'd be blasted out of the waters. The Perkunishan air force would take care of that. No, there's no hope from Ikhwan."

"I thought so," the Protector said. He spoke to Raske, "You're going to the guardhouse while I decide what to do with you. Your wife will be lodged in a house, where she'll be treated well. After all, she's the Kassandrash's daughter. What happens to you, Raske, depends upon the outcome of the battle tomorrow. If we lose, Perkunisha will have you, and I suppose you'll be shot on sight. If we win . . . well, I may shoot you. Because of you and your flying machines, Blodland is denied a chance to arm itself again in Bamba."

As Raske was escorted from the tent, Two Hawks said, "Tough luck, my kraut friend. You lived high on the hog for a while, higher than you ever would have on Earth 1. Be content with that."

Raske grinned back at him. "Red-skin, I'm

not dead yet. I'll see you later, that is, if you're alive."

Two Hawks watched him being marched off and thought that Raske's words were more than bravado. Tomorrow's battle might be Two Hawk's last. As it turned out, it was almost—but not quite. Four times during the day, he was slightly wounded by shell fragments, by grenade fragments, and once by a bayonet during hand-to-hand combat. Dusk came, and with it the Blodlandish retreated northward. Two Hawks and Kwasind walked west, since they thought that the main part of the Perkunishan army would be streaming upland, hot for the kill.

"We could take to the hills and lead a miserable life as guerrilla fighters," Two Hawks told Kwasind. "Eventually, if we didn't starve, we'd get caught. So, it's to the coast for us and a boat to Bamba. What the hell, we don't owe these people anything! It's not our fight; it's not even my world. I'm getting to Hivika—somehow."

They arrived at the port of Lefswik on the edge of the Bambish Sea. Lefswik was crowded with refugees, all wanting to take passage on the four large steamers and the score of smaller ones. Two Hawks did not have much hope of being allowed on board unless he could find some important official to secure a berth for him. He had, however, not even gotten to the docks before he heard his name called. He turned to see fat Humphrey Gilbert pushing through the crowds. Gilbert was smiling and waving a handful of papers.

"Two Hawks! My fellow Earthman! What

luck! I've been looking for you, hoping that you'd show up, despite all the odds against your doing so! I can get you into my stateroom! You'll have to sleep on the floor! But hurry! The ship leaves in thirty-five minutes! I'd just about given up all hope!"

"Did you see Ilmika Thorrsstein?" Two Hawks said.

"Did I see her?" the fat man jumped up and down in glee. "She's in my stateroom, too! She ... never mind ... she came looking for you, and she's all right! Lovers reunited, joy requited, and all that!"

Two Hawks was too happy to reply. He heard only half of Gilbert's chatter. They were stopped at the bottom of the gangplank where an official took an exasperating amount of time going over the papers. He did not, however, give them an argument. If he had, he would have found himself thrown into the water by Kwasind's huge hands. Two Hawks would have stormed the ship to get to Ilmika, a foolish move, since the marines at the upper end of the gangway would have shot him down.

He was not so caught up with his rapture, however, that he did not see a familiar face in the mob on the foredeck. He stopped, looked again, and then shook his head. It could not be.

But he was not mistaken. Blond, curly-headed, handsome Raske was grinning at him. The German waved his hand and then turned and disappeared into the crowd. His feeling that he would not be betrayed by Two Hawks was correct. Two Hawks wondered how Raske had

gotten out of the guardhouse and made his way
here and on board a vessel which was taking
only the elite of the refugees. He would find out
later. Meantime, if Raske was clever and quick
enough to make good his escape, he could have
it. For the time being, anyway. All Two Hawks
wanted now was to hold Ilmika in his arms.

This he did, although with no privacy. Besides
Gilbert and Kwasind, there were five others in
the cabin. They pretended to ignore the two lov-
ers and talked on as if nothing were happening.
Looking up momentarily from between kisses,
Two Hawks saw them glancing covertly at him,
their amusement or embarrassment apparent.
He did not care.

The ship left the harbor and gained speed as
swiftly as its laboring engines would allow. It
was not safe now nor would it be even after it
docked in Dublin. At any moment, Perkunishan
planes could appear to strafe and bomb. Then, a
fog set in, and they were secure—provided they
did not ram another ship or run afoul of reefs
close to the Bambish shore.

Two Hawks hated to do it, yet he had to find
Raske and determine what he was up to. He still
was not sure that he would not turn the German
in. Raske represented no genuine threat to the
Blodlandish at the moment. He could do little
against them or for them, although he might
possibly be very valuable later on. Or he might
end up being a Blodlandish nobleman or even
their ruler. Two Hawks would put nothing past
Raske.

He found him sitting on a blanket on the deck.

There were others close but half-hidden by the thick fog. Two Hawks called his name until the German answered. Two Hawks said, "Where's Persinai?"

"She's dead," Raske said unemotionally. "Right after we escaped—and I must tell you about that some time, my red-skinned friend, you wouldn't believe how I got out . . . well, I had weapons; I gave her a gun. And she killed herself. She'd been despondent ever since she was put in the guardhouse; conscience, I think. She felt guilty because she'd deserted her people. And she blamed me for her father's death, hence herself, for having fallen in love with me."

Two Hawks was silent for a while. Raske's story could be true. On the other hand, he was capable of abandoning her if he thought she would hinder him. Whatever the truth, it would probably never be known by any but Raske.

"What do you think the future holds for us— for us two Earthmen?" Raske said. "We might be safe in Bamba for a while. I know that Perkunisha doesn't intend to invade it until next year, maybe not for two years, if Bamba gives no trouble. Perkunisha is overextended as it is; it wants no new wars."

"If—when—Perkunisha finds out we're in Bamba, it'll demand we be turned over to it." Two Hawks said. "You know as well as I do that they won't want us floating around. They think we're too dangerous to them. Which is a laugh."

"What do you mean?" Raske said. His hurt pride showed in his voice.

"This world has already sucked us dry of our

—admit it—limited knowledge. We really have nothing more than some technical assistance to give it. It's true the Blodlandish have rejected what I told them about the origin of disease. But they'll come around to it in time. They would have done so in a few years anyway, when some native Pasteur stood up to their superstitions and fought them down. Just as all we have told them would have come about in twenty years or less, anyway. We just accelerated science a little bit, that's all."

Raske chuckled. "You know, Two Hawks, you're really right. I was hurt for a minute, but I can recognize the truth when I have to. Only . . . well, I did have what they wanted, and I was parlaying my advantages into an empire for me. If things had gone just a little bit differently."

"They didn't. So here we are. Doomed to be hounded to the ends of the earth because of something we don't have. But try to convince them of that."

He hesitated a moment, then decided not to tell Raske his plans. Raske might be harmless, even useful. However, if he saw a chance to advance himself at Two Hawks' expense, he would not hesitate a moment. He had proven himself capable of murder and, perhaps, even abandoned the woman who had given up her country and title for him. Yet, Two Hawks found it hard not to confide in Raske. There was the tie of Earthkinship between them, and the fellow was so charming. He would smile at you just before putting the knife in, and the strange thing about it was that the smile would ease the pain a little. Or anaesthetize the victim.

Two Hawks thought that, if he could be realistic, he would tell the captain of the ship to throw Raske into the sea.

He sighed and rose, saying, "I won't turn you in. But if I hear of any skullduggery on your part, you're done for. And this is goodbye. I don't want to see you anymore, except at a far distance."

"Two Hawks! You hurt me! Why?"

Raske actually did sound as if he had been cut deeply. Two Hawks walked away, knowing that he was possibly letting a wolf loose on this world but unable to sever the bonds of a common universe. Strange as it sounded, Raske's death would be like cutting out part of his own heart.

The rest of the journey was in fog. Dublin was just as mist-shrouded. The passengers disembarked in a wet dusk. Gilbert led Ilmika, Two Hawks, and Kwasind to the home of a friend. They were there only one day when news of the plague came.

It was just as it had been thirty years ago, when Perkunisha was on the verge of conquering the Western World. The piles of rotting bodies all over the land, the weakening hunger and deadly winter, the lack of cleanliness, and the thriving of the rats had brought the Black Plague once again.

"Europe is saved from the Perkunishans; God save it now from a far worse fate," Gilbert said. His normally red face was pale, and he was no longer smiling. "My own parents and three of

my brothers and two sisters died the last time
the scourge struck. My aunt brought me to Bamba to escape it, but it followed us, and she, too,
died. God help mankind. Now you will see such
a slaughter as the Perkunishans could envision
only in their nightmares. They, too, will die; half
of mankind will die in two years."

"If they had listened to me . . ." Two Hawks
said. He stopped, shrugged, and resumed. "Do
we stay here and die?"

Gilbert said, "No! One of my ships is in port,
in fact, the last of my ships. It's provisioned for
a long voyage. We'll sail tonight for Hivika!
Only, let's hope we get there before Hivika hears
of the plague! Otherwise, we'll never be allowed
on shore!"

Two Hawks knew what was in his mind
besides escaping bubonic plague. He said, "I'd
like to hope, but I don't have much faith in the
tales of superstitious witch-doctors."

"Why not?" Gilbert said.

And indeed, why not?

Nevertheless, as the days went by and the Atlantic was the only thing to be seen, the cold
gray and sometimes angry ocean, Two Hawks
grew less optimistic. Even if there were a 'gate'
in a cave on top of that high mountain in Hivika,
it probably would not be open. The sorcerers
themselves had stated that it only opened every
fifty years or so and then only for a few seconds.
The last time had been thirty years ago.
Moreover, there was the problem of gaining access to the cave. Of all the many tabu places on
the island, the cave was the most sacred. No one

except the few high priests and the king were ever allowed there; the mountain itself, though close to the sea, was walled halfway up its slope and heavily guarded.

Despite his misgivings, Two Hawks enjoyed the trip. He and Ilmika had a chance for a long honeymoon. For the first time, they really became acquainted and found, much to the surprise of both, that they not only loved each other —that is, had a mutual passion—but actually liked each other. They had, of course, certain ways of thought and behavior that aggravated the other. These were both personal and cultural. But they were willing to tell one another when the partner did something to offend, and the friction would be smoothed out. Two Hawks was happy, although he was realistic enough to know that she would always have a certain amount of arrogance. She could not help it, since she had been brought up as an aristocrat in an undemocratic world.

Two Hawks really began to feel uneasy for the first time when the vessel crossed that invisible line which would have been the shore of North America on Earth 1. Almost, he expected the ship to shudder, then rise up out of the water on a slope of land with a great crash and grind. But the *Hwaelgold* continued on smoothly while somewhere below was New Foundland. It went over the area in which the city of New York would have been; he imagined a sunken metropolis of skyscrapers and human bones on the streets, over which fish swam. It was sheer fantasy, of course, since in this world no man had ever seen that area. It was at least 6,000 feet below the surface, cold and dark and covered with slimy mud.

There was no part of the North or South Americas above water which had not been, on Earth 1, at six thousand feet above sea level. In the Northern Hemisphere, only a few small islands in the east (the highest part of the Appalachians on Earth 1) and a chain of islands, some rather large, in the west, existed. These were inhabited by Polynesians, presumably immigrants who had arrived 750 years ago. The South American chains, bigger in area and longer than the North, were populated by colonizers from, presumably, that island known on Earth 1 as Easter Island.

The main island toward which the *Hwaelgold* was heading was composed of highland which, on Earth 1, would have been the mountainous parts of Colorado. The capital city of Kualono was on the eastern sea coast and was a harbor with great stone temples and palaces and massive granite idols, light airy houses ill-adapted to the cold winters, highways of huge close-fitting stone blocks, and vegetation peculiarly North American. The natives wore few clothes in the summer time and played and swam much like their Hawaiian cousins. In the winter, they wore heavy clothes of spun fabric and feathers. There were also iron mines and smelters and factories now, and automobiles on the roads. Despite the increasing industrialization and trade (mainly with the South African Arabs), the Hivikans lived much as they had in the past: easy-going, laughing, playing, and only vicious in their wars. The last one had taken place some fifty years ago and had made more than enough elbow room in an overpopulated land.

Two Hawks spent much time on the bridge with Gilbert. Ilmika sat on a chair in a corner and knitted; Kwasind stood like a bronze statue of Hercules in one corner. Two Hawks, who had drawn a map from memory of the North America of his native world, indicated the Mississippi River.

"We should be about over it," he said. "Rather, where it would be if it existed here."

At that moment, the captain exclaimed. Two Hawks looked up to see him staring through a pair of binoculars to the north. He picked up a pair given him by Gilbert and searched the same quarter of the sea. There, so low on the horizon it could only be viewed with glasses, was a small cloud. The captain, after studying it for a while, gave orders to increase the speed of the *Hwaelgold*. He explained that the vessel might be peaceful, perhaps a merchantman from South Africa. But if the contact with the ship could be avoided, it would be best.

By dusk, the smoke had come closer. Its estimated speed placed it out of the category of merchant; it could only be a warship, either a destroyer or cruiser. "The direction from which it comes should make it an Ikhwani. But it could be a Perkunishan raider."

At the end of the second day, the pursuer (if it was one) was a little over a mile away. It glit-

tered whitely in the sun and was identifiable as
Arabic.

"I don't think they'll sink us," the captain
said. "We are too valuable a prize, a large well-
built lander the Ikhwani can use to enrich
their merchant fleet. But they can't put a prize
crew aboard and take the *Hwaelgold* back to
South Africa. It doesn't have enough fuel or
provisions to make the voyage. So, the only thing
the Arabs can do is to sail us into Kualono and
refuel it there."

"What will happen to us?" Ilmika said.

"The Ikhwani might make some of the sailors
help sail the *Hwaelgold* to Ikhwan," he replied.
"The rest of us should be left on Hivika, free to
make our way back to Blodland as best we can.
The Ikhwani won't want to take more prisoners
than they can help. After all, they'd have to feed
us. Unless we could be used as slaves. That's a
possibility. Tell the truth, I don't know. It's up
to God and the Ikhwani."

Night fell. The cruiser kept a quarter-mile behind the *Hwaelgold,* its searchlights pinning the
merchantman. The captain took no vain evasive
action but continued to run his vessel at top
speed. He could do nothing else unless the
Ikhwani sent a shell over him and ordered him to
stop. This the cruiser would undoubtedly do
when dawn arrived.

At midnight, the rainstorm that the captain
had been praying for swept like a dropped net
out of the west. With it came rough seas. Two
seconds after the rain and darkness struck, the
captain ordered the *Hwaelgold* to turn sharply

southwards. In a short time, the lights of the cruiser had disappeared. When the sun came up, it shone only upon the Blodland ship. The captain ordered a normal cruising speed, since he had been worried about his engines giving way under the long strain.

18

THE SEAS WERE EMPTY of alien smoke for the
next five days. The dawn of the sixth day, the
captain took a reading and verified that their
position was only a hundred miles east of
Kualono. Within an hour, they should be sight-
ing Miki'ao, a small island. Exactly forty
minutes later, the 500-foot peak of Miki'ao
reared above the horizon. The captain's grin of
pride, however, was wiped off when smoke was
sighted to the rear. He gave the orders for full
speed ahead and spent most of the next two
hours watching to the aft. This time, the
Ikhwani had approached much closer before
being detected. It was coming up fast to the
southward and at an angle that would intercept
them long before they reached the safety of
Kualono.

The captain conferred with Gilbert and then
ordered the *Hwaelgold* to turn at a 45-degree angle northward. "There are dangerous reefs just
above the harbor," he said. "I know them well.
We'll make a run through them; perhaps the
Ikhwani will pile up on them. If they don't we'll
run it ashore, if there's a place on those forbidding cliffs to do so. In any case, the Arabs won't

get their hands on my ship."

Gilbert said, "He's making for Lapu Mountain, where the Cave of the Outer Gods is. If we land there, we'll have a good excuse for trespassing on tabu property. We won't get there until a little before dusk. So, if the Hivikans don't see us . . ."

Two Hawks replied to Gilbert's smile with one of his own. "We bulldoze our way in then? Great! And what if the Ikhwani respect the marine sovereignty of Hivika and refuse to follow us in? What do we use for an excuse?"

"If they respected the Hivika sovereignty, they would have quit long ago," the captain said. "Hivika claims extend to fifty miles out from the coast. No, they're not going to quit unless they come across a Hivikan naval ship. Maybe not then. Ikhwan would like an excuse to go to war with Hivika; it has coveted Hivika for a long time. Only the threat of war with Blodland and Perkunisha kept them from conquest. Now, I don't know."

The *Hwaelgold*, her engines pounding, beat northwestward. Its pursuer steadily cut down the distance between them. By the time that the black headlands of the coast had become quite high, the cruiser was only a half-mile behind. Then smoke flared out of the muzzle of one of its eight-inchers, and a geyser soared up twenty yards off the starboard bow of the *Hwaelgold*. Twenty seconds later, a second waterspout appeared fifteen yards off the port bow.

By then, the captain was taking his ship on a zigzag course. The path was not chosen at random, however, since the vessel was steering through the narrow channels between the reefs. Some of these were evident only by the darker blue of the water; others were near enough to the surface to cause the seas to boil.

By then, the cruiser had quit firing. Evidently, it had not meant to hit its quarry but only hoped that the shells would make it surrender. Seeing that the *Hwaelgold* intended to make a run for it, the Ikhwani went after them. It, too, zigged and zagged but at a more cautious pace. Two Hawks wondered why the Arabs were taking such chances. Why should they be so determined to capture them? What was special about the merchantman? Perhaps, their espionage system in Blodland had learned that he was on his way to Hivika. It would then have sent a radio message, by spark-gap transmitter, to an Ikhwani vessel somewhere in the vicinity. And the message would have been relayed by various ships until the cruiser had received it.

This would explain why the *Hwaelgold* had not been sunk. He was wanted alive so that the Arabs could use his knowledge, just as the Perkunishans and Blodlandish had. That would explain not only their hunting through the reefs but their ignoring the Hivika sea-domain.

The mountain of Lapu was at the very edge of the waters. It rose steeply on both the south and north sides; on the eastern, it sloped much more gently and terminated in a wide black-sand beach. Towards this, the captain steered the ship after it had slipped through a narrow channel. There was a slight scraping of the plates of the keel on the rocks, and the vessel was in calmer waters. Captain Wilftik heaved a sigh of relief and grinned.

"The cruiser won't make it through there without tearing her bottom out. I hope she tries it."

He gave orders to stop the ship and to lower two lifeboats. The cruiser did not attempt the passage; it slid on by alongside the reef, turned as closely as it could to avoid another reef, and then pointed her nose outwards. While her engines kept her from drifting backwards against the reef, it lowered two power launches. Two Hawks, observing them through his binoculars, saw that the launches were equipped with several two-inch cannons and mortars. Each held about thirty marines, in addition to the crews. The marines looked like medieval Saracens with their turbans above which rose the gleaming points of the helmets, steel cuirasses, great leather belts, scabbards containing scimitars, scarlet baggy pants, and calf-length boots with turned-up toes. Each had a large blue sack strapped to his belt and carried a rifle.

Captain Wilfrik wanted to run his ship back through the entrance between the reefs and smash the launches just as they came into the passageway on the other end. Gilbert objected. "The cruiser will blow you out of the water. And it will then send another launch with marines. Hold your fire; permit the landing-party to go after us. The sailors in our party will ambush them, but I'm not asking them to give up their lives for us. They'll do it from a place which the

Ikhwani can't take—if they can find one."

Two boats took Two Hawks, Ilmika, Kwasind, Gilbert, and officers and crewmen ashore. They went quickly across the beach and began climbing. The sun had gone down behind the mountain by then, shrouding this side in twilight. Above them and out to the sea, the sky was a bright blue and the waters green. The Ikhwani launches drove their prows onto the sand, and the white and scarlet (twilight-browned) figures were little dolls. The pursued had a twenty-minute headstart and had taken advantage of it. Although they were soon in a dusk so thick it made climbing difficult, they continued. Then the sun plunged down in the sea, and they were slowed even more. They caught hold of bushes and pulled themselves up, occasionally slipping but always able to stop their backward slide by grabbing the vegetation.

Now and then, they came to great gnarled oaks, which Gilbert said had been planted here two hundred years ago by King Mahimahi. "The mountain above the guard-wall is a thick forest of oaks. We'll be well concealed then—if we can get past the Hivika sentinels."

"I wonder why they haven't spotted us yet?" Two Hawks said. "I know it's dark now, but the guards should have been able to see both ships."

"I don't know," Gilbert replied. "Perhaps they're planning on ambushing us, just as we are the Ikhwani."

Gilbert's fat was telling on him; he was breathing heavily. Aside from his panting, it was quiet on the mountain, with the only sounds

being the wind through the oak leaves and the
noise of their progress: twigs cracking, wet leaves
squishing, a branch springing back with a
swishing sound, muffled curses as a man slipped.
When they stopped to rest, and Gilbert regained
his breath, the silence was like that in a huge
cathedral, in the moment when all have bowed
their heads and just before the minister launches
into a prayer. However, it was no prayer that
was to come, Two Hawks felt sure of that. It
seemed as if lightning would leap out from the
very rubbing of the air against it, or a curse instead of a prayer would crackle down the mountain.

They struggled on up, their path lit only by
the stars. Two hours went by, and the moon
came out. Three-quarters full, she bounced a
bright mercury over the mountain. Thereafter
they climbed more surely and more rapidly. The
illumination, although advantageous now,
would be a danger when they reached the sentinel wall. Two Hawks hoped that the vegetation
had not been cleared off between the wall and
the oaks and bushes. To venture across a clear-
ing in this brightness was to be revealed at once
to any watcher.

Twenty minutes later, they came to the edge
of the woods. As he had feared, there was a bare
space of forty yards. At its other end, above them
at a 50-degree angle, embrasured walls loomed.
These were about 20 feet high, composed of huge
stone blocks, grey and veined in black, and fitted
together without mortar. Every thirty yards
along the top of the wall was a slender twenty-

foot tower, round and capped with a cone of small mortared rocks.

"Where are the guards?" Gilbert whispered.

The moonlight coated the wall with soft metal; the shiny grey looked as if it would ring at the blow of a hammer. But there was no sound except for the shush-shush of wind through the leaves.

Two Hawks, looking at the dark, narrow, arched entrances on the sides of the towers, said, "If the guards are in there, they're hiding. Well, here goes. Don't anybody follow me until the coast is clear."

With the coil of the rope in his left hand and the three-pronged catching hooks in his right, he ran out from under an oak's shadow. He expected to hear a shout from the black interior of a tower, followed by a tongue of flame and explosion. However, the walls remained as still and shiny grey as before. Reaching the bottom of the ramparts, he paused, gauged the distance to the top, and cast the hooks, the rope uncoiling after them. The hooks sailed through an embrasure just above him and struck with a clank. The noise shocked him. Until that moment he had not realized how unconsciously strong the impression of the *sacredness* of the place had been.

He pulled on the rope, and it became taut as the prongs dug in. Hand over hand, his feet against the wall, almost parallel to the ground, he climbed up. He gripped the lip of the stone and pulled himself up and over and then crouched in the shelf of the embrasure. He waited for an outcry from a guard. When a

minute had gone by, he eased himself down into
the passageway that ran the length of the wall. It
was six feet across and high enough to reach to
the top of his head.

He drew his revolver and ran to the stone steps
which led up the wall and to the nearest watch
tower. Up the steep flight he went and hurled
himself through the narrow pointed arch into the
tower. Moonlight beamed through a small narrow hole in the roof and thinned the darkness
enough so that he could see that no one was
within. A wooden ladder against the wall of the
tower led to a wooden platform. From this, a
guard could observe—and shoot—through any
of six ports and cover 360 degrees.

He went out of the tower into the moonlight
and signalled. The entire party was soon up on
the wall, aided by the ladder which Two Hawks
removed from the tower. Gilbert spread his men
out so they covered a hundred yards of wall. If
the Ikhwani marines tried to scale the walls at
this point, the Blodlandish could concentrate a
strong fire. Should the Ikhwani try elsewhere
along the wall, a sailor in the tower would spot
them, provided the Ikhwani were not too far
away.

Gilbert, Kwasind, Ilmika, and Two Hawks
walked along the passageway until they came to
a point beneath which was a gate. Inside the
walls was a path that led from the gate on up the
mountain. They decided to follow the path. The
chances of being ambushed seemed few. It was
evident that the Hivika guards had abandoned
their posts, the reason for which would have to

be determined later.

The path made for easier going even if the slope was as steep as before. By dawn, they were only several hundred yards from the top of the mountain. And here they came across a Hivikan. Sprawled face down by the side of the path, he was dressed in a cloak of brilliant many-colored feathers, a feathered headdress, and a wooden mask set with garnets, turquoise, emeralds. Two Hawks turned the body over and removed the mask. The face of the priest was dark grey. Two Hawks took off his cloak and breastplate of bones and feathers and the cotton skirt. There were no wounds.

Two Hawks' skin prickled, and his head and neck chilled as if a helmet of ice had been placed over them. The others looked as apprehensive as he—all except Kwasind, stolid as ever. Yet he must have been quivering inside, since he was so sensitive to the terrors of the unknown.

Two Hawks started on up but stopped again. The grey light of dawn seemed to be rushing towards certain spots and solidifying. The concentrations, as the party neared them, turned out to be huge statues of grey granite or black basalt or grey porous tufa. They were squat, toadish, and scowling. Most had faces, distorted or misshapen, of men or of gods. Some were of beasts: big-eared, long-snouted, wide-fanged. By the hundreds, they crowded the mountain slope, most of them glaring down the mountain but a few looking upwards.

Kwasind followed Two Hawks so closely he stepped on his heels several times. Two Hawks had to order him back a few paces. "They're only stone," he said. "Dead rocks."

"The rocks are dead," Kwasind muttered. "But what lives within them?"

Two Hawks shrugged and kept on trudging up the steep path at the head of the file. As he ascended, he felt more strongly the brooding-ness, the almost tangible resentment from the idols. He told himself that it was his own fears working on him; he expected trouble, perhaps death, and the squat grey figures symbolized them. Nevertheless, he was being squeezed around the chest; his breath was coming with more difficulty and his heart was beating harder than the exertions of the climb warranted. He could appreciate and sympathize with the oth-ers. Superstitious as they were, they were show-ing great courage by refusing to bolt.

The rattle of rifle fire broke out far below. It was as if they had been released from a rope that was pulling them the wrong way. All jumped into the air, but their faces showed relief instead of the anxiety that might have been expected. The crack of the battle was such a human, and, to them, mundane phenomenon that it dis-sipated the strangling psychic air.

Two Hawks looked up and said, "Another hundred yards and we'll be at the cave."

Abruptly, the brown-black, hard-packed dirt of the path ceased. Ahead of him was a dully grey substance that spread out over the moun-tain from that point up. It felt warm through the sole of his shoe. He told the others to halt.

"Lava," he said. "Still warm."

The stone had flowed down from the mouth of the cave and fanned out to form a triangular apron. The huge entrance to the cave was half-choked with the grey stuff.

"Now we know what scared everybody away," he said. "The Hivika must have thought the mountain was going to blow its top. Or that the gods were angry. Or both. That priest may have died of a heart attack. There's no evidence of poisonous gas."

As they neared the cave, slipping somewhat on the lava, the heat became more intense. Their clothes were soon soaked with sweat, and the bottoms of their feet began to get uncomfortably warm. By the time they reached the entrance of the cave, they knew they could not stay long.

They did not have to linger. The beam of Two Hawks' flashlight into the interior showed the lava sloping sharply upward from the mouth of the cave. Only twenty feet from them, the cave was entirely filled. The eruption—if it was an eruption of Terrestrial origin, had filled the inside. Two Hawks knew from Gilbert's description that the cave extended at least a hundred yards into the stone of the mountain. At the end was—had been—the 'gate.' That is, if it had ever existed.

There was nothing to do now but to forget about the gate and to get away from the Ikhwani. They went back down the path towards the wall. Before they had gotten halfway, they heard the firing cease. Two Hawks stopped them.

"If the Ikhwani have gotten through, they'll

be coming up after us. If they're still being held outside the wall, we can afford to wait a while until we know for sure."

They hid behind a huge stone idol, fifty yards from the path. They leaned against its broad base, ate some dried beef and hard bread, and talked softly. The sun warmed away the chill of night. From time to time, Two Hawks looked around the idol and down the path. He saw nothing for half an hour. Then, he stiffened. Many small figures, shining white and black and scarlet, were toiling up the path. And the sun also twinkled off the barrels of guns or from drawn scimitars.

"Your men have been killed or captured," he said to Gilbert.

Gilbert looked through his binoculars. He swore and then said, "There's a man down there in Ikhwan uniform but wearing Perkunishan medals! His head is bare; he's a blond! From your description, I'd say . . . no, you better look for yourself!"

Two Hawks took the binoculars. When he put them down, he said, "It's Raske."

Ilmika gasped and said, "How could *he* be *here*?"

"Obviously, he got in touch with the Ikhwani embassy in Bamba. He knew where we were going, and he got the Ikhwani to come after me. They want me for the same reason Perkunisha and Blodland did. And if the Ikhwani can't have me alive, they'll have me dead!"

He used the binoculars again and counted thirty-two enemy. There were six men far behind the main body, slow by reason of the two mortars they were carrying. Out on the lagoon, the *Hwaelgold* still rested at anchor and beyond the reef the cruiser prowled back and forth like a restless wolf.

He swept the horizon of the sea. Far out were two plumes of smoke. If only, he prayed, the smoke could be pouring from the stacks of two Hivika warships, hastening to challenge the unauthorized vessels . . . If only . . .

He quit looking. Now was the time to seize all the time they could. He led them back up the mountain until they came to the lava, then turned northward, skirting just below the lava. When they had gotten past it, they began climbing up again, diagonally across the slope.

On rounding the peak, they stopped. The mountain was sheared off here. It fell straight for three thousand feet into the waters of a deep fjord. They would have to climb directly over the top of the peak at the first scalable point—if any.

The Ikhwani had seen them by now and were climbing towards them. They were pushing themselves to the limit and were only three hundred yards below them.

Two Hawks said, "I don't suppose it'd be any worse living in South Africa than elsewhere. But I sure hate to think about learning Arabic; I haven't even mastered Hotinohsonih, Perkunishan, or Blodlandish."

He said to Gilbert, "I'm sure the rest of you will be let go if I surrender to them."

Ilmika said, "What about me, Roger? Would you leave me?"

"Would you come to Ikhwan with me?"

She went into his arms and whispered, "I'll go anywhere you go. Gladly."

"It'd be a miserable lonely life," he said. "The Ikhwan practise a strict purdah, you know."

He released her and swept the sea again with the binoculars. The *Hwaelgold* was aflame; boats were being lowered from it. Water spouts were rising near the merchantman, and smoke puffs from the cruiser. A white sliver with a white wake was departing from the cruiser, headed towards the break in the reef. More Ikhwani marines were on their way. But they'd have to fight through the Blodlandish sailors, who would have established positions by the beach.

The twin smoke feathers on the horizon did not seem to be getting any closer. At this distance and in such a short time, he could not determine how fast or in what direction the unknowns were traveling.

He put down the binoculars and swore. He said, "To hell with the Ikhwani! I'm tired of being passed around like a piece of merchandise! I'm for trying to escape, or, if we're cornered, making a fight of it! The Hivika are bound to come nosing around sooner or later. We can throw ourselves on their mercy!"

Gilbert said, "We'll make them know they're dealing with Blodlandish."

Two Hawks laughed, since there were only two Blodlandish in the group, and one of them was a woman. However, Ilmika was not to be lightly considered. She could outshoot any of the men.

They went back to the point where the mountain became a monolithic verticality. There was a small plateau here about forty yards long and twenty deep. Behind it was a cliff 300 feet high. Below it, the slope was at a 50-degree angle. There were only a few large boulders for cover for the Ikhwani and none whatsoever for a hundred yards just below the plateau. If the marines tried for an approach on the right flank of the defenders, they could get no closer than fifty yards without exposing themselves. And they could get above the defenders only by climbing around the peak. If this were possible, it would still take them many hours.

19

AT ABOUT 1 P.M. the Ikhwani, crawling on their bellies, ventured towards the four large boulders which gave the only protection anywhere near the plateau. By then, the three men had rolled all the smaller boulders on the plateau to its lip. There were ten in all. The defenders placed themselves between some of these and waited. Two Hawks had counted their ammunition and found that there were thirty rounds apiece. He cautioned them against wasting them.

The marines opened the fight with a fusillade that lasted about three minutes. Their bullets keened over the defenders' heads, richocheted off the boulders, or struck on the rock below the lip of the plateau. The defenders did not fire back once.

Encouraged by this lack of response, ten marines climbed to the boulders while the rest continued their covering fire. Two Hawks stuck his head out over the lip long enough to see them crawling up. He also observed that the men carrying the mortars had a long way to go. These were very heavy pieces evidently, not like the easily portable field-mortars of his own world.

Two Hawks waited for a few minutes. The firing stopped, but he did not look out. When it resumed even more furiously, he counted until he thought that the forward line should be at least fifty yards below them. He looked quickly; it was as he had expected. Ten Ikhwani, each separated from the other by ten feet, were advancing. They were on their feet now, crouching, holding their rifles with one hand and getting a grip on rock projections with the other.

He gave a signal. Kwasind and Gilbert got on their knees behind a boulder and shoved it over the lip. It bounded down the mountain like a fox after a hare but struck no one. It did make the marines scatter away from it, however. Two lost their footing and rolled down the slope. By the time they had managed to stop themselves, they were out of the action.

The second boulder knocked an Ikhwan into the air, flipping him over twice before he hit the ground. He did not move thereafter. The marines who had been providing a covering fire were too busy trying to guess which way the boulders would travel. They stopped shooting, and in the interval Two Hawks and Ilmika carefully squeezed off three shots apiece. Four marines were hit. The three survivors started back down the slope. One of them slipped and slid on his face for thirty yards before ramming his head into a small boulder.

"Now they know," Two Hawks said. "If they're smart, they'll wait until the mortars arrive. Then it's good night for us."

Ilmika said, "They don't want you alive, Roger."

"Yes, I know. Raske must have it in for me."

The Ikhwani contented themselves with firing an occasional shot. The mortarmen continued to make progress slowly, even if a number had been sent down to relieve them. Two Hawks estimated that the mortars would not be delivered until close to dusk. Not that night would make much difference in the accuracy of the mortar fire.

He could not see the men from the *Hwaelgold*. The launch from the cruiser had landed long ago and the marines had disappeared into the oak woods. The merchantman had rolled over on its side but was still afloat. And the two pillars of smoke were definitely nearer.

Gilbert told him that the mortars probably had a range of about 200 yards. Two Hawks grinned at this news. To bring the weapons within effective range, the mortarmen would have to leave the protection of the far boulders to station the mortars behind the nearest boulders. He doubted that they would try to do so except under cover of night. They would have too much respect for the stone missiles the defenders could roll down on them.

The sun dropped behind the peak. The blue sky darkened. Two Hawks said, "The moment it gets dark enough, we leave here. The Ikhwani will take some time getting the mortars to those boulders. The others may or may not set up a firing cover for the mortarmen. In either case, we have to take a chance. We'll cut to the right across the slope and hope we can get around the line while they're shooting us up—they'll think."

Clouds from the west came over the mountain, gladdening the defenders. The sun's influence disappeared entirely, and a darkness thick as charred jelly covered the mountain. The four let themselves gingerly over the edge of the plateau and began crawling down the slope. Approximately a minute later the night became noisy and flame-shot. The marines were trying to keep the defenders busy while the mortars were carried to the new positions.

Two Hawks, observing that they were below the line of fire, changed his mind. He told the others what he wanted to do but said that they would keep to the original plan if they preferred. They said they would do what he ordered.

The four began to crawl northeastward, towards the nearest line of boulders. They arrived there a few minutes before the mortar crews. On the opposite side of the two boulders, they listened to the rasp of Arabic while the mortars were being set up. It was impossible to determine whether only the mortar crews were there or if others had come with them. Deciding that the longer he put off action, the less their chance of surprise, Two Hawks crawled around the huge rock. He and Ilmika were behind the one; Gilbert and Kwasind behind the other, ten yards away.

Everything went even better than Two Hawks had hoped. He shot from one side of the boulder while Ilmika fired from the other. Kwasind and Gilbert went into action as soon as they heard the first shot. Although it was dark, the white trousers and turbans of the marines made for

easy shooting. The four aimed at the dark areas
between the white.

There were eight men with each mortar. Four
fell at each mortar before the survivors could
bring their revolvers into play. Several tried to
run, slipped, and rolled away out of the fight.
The others died where they stood.

Ilmika and Two Hawks started around the
boulder for the mortar but had to dive for cover.
The marines further down, guessing what had
occurred, opened up. Two Hawks' plan of using
the mortars against them, of blasting them off
the face of the mountain with their own weapons, was no longer feasible. Worse, the marines
were advancing towards the boulders, intent on
recapturing the mortars.

The four risked sticking their heads around the
boulders and shooting now and then. But the
hail of bullets, screaming just over their heads,
throwing rock chips off the sides of the boulders,
made it suicide to keep on trying a return fire.

Two Hawks cursed. He should have stuck to
his original plan. They might be on their way to
safety now, if he had not been carried away with
his overbold, damned foolish counterattack.

Suddenly, the racket from below redoubled,
tripled in intensity. The bullets stopped flying
around them, but the barking bedlam below
continued. There were whistles and shouts in a
non-Arabic speech. Two Hawks did not understand the words, but he recognized the language
as Polynesian.

The Hivika had come.

The battle lasted for about five minutes. Then

the surviving Ikhwani surrendered. The Hivika, having been told what was going on by their prisoners, called up for the four to surrender. The officer's Blodlandish was heavily accented, but he could be understood. Gilbert answered in Hivika, and a moment later the four were also prisoners. They joined the others down below.

Raske was there, his hands clasped behind his neck. He laughed when he saw Two Hawks, and he said, "You slippery devil! By the skin of your teeth, heh? You have all the luck of Hitler himself!"

Two Hawks said, "Who's Hitler?"

20

THE NORWEGIAN dawn was paling the windows of the hotel room when Two Hawks stopped his narrative.

I said, "Surely you're not going to quit now? Just before the end?"

"I forgot," he said, "that Raske's words would not mean anything to you. At the time he said them, they meant nothing to me. I was too concerned about what was going to become of us to think much about it. All of us, Ikhwani, Blodlandish, Kwasind, Raske, and myself were being tried for illegal entry, a noncapital crime, and for trespassing on sacred ground, a capital crime. But Raske and I had something valuable to offer Hivika in return for our lives. And I got Kwasind and the Blodlandish off, too. However, the king of Hivika wanted to make an example of somebody, so he hung the Ikhwani marines and also the sailors who had survived the sinking of their ship. Those two smokeplumes I saw came from Hivika cruisers. They sank the Ikhwani ship, although not without heavy casualties themselves.

"We spent a year on Hivika, a very busy year, a repetition of what Raske and I had gone

283

through in Perkunisha and Blodland. By the time we got our freedom, the war was over. The plague had finally died out, although not before killing four times as many people in three months as a year of war had done. Perkunisha fell apart; a part of its army and many civilians revolted, a commoner by the name of Wissambrs became head of a republic . . . well, you know all this."

"But what's this about . . . a Hitler?" I said.

Two Hawks smiled. "Raske answered that same question for me while we were in the Hivika jail. And he told me about the world from which he had come. As I said, we had always been working too hard while in Berlin to have much small talk or conversation about our lives on what we *thought* had been the same Earth. Besides, both of us avoided discussion of our ideologies or goals of our countries. We felt there was no use carrying on the disputes of a world lost forever to us.

"It was not until we were in Hivika that we learned that we had come through the same gate, simultaneously, but from *different* earths."

"Amazing!"

"Yes. The ruler of the Germany of my world was the Kaiser, grandson of the Kaiser of Germany of World War I. Raske said that, in his world, the Kaiser had been exiled to Holland, after World War I. By the way, his World War I took place about ten years after that in my world, if your relative chronologies are correct. In Raske's universe, an Austrian commoner named Hitler became dictator of Germany and led it into World War II.

"Of course, the Kaiser of the World War I of my world and of Raske's were not the same people, you understand. They didn't even have the same personal names. Yet, the course of history on his world and mine were amazingly similar; the people were just different. The coincidences between the two are too many and too close to be coincidences. So, out the window goes my theory of this earth being populated by humans who had passed through gates from my earth.

"Did you know?—no, you wouldn't, of course —that American Air Force raids were made on the two Ploestis on the same day? Raske was in a Messerschmidt, a type unknown to me, about to attack an American Liberator, much like my own bomber, although mine was classed as a Vengeance.

"So—we now know that a 'gate' can open onto more than two worlds at once."

There was a knock on the door. He opened it, and the beautiful Ilmika Thorrsstein entered. She said, "Pardon me, gentlemen, for interrupting, but it is time for us to go."

A moment later, two men came into the room. Two Hawks introduced me to the herculean Kwasind and the blond and handsome Raske.

"Where are you going now?" I asked Two Hawks.

"We've heard of something very curious in the glacier country of upper Tyrsland," he said. "The Wakasha nomads have stories of strange things in a valley there, of something that sounds to us like a gate. If the tale has any foundation, you may see us no more. But if it's baseless, as I expect it will be, then we're staying in this world. Raske would like to get back to his world, if possible. If he can't, he's going to Saariset. He's had a magnificent offer from them; he'll be the next thing to a king if he accepts. Raske, I'm afraid, is the leopard who can't change his spots. As for me, I'll go back to Blodland with Ilmika."

He smiled and said, "This may not be the best of all possible worlds. But it's the one we're in, so we'll make the best of it."

21

Tva Havoken Fra Erthe, Off Aethelstan Porsena, was published sixteen months later. Roger Two Hawks received an autographed copy through the mail the day he returned from the Wakasha country in the northern part of Norweg and Tyrsland. That evening he sat down in the library of the mansion in the Kimbran shire and wrote a letter of thanks to Porsena, who was in Bammu. He commented that he thought it was an accurate report, though it did leave out at least half of what he had told Porsena. Perhaps the second edition could have an addendum which would explain his, Two Hawks', world more fully. He also said that he was happy to hear that the book would soon be translated into Rasna and Kerdezh.

In the final paragraph he stated briefly that he had failed to locate another gate.

The book turned out to be the best seller of the year, though many readers thought it was fiction.

In the meantime, Roger was busy supervising his estates and conferring with various government and private scientists and technologists. He'd been ennobled with the title of *gerl* (pro-

nounced *yerl*), a rank just below that of *melik*, the
highest of the nobility. With the title had come
the estates of the late Gerl Lars Volfrik, who had
left no direct heirs. His mansion stood by a
ruined castle near a town that was, in his native
world, called Pembroke, Wales. Ilmika was of
great help in this time-consuming labor of ad-
ministering the estates. Like all noble women,
she had been trained from childhood in such
tasks. The war had caused much hardship
among his tenants, whose life had never been
easy during the best of times. Moreover, the
problem of what to do with the freed slaves
caused Roger much trouble and many heart-
aches. Most of them wanted to stay on as
farmers or house servants, but they had no land,
and Roger, who was not wealthy, could afford
only so many servants. The dark-skinned
Caucasians, descended from West African
aborigines, were resented and despised by the
farmers and townspeople. Those who could hire
the enfranchised were able to pay a bare sub-
sistence wage, if that. Thus, the majority of the
slaves, though very reluctant to leave the only
area they knew, drifted towards the big in-
dustrial cities.

Then the local people regretted seeing them
go. The plague had caused a labor shortage, so
much in fact that the citizens had demanded
that Leonitha's freeing of the slaves be canceled.
The Thekker (Protector) had stood firm against
them and had managed to get a slight majority
in the Blodlander parliament to back him.

There were hard times in the Six Kingdoms,

shortages of almost everything, high taxes to re-build the country, riots, other diseases taking their toll on the enfeebled survivors of the plague, and much political unrest. The northern shires were demanding that the nobility be abolished along with the poll tax and that Leonitha be the elected head of a republic. Blodland was on the verge of civil war.

On the continent, the situation was no better. The slaves there had heard about the freeing of the Blodlanders and were demanding that they too be made citizens. The inevitable riots and massacres on both sides had occurred.

Then Kwasind came to Two Hawks and said that he must leave him.

"My country has freed itself from the Perk-unishans. But they are assembling many armies along Kinnukinuk's borders and intend to take it back. I must help my people to fight against the *matcheswomp* (evil doers)."

Both men cried when they said farewell. Just before Kwasind boarded the steam train, Roger said, "We'll see each other again. Soon."

The giant said, sadly, "No. I don't believe so. My guardian *mantowak* came to me the other night while I slept, and they told me that I will die fighting against the Perkunishans and you will not be long in this world."

Seeing Roger's shocked expression, Kwasind said, "I do not think that they meant that you will die soon."

He embraced Roger again, murmured, "Goodbye, friend," and got onto the coach. Roger waited a while to wave to him, but the train pulled out without a glimpse of that broad dark face.

Roger grieved, but he did not have much time to think about Kwasind. Besides, his duties as the gerl, he had to confer with the savants who came to him. These wanted to drain him of all the information he had concerning the science and technology of his world. He told them all he knew, and he was pleased that the data he furnished were going to provide this world with many things it desperately needed. He wasn't pleased with the use that would be made of his knowledge of military machines.

However, he had finally convinced some eminent scientists that bacteria were responsible for many diseases. Actually, he wasn't the first to tell the world this. A Rasna doctor had done so ten years ago, but he had been ridiculed and hounded and had ended up in an insane asylum.

During these busy times, Roger's married life began to deteriorate. Some of this change for the worse was caused by his fatigue and the lack of time to spend together. Most of it derived from the clash of their widely differing cultural backgrounds. Ilmika was kind and even soft-hearted towards her servants, but her attitude towards the lower classes distressed Roger. She was furious when he used his influence as the local lord to get a judge to give an eleven-year old boy a five-year jail sentence instead of death by hanging. The child, one of the many half-starved orphans wandering around, had stolen a loaf of bread, a pot of butter, and a small ham. Roger had even offered to take the boy in as a servant and be responsible for him. The judge, however, had refused to permit this. He said that he was being far too lenient as it was. To let the criminal go unpunished would loosen the foundations of a society which was already too unstable.

Ilmika and Roger quarreled violently over this, the worst of a long series of disputes. Instead of reconciling afterwards, as had always happened, they separated for awhile. He went to Bammu, and she visited a cousin in a southern shire. When they returned to their home, they both made an effort to regain the tenderness and passion of their first six months of marriage. It failed, and Roger thereafter slept in another bedroom.

Another major factor in his increasing unhappiness was the attitude of the other nobles towards him. Theoretically, he was their peer. In actuality, though they were polite to him, they could not entirely conceal their prejudices against the foreigner and the dark-skinned. Roger was both, and though he was regarded as a national hero, he was still an upstart from a different race. He was excluded from many social events to which he should have been invited, and at those he did attend he was subtly snubbed.

Roger could have endured this if Ilmika had given him her full support. But now she was seldom with him, and after two years she divorced him. He could have won if he had fought her in court, but he didn't see why he should. She packed up and left, though not without weeping, and took the train to Bammu, where she had a mansion. A year later, her engagement

to her third cousin was announced. Roger sent
her a wedding present, a coat of polar bear fur
and a small diamond-studded gold chest, five
hundred years old and of New Cretan make. He
could ill afford to do so, but he wanted her to
know that he did not hate her.

Five months later, just as he was leaving the
parliament after a stormy session, he was hailed
by Humphrey Gilbert. Fat and jolly as ever, Gilbert insisted that they celebrate their reunion by
going to the nearest tavern. Roger was happy to
see him. The fellow genuinely liked him and
was, in fact, the only "friend" he could trust.

Roger ordered a beer; Gilbert, a tall glass of
Bambish whiskey. They toasted each other, and
then Gilbert said, "You look as if you need a
long vacation."

"I do."

"Then come with me to Hotinohsinoh."

"You're going *there?* Why?"

"Business, my boy. Business which it is better
for you that you know nothing about."

Roger smiled. Gilbert's wealth had been lost
during the war, his warehouses burned and his
ships sunk. But he had turned to smuggling, a
lucrative but dangerous profession, since he
could end up in a hangman's noose. After amass-
ing considerable capital, Gilbert had quit smuggling and gone into the import business. And
only two months ago he had been knighted by
the Huskarl Tekker himself.

"You need not concern yourself about my
projects there. Or I should say, you should ignore all but one of them."

Gilbert looked both happy and secretive.

"And what is that?"

"I have agents there. One has reported an interesting phenomenon, a most interesting one."

He leaned back, his eyes twinkling, and downed some more Bambish. Then he leaned across the table.

"It could be another gate!"

22

HUMPHREY GILBERT, panting heavily, said, "There's no hurry, Roger. Let's rest a while."

Two Hawks also felt like a breather, but he did not sit down. He looked back down the steep craggy mountain up which he, Gilbert, and the interpreter, Wentasta, had climbed. Another three hundred feet would bring them to the peak. This land was rough, craggy, and had a desolate forbidding appearance. Something seemed to brood over it, a something which it was best not to offend.

That the area was the Transylvania of his world and that they were not too many miles from the site of Dracula's home on Earth 1 may have been responsible for this impression. On the other hand, the tales of the locals, as relayed by the interpreter, were as spooky as those about Dracula. Here, according to the villagers, roamed witches, giants, a man made of stone, and a beast with a lion's shape but covered with feathers and beaked like an eagle. There were also bloodsucking pygmies and hairy dwarfs who rolled boulders down on intruders.

The man they'd hired as guide and interpreter of the many dialects spoken here claimed that he did not believe such superstitions. But he was obviously uneasy. And he'd refused to take them beyond a certain point.

Gilbert, mopping off his sweat and wheezing, removed his backpack and rifle and then sat down. Wentasta presently squatted by him. His jaw moved as he chewed a piece of resin. Since there was no chicle in this world, the substitute for gum was resin from mastic or spruce trees.

When he'd regained his wind, Gilbert said, cheerily, "Well, this is undoubtedly a wild goose chase. But it's been beneficial in that it's made me lose weight."

Wentasta grinned and said, in broken Blodlander, "That reminds me of a joke. There was this fat traveling salesman, see, and he . . ."

During their trip the interpreter had told at least two hundred jokes, all dirty. Their frequency and grossness had increased the closer they got to their goal. Though he denied it, he was scared, and the Rabelaisian tales were a means for keeping his spirits up.

At the end of the story, Gilbert and Wentasta bellowed laughter. Two Hawks smiled, but he walked away when Wentasta began another one. Gilbert protested that he needed more rest. Two Hawks called back, "I'll wait for you on top."

On the way, he thought about what he'd done since he had landed in Hotinohsinoh. While Gilbert attended to his business affairs, Two Hawks had roamed the seaport, observing everything and at the same time improving his use of the language. He was aware that he was being shadowed by the secret police, but he didn't allow himself to be bothered by it. Gilbert had taken care of any charges that might be brought against him because of the incident at the sanatorium.

This was the city of Shikelami, which was on Earth 1 Constanta, Rumania. Once it had been inhabited by colonists from Wilios or Troy, which had a different history here. The colonists, called Darians, had established a kingdom which had lasted three hundred years and then had perished.

Gilbert's business took three months, but halfway through it he'd told Roger that he'd located the site of what might be a gate.

"Of course, I'm going on just rumors and the tales of the superstitious mountaineers. It's likely that we'll be very disappointed. Even if there is a gate, what then? What's on the other side? Your native world? Or another Earth which will be even stranger to you than this one?"

"If there is a gate," Two Hawks had said, "and I doubt very much that there is, then I'll take my chances. I'm homesick. I've toughed it out far longer than O'Brien did. He was alienated from the beginning and was never able to overcome his longing for his own world. I think that was why he made that suicidal attack on the Itskapintik police when they were raping Ilmika. He just didn't want to live here, and there seemed no way he was going to get back to his Earth. I was far more adaptable, but now I'm suffering, too. The feeling of being not quite locked in with reality gets a little stronger every day. And I long for home."

Even though the venture seemed hopeless—how many gates could there be?—he was determined to go all the way.

He crawled over the edge of a little plateau, stood up, and walked to its other side. This side of the mountain was far shorter than the other. About five hundred feet below was a little valley. The foot of another mountain began a mile away, and halfway up it was the large dark mouth of a cave.

On the ledge in front of it was a building.

After a few minutes, Gilbert and their guide joined him. Wentasta said, "See. I was not lying. There is the witch's house and behind it the cave. It is said that near its back is a place through which she enters the kingdom of demons. Or some such nonsense. Anyway, the mountaineers claim that she gets rid of her enemies by pushing them through the door to the demons' place, though why they should visit her just to be gotten rid of I don't know."

He added, "It is said that people who want to murder others and would like to do away with the bodies so that they can't possibly be found bring the corpses here. For a fee, she throws the bodies through the door, which is invisible, and thus there is no evidence. The tales are ridiculous, of course. Who'd be able to lug a body up these steep mountains?"

"Haven't the police investigated her?" Two Hawks said.

"Nobody is brave enough to bring charges against her. Moreover, the local police are as scared of her as the others are."

They sat for half an hour. A bear ambled down the slope towards a berry patch. Three deer, tiny figures, drank from the stream running across the bottom of the valley. Finally, Wentasta stood up.

"This is as far as I go. I'll make camp under that ledge we passed, the one by the twisted tree. If you don't come back within two days, I'll go home."

"We'll be back," Gilbert said. "At least, I will."

Wentasta didn't look as if he felt that it was a certainty.

By the time they had reached the building, the sun had set behind a peak, though the sky above was still quite light. They were greeted with silence. Either the tenant of the two-story log house was watching them from inside it or was elsewhere.

They switched on the electric flashlights which they'd brought from Blodland, devices that Two Hawks had introduced. The rays played about the many windows and the closed front door.

"She didn't build this by herself," Gilbert said. "She must have had a lot of help."

"Why are you whispering?" Roger said.

Gilbert laughed nervously, and he said, "This place is eerie."

Two Hawks called out, "Nemata! Nemata! You have visitors!"

There was no answer. Could she be in the cave?

He went around the building. Behind it were

what looked like wooden chicken coops. But the fowl were long gone.

His flashlight played about the entrance to the cave. Far back was a table and some chairs and some stone goblets on the table. Beyond that was a curtain of what seemed to be leather, fringed on the bottom.

Gilbert joined him.

"It's stupid, of course. But I don't like being alone here."

Roger said, "I don't blame you."

He called into the cave. No answer except for the echo.

They returned to the front door, and he shouted her name again. Perhaps she was somewhat deaf, though the guide had described the "witch" as being young and beautiful. However, he'd admitted that he'd never seen her and that she was supposed to have lived here for fifty years.

Two Hawks beat on the door. Receiving no response, he lifted the latch and pushed. The door swung inward on wooden hinges. His beam acting as vanguard, he entered. The dust was thick on the floor and on the few pieces of furniture. There were no footprints.

They found her in a large back room. She was bones under a moldering blanket, a skull staring at the ceiling, a mass of dust-covered black hair.

"The witch is dead!" Roger said, thinking of the movie about the Wizard of Oz.

"And a long time, too," Gilbert said. "Those tales we heard about her must have been about her activities far in the past. If they were ever true."

They searched the rest of the house and then went outside. Things small and black swooped by them. One shot through a beam. A bat.

"Maybe her spirit has gone into one of those," Gilbert said. He sounded half-serious.

"You know what the locals say."

They entered the cave and walked through the bat-droppings to the curtain. Two Hawks went to pull it to one side along the wooden rod. The rotting leather tore in his hand.

Beyond was a long wide tunnel. Near its end was a door set in the stone of the wall. It was so massive and heavy that it took both of them to open it. The door itself was of oak, but the hinges were bronze. Iron nails secured the outer leaves to the wood; the other leaves were secured by iron nails which had been driven into smaller holes drilled into the rock.

"She never opened this by herself," Gilbert said.

"Maybe she never opened it at all," Two Hawks said.

Inside was another tunnel, cut out of the stone, wide enough for only one person. There was inch-thick dust on the floor. Along the wall were niches from which the skulls of human beings and animals stared. At the end was another curtain, but this one was made of strings of sea shells.

"She's a long way from the Black Sea," Gilbert said.

Two Hawks stopped by a skull. He peered at it, then took it from the shelf and blew the dust off.

"Fossilized," he said. "I'm no expert, but it

looks Neanderthal to me.''

Gilbert said, "Neanderthal?"

Two Hawks explained.

Gilbert said, "Ah, you mean the Gelsomedian Man."

The curtain rattled as he stepped through it. His light played on twenty more feet of tunnel. He felt very disappointed, though he had not really expected to find anything.

The seashells struck against each other as Gilbert poked his head through.

"There's a mystery here, my friend, but not the one you're looking for."

"It really was too much to expect."

Two Hawks walked towards the end anyway.

He was within two feet of it when he felt dizzy and then a sense of intense dislocation, a wrenching, a sickness. And then he was falling in sudden sunlight.

He struck something.

23

WHEN HE awoke, he knew he was in North America.

High on a branch of a tree near him was a bald eagle.

What most interested him, though, was the pain in his head. He reached up and felt a knot on the right side of his head near the hairline. He winced as his fingers touched it.

The eagle, finding that he was alive, flew off to look for another meal.

Two Hawks then became aware that he had a lesser pain. He'd landed on his back, and the backpack and the rifle under him were causing his spine to bend most uncomfortably. He rolled over, groaning, and rose unsteadily to his feet. Before him was a spire of granite. He looked upward, feeling a pain in his neck as he did so. The rock was about thirty feet high, which meant that he'd fallen through the gate from a height of at least thirty-five feet. He was lucky he'd not broken any bones.

On top of the rock was more evidence that he was in the New World. A big red-breasted robin. It must have alighted shortly after the eagle had left for a better hunting ground.

Two Hawks unfastened the straps and let the
heavy pack to the ground. After examining the
semi-automatic .36 caliber rifle (which he'd had
made in Blodland) and checking the .36 revolver
he wore in a holster, he observed more closely his
surroundings.

He was on top of a high hill on which and
around which grew evergreen trees of various
kinds, spruce, and larch. Through an opening he
could see a large creek.

A thud behind him made him whirl, his heart
beating hard, and the sudden motion shot pain
through his head and back. Two feet away lay
another backpack and a rifle. Attached to the
pack was a folded sheet of paper.

He looked upward again. There was no
evidence that a gate was there, but Gilbert had
heaved his pack through it. Evidently, he wasn't
going to stick his head through it to check on
what had happened to his suddenly disappeared
companion. Two Hawks didn't blame him.

The note said: "Wherever you are, God be
with you. I hope that you find whatever you're
looking for. You may need the ammunition and
provisions in my pack, so I'm sending them
through. I feel like a coward, but I'm doing all
right in this world. Anyway, you know that I
never promised to go with you.

"I'm going to block up the entrance to this
cave. I'll bring explosives and tools to do the job.
However, I will leave a narrow opening for you
to crawl through if you do come back. I doubt
that you will. I have a feeling that the gates are
all one-way.

"In any event, God bless you and bring you happiness.

Farewell.
Humphrey"

Two Hawks searched until he found some small stones. He threw them towards the area through which he must have fallen. Five stones sailed into the trees, but the sixth bounced back from an invisible object, if a gate could be called an object. Gilbert was right. Gates were one-way. Or, at least, this one was.

Raske had proved, however, that a gate could admit people from two different parallel worlds into a third at the same time.

He drank from his canteen and then shifted the boxes of cartridges to his pack and removed more from the bandoliers in Gilbert's pack. He stuffed as many cans of preserved meat and fruit as he could from the pack into his own. Other cans he jammed into his jacket pockets and boxes of matches into his pants pockets. Then he started down the hill.

Thirty days later, he was about 210 miles southeastward of his point of departure. All except two cans, saved for emergency, were gone. He'd expended twenty of his bullets, six to get meat, the rest in self-defense. He'd encountered bears, cougars, bison, and mastodons. Besides his firearms, he now had a bow and a quiver full of arrows. The shafts of these were tipped with chert. He was thankful that he'd once taken the trouble to learn how to work flint and chert from a Texan anthropologist while he was in college.

The forest seemed to go forever, though he

now and then came to small plains. He'd crossed
two broad rivers on rafts made with his handaxe
and wood chisel. When he came to a river which
flowed south instead of west he'd make another
and float as far south as it would take him. He
hoped that it would also go eastward, since he
wanted to get to the coast. But just now his main
desire was to get to a warmer climate. He didn't
want to get caught in a severe winter.

So far, he had seen no human beings or any
evidence that there were any. He was beginning
to wonder if this world was in an era before the
Indians had entered North America from Asia.
When, on the thirtieth day, he came to some
great plains and saw imperial mammoths and
camels and sabertooths and giant sloths and
horses, he was sure that he was alone, the only
human on two continents.

He was lord and master of all he surveyed, as
long as he stayed away from the great herbivores
and carnivores. But he didn't like it one bit. This
was a paleontologist's and hunter's paradise and
fascinating to him. Yet, he thought he'd go mad
if he didn't see a human face, hear a human
voice soon.

The next day, he thought he'd die from happiness. While hunting on the edge of the plain,
hoping to shoot one of the giant rabbits abound-
ing here, he was startled by shouting. It came
from beyond a small hill. He hurried to its top
and looked from behind a tree. About a quarter
of a mile away twelve men, Indians, had cornered a small camel. Its left rear leg was bleeding heavily, evidently so badly wounded that it
couldn't be used. Nevertheless, it roared and

spat at its tormentors and struck out with its front hooves when the men in front of it got too close. Then it would whirl as those behind it ran in, thrusting their flint-tipped spears.

The hunters were tall and well-muscled, their skins darker than Two Hawks', their hair long and free and blue-black, the faces broad and high-cheekboned, the noses aquiline. There was one who could have passed for Sitting Bull. They wore very short skin kilts, cords around their necks which held perforated mussel shells, and they were shod with furry moccasins. Their only weapons were spears and stone axes and knives.

"They don't even have bows," Two Hawks muttered. "Not even atlatls."

About twenty yards from them, slinking through the bushes, were two sabertooths, a male and female. They wouldn't be planning to attack the hunters, but they would hope to scavenge what was left after the men had departed. But they'd have to run off the big vultures that had settled on or around a tree closeby.

Presently, the camel was hamstrung, and the hunters closed in. A moment later they were butchering the animal. They smiled and chatted happily while they worked. The tribe would feast well tonight, stuff their bellies until they could hold no more. Now would be the proper psychological moment for Two Hawks to introduce himself. The hunters would be in a very good mood.

But what would their attitude towards strangers be?

Very suspicious, of course. No doubt, they

warred on other tribes, had their hereditary enemies. But his strange garments and his weapons
would identify him instantly as anything but a
member of a known hostile group. He would be
completely alone, and if he approached them
without showing fear, seemingly full of con-
fidence, they would react very cautiously.

If he shot one of the sabertooths, preferably
the male, since the female might have cubs, he
would show them that he was to be feared, that
he was a magician or perhaps even a spirit.

Still, he hesitated. Not because of his ap-
prehension. He had to take this step sometime,
and it might as well be now. What made him
pause was a certain disappointment. None of his
fantasies were to be realized. He'd visualized a
number of worlds, all of which had been shaped
according to his desires and all of which could be
possible. One had been a continuum in which
the French had won the French and Indian War.
In this, the Iroquois tribes had sided with the
French against the British colonists instead of
with the British, as they had in his native world.
The French had gained control of eastern North
America and in gratitude had given the Iroquois
all of upper New York and adjacent parts of
Canada. And so, when Two Hawks had arrived,
he had found that Iroquoia was a sovereign nation. He would happily become a citizen, take a
wife, raise children, work, perhaps as a pilot for
his own people's airline, grow old, and be buried
in his native soil. Well, an approximation of it,
anyway.

Another fantasy, but one which could also be

realized, was a world in which the Roman Empire had not fallen until, say 800 A. D. In this the Romanized Britons held off the Anglo-Saxon invaders. Their Latin speech gradually became a separate branch of the Romance family and they became independent of Rome. British explorers discovered America about five hundred years earlier than it had been in his world. They had established colonies, but these had grown far slower than on Earth 1. The Amerinds had not suffered from such a swift and terrible cultural shock; they had been able to learn the technology of the invaders and to keep up with it.

And so, when Two Hawks got to this world, he had found that the Iroquois held all of New York and Ohio and perhaps Pennsylvania. And other tribes, the Cherokee, the Shawnee, the Creek, the Choctaw, and so on were populous thriving technologically advanced powerful nations. Or perhaps members of a Confederacy or Union of America. The whites had been driven out, and all of North America, South America, too, was red-skinned.

This wouldn't necessarily make the world, taken as a whole, a better world. But it would certainly suit Two Hawks.

If these worlds did exist somewhere, he was not in them.

Nor was there much chance that he would find another gate. He had been extraordinarily lucky—or was he?—to locate a second gate.

Now, watching the hunters cut up the meat after stripping off the camel's hide, he had another fantasy. He would become this tribe's leader. He would teach them the use of the bow, proper sanitation (though they might be one of the cleanly tribes), domestication of animals (especially the horse), and agriculture. He would lead them to the coast, to Georgia, say, where it would be warmer. He would take a wife and found a dynasty. His tribe would expand. He might even be able to make iron tools and weapons. And if he established metalworking, then he would give his people the opportunity to leap forward, what, five thousand years, ten, twenty?

And when this world's equivalents of Columbus, Cortez, Pizarro, Cabot, Hudson got here, they would find a nation with a far superior science and technology. And the Americas would remain Indian.

Or, probably, it would be the Indians who would discover Europe, the New World to them, it would be they who would conquer the barbarians.

Unless, by then, the Americans had become a wise and humane people and treated the lesser beings well.

"You're a fool!" he said.

Nevertheless, he walked down the hill. He wasn't observed until he was within a hundred yards of the hunters. Suddenly, the chatter and the horsing-around stopped. They ceased work and rose to face him, their spears ready, and they moved towards each other.

When he was fifty feet from the nearest, he stopped. He smiled, and he cried out a greeting in Onondaga. They wouldn't understand this, of course. Even if by some wild chance they spoke a tongue which was destined to become Iroquois or Cherokee, they wouldn't recognize a single word of his. But they might feel the lack of hostility in the tone.

And they might respond to the vibrations of loneliness.

They were still hard-faced and silent.

He pointed to the two smilodons, who had come within seventy feet before stopping.

He raised the butt of his rifle to his shoulder, took aim, and fired the first shot ever heard in this world.

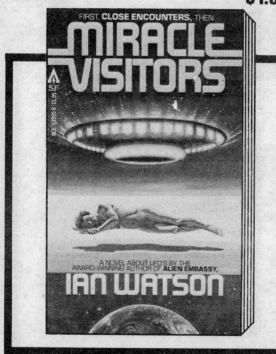